I0784081

The
Fine Art
of
Deception

A Provincetown Mystery

Jeannette de Beauvoir

"Perhaps the suspicion of fraud enhances the flavor."

-C. S Forester

1

The nightmare came—appropriately enough—in the night.

We've all had it. Someone is chasing you, someone dangerous, and you're trying to punch a number into the phone to get help, but you keep punching in the wrong digits, and the person chasing you is coming closer and closer and...

I screamed, of course, and my boyfriend was half out of bed before either of us was fully awake.

Ali's in law enforcement. You don't scream your head off in the middle of the night and not expect a reaction. I was probably lucky he hadn't drawn a gun or something.

***

Mirela was sitting at the tiki bar near the pool when we got to the Race Point Inn, talking to her nanny on the telephone. "She knows she can't go to the beach if she doesn't take her nap," she was saying, turned slightly away from the bar, one long, tanned leg crossed over the other for maximum effect. Since she'd broken up—for the second time—with Guy, her English sometimes-boyfriend, Mirela had been advertising her availability. Ali thought she was lonely.

I thought she was having a midlife crisis.

She clicked the phone off and turned to us. "My daughter," she announced, "has transformed herself into Kid Zhivkov. She wants what she wants when she wants it. I did not know that five years old would be as bad as when she was two."

Ali snagged a couple more stools for us to perch on with her. "Hi, Mirela," he said.

She offered him a cheek to kiss. "Ali. When did you get into town?"

"Evening ferry last night," he told her.

I said, "Who's Zhivkov?"

Mirela blinked. She forgets sometimes the rest of us don't live inside her head. "Comrade Todor Zhivkov," she said. "It was his birthday a few days ago. Lily celebrates by becoming a pest."

I stared at her. "Comrade? Bulgaria hasn't been communist since last century." I was dredging up one of the few facts I knew about Communism, adding for good measure, "*tovarisch*."

"That is Russian, not Bulgarian," she said and shrugged. "It is still a celebration," she added.

Mirela came to Provincetown the same way dozens of Bulgarians do every summer, to work full-on hard at three or four jobs, party with the stamina of the very young, and leave in time for the fall semester at home. Mirela, however, found the oldest art colony in the United States to be her soulmate and ended up staying on, eventually becoming a well-known and well-respected painter with work in galleries here and in New York, as well as in her native Plovdiv.

"You celebrate a dictator?" I asked.

Ali signaled the bartender. "She's referring to Lily," he reminded me. "What do you want to drink?"

"He knows," I said, nodding to the handsome young man behind the bar. Glenn and Mike, respectively, the Race Point Inn's owner and manager, have a habit of hiring the best-looking guys for the tourist season. With P'town a gay summer destination, this served them well. I gave up at some point each summer trying to keep all their names in my head—Brad, Pete, Jim, Todd—and generally just thought of them as Kevin. All of them. A lavender army of Kevins.

And, yeah, I've worked out a discount system at each of the inn's four bars. I'm no fool.

"So," said Ali to Mirela, as though picking up a conversation they'd just left off, "we're invited to your opening, right?"

She smiled for the bartender, picked up her cocktail, and took a sip. "Why should I invite you?" she asked innocently. "You do not know much about art."

"Don't do that to him," I implored. "It's just plain cruel."

Mirela smiled.

Ali drank some of his juice. He's Muslim, and while he doesn't do a lot of things good Muslims are supposed to do—I don't think he even owns a prayer rug—he doesn't drink alcohol. "I know you wouldn't break my heart," he said easily.

"Perhaps you could learn something about art from looking at my work," she conceded. Mirela and Ali are the best of friends. Sometimes even I could forget that.

The bartender drifted our way, polishing a glass. "Heads up," he said to me quietly. "He's in a mood today."

"Who?"

He inclined his head toward the pool area. It was just Glenn, the inn's owner, looking irritated. He'd been looking irritated for the better part of a week now, so I wasn't particularly alarmed. It was September, after all, and we're all exhausted as the tourist season winds down.

Not that said tourists had shown any indication of going away, not yet. Things in Provincetown don't truly calm down until January when we'll get two or three months' respite before the second-home owners and day-trippers start descending again *en masse*.

Glenn came up to the bar, a hulking presence even when he wasn't "in a mood." Glenn is what is known as a bear, a large hairy gay man, and—well, you *notice* him when he comes into a room. Or up to a bar. "Don't you have work to do?" he asked me.

"Nope," I said cheerfully. I had two weddings to orchestrate that week and had been on top of them for what felt like forever. It's generally assumed wedding planning is stressful, and that's probably true in places like Boston or Miami, but P'town is laid back.

Plans are flexible, expectations are set around what is fun rather than what someone's mother wants, and everyone is up for a good time.

I was, truth to tell, getting a little bored with my current chosen profession.

Glenn glowered. "You don't seem to be worried," he conceded, but even the concession sounded begrudging, like he was reserving judgment. "I don't want anything going wrong."

Not like him to micromanage, I thought. "Nothing will go wrong."

"Hi, Glenn," said Ali easily. "Care to join us?"

Glenn seemed to finally notice I wasn't sitting alone. He raised a hand in refusal. "Thanks, Ali, no," he said. "Things to do. Hi, Mirela."

She smiled prettily. Mirela does everything prettily. "But it is the cocktail hour!" she protested.

"It's always the cocktail hour," Glenn said sourly. Okay, he *was* in a mood. That's the other thing about working in a tourist town: while everyone else is on vacation, partying, and having fun, you're working. You aren't on their vacation, but they're making sure you know they're having a good time. Sometimes it can get to you.

I'd never seen it get to Glenn like this, though. "Just make sure you take care of the weddings," he said to me.

"Aye, aye, captain," I said, saluting. Maybe I could prod him out of it with sarcasm, my favorite mode of communication.

No such luck. He scowled at me, scowled at Mirela, turned, and walked back into the inn. As he passed the pool, he called to the hapless pool-boy. "You, there! I see a leaf in the water!"

The bartender, who had conveniently disappeared while Glenn was talking to us, drifted back over again. "See?" he said. "I told you."

I was staring after Glenn. "That's so not like him," I said. Like most bears, Glenn is generally the very model of laid-back bonhomie. "I wonder what's wrong."

"Whatever it is," said Ali, "let's hope it doesn't affect dinner."

I transferred my gaze to him. "What?"

"Your father's going to be here," he reminded me. "Dinner in the restaurant. Unless Glenn gets into it with Adrienne."

Adrienne the diva chef, the reason we had a Michelin rating... and all-around dragon lady. She had a short fuse and required absolute calm around her at all times. Given that requirement, her decision to work and live in Provincetown was still a mystery to me.

"If that happens," prophesied the bartender, "the whole place will explode."

All of which made it, so far, just a normal day.

2

Mike, the inn's manager, was also worried.

"There's nothing to suggest he's ever done anything this *outré*," he said to me, *sotto voce*, as though we were talking about someone recently deceased. "For heaven's sake, there's nothing to suggest he even knows what *outré* means."

"Never done what?"

Mike gestured behind him. We were standing in the small cubicle beyond the inn's reception area I euphemistically refer to as my office. Beyond it are three doors: a restroom, Mike's office, and Glenn's office. Glenn's door was closed.

The last time I could remember that door being closed, we had been negotiating a ransom demand from a kidnapper. Mike wasn't there—he'd been away on sabbatical. Glenn had tried to save an old friend, and I had tried to put an old ghost to rest. "The last time he closed his door—"

"I know," Mike said. "Last summer."

"Last summer," I echoed. Almost a year ago. I'd nearly gotten killed. That was something I didn't like to spend a lot of time thinking about. "Do you know what's going on?"

He shook his head, worried. Mike worries a lot; it makes him an excellent manager. Between him and Martin, the restaurant's maître d', the Race Point Inn nearly ran itself. Well, there was me and Adrienne, too, of course. But still… we were a good team. There wasn't a lot for Glenn to be concerned about. Certainly not anything to put him in a *mood*.

"It's nothing financial, is it?" I asked. Finances make everyone a little crazy, and company towns are always a little crazier than others. When you only have one industry, fluctuations in its popularity affect everyone. The Race Point Inn didn't have to deal with the staffing problems other places in Provincetown encountered: we provided housing, and we paid above the average rate, enough to keep us in Kevins, in-season and out. But that didn't mean that everything was lovely—or always running smoothly.

"There were auditors in," he said. "Back in the spring, remember? But it's all fine. It was just around the time he was thinking of adding a stage to the dining-room. He said then he needed a full audit, though honestly, Sydney, I don't know what that connection was."

"I remember," I said grimly. None of us had been very happy back in the winter when Glenn proposed the Race Point get into the entertainment action—mostly Broadway performers and drag shows—that bring in so much money during the season. We were all relieved when it turned out to not be terribly feasible, and Glenn had let it go.

"Well," said Mike, shrugging, "that's the only financial thing that's been happening. I do know he spent more time with them than I did, and his attorney was involved, but that could have meant anything. The point is, the inn's on an even keel. I'm the manager, remember? If there were something desperately wrong, I would literally be the first to know. There's nothing there."

"Maybe it's his love life," I suggested. Glenn had become the inn's owner when his partner and my first boss, Barry, was murdered. Since then, he'd had a couple of relationships, but they'd come and go—the way summer romances tend to do.

Mike nodded. "You might be on to something there," he said. "There have been late-night telephone conversations. *Murmured* conversations. And he's been traveling more, hadn't you noticed?"

I shook my head. "I don't keep up," I confessed. When I was at work, I was at work. When I was home, it was my boyfriend and my cat I was thinking about.

"We'd know if there were anyone serious, surely," he said, though he didn't sound all that sure. But it was true: Glenn pretty much wore his heart on his sleeve. "Whatever it is, it had best resolve itself soon, or no one's going to want to work here. He's been positively *tyrannical* to the staff."

That was a bit of an exaggeration, of course. The Race Point Inn is, in fact, a fabulous place to work, and not only because of Glenn's usually jovial presence. Besides providing or finding worker housing, the Race Point is genuinely nice. Most of us are proud to work here. It's well-run, the pay is above what any other lodgings in town are offering, and it looks good on a resume, what with the Michelin star Adrienne the diva chef consistently earns.

"Everyone wants a job here," I said automatically. "They just want to avoid Glenn." A terrible thought took shape. "Mike, you don't think he's going to *sell?*"

A few years back, Glenn had flirted with the idea of selling the Race Point to one of the ubiquitous national—and even international—corporations that, for the past few years, had been quietly buying properties in Provincetown. He'd decided against it, much to everyone's relief, but that didn't mean the idea was off the table forever.

"I don't know," said Mike, sounding helpless, and I felt fear for the first time. Yeah, I was a little restless in my job, but I loved the inn and couldn't imagine life without it. Or without Glenn, for that matter.

I wanted Mike to *know.* I wanted him to have a reasonable explanation, something plausible I could take with me and hold onto until whatever storm Glenn was experiencing would pass.

It was never going to be that easy.

***

My father didn't generally visit me without my mother in tow, and this week—to be fair—she was supposed to have been arriving with him, were it not for a fortuitous set of circumstances involving my hypochondriacal aunt, her husband's absence on a fishing trip, and a bee sting. Aunt Germaine had insisted she was dying (not, it should be noted, for the first time), and my mother went to see her to "snap her out of it."

Whether she's trying to run my life or bring her sister back to reality, my mother can be ruthless.

My father, recognizing the signs—and not wanting to be deprived of a couple of Race Point Inn dinners—had come on without her. He said he actually had some business to take care of on-Cape, but I hadn't really been listening; I was still in the relief stage of oh-thank-God-my-mother-isn't-coming.

We kept the table reservation for four, with Mirela substituting for my mother. *She* wasn't about to be deprived, either.

It was an early dinner—which the European-trained kitchen staff would never get used to—as we were headed over to the Provincetown Art Association and Museum for an evening lecture Mirela had recommended. "You," she had said to Ali, "need to see more art."

"How can I help but see art when I'm here?" he countered.

Now my father was politely taking up the conversational baton. "How did this town get so much art in the first place?" he asked. The inquiry was courteous; I thought he was probably far more interested in his smoked corn custard with seared scallops than he was in the conversation. In retirement, my father has become a gourmet diner.

I knew the answer to this one, anyway, which isn't always the case. Well, sort of knew it. "It's the light," I said. "Back in the late 1800s, artists started coming here because of the light." I'm no artist, and I honestly have no idea what people are talking about when they say that, but apparently, it's a Thing, this Provincetown light, a mixture of sky and water and the resulting humidity that for a century and a half has drawn people here to paint or sculpt or sketch. They say it reverently: "The Light."

Ali, infinitely more practical, said, "That's when the railroad was built, so the town was accessible to everyone, even artists on limited budgets." He smiled at Mirela when he said that: she, too, had had a limited budget when she'd started out.

Those days were long gone.

"And then came the summer of 1916," I said. "All the Greenwich Village bohemian artists and writers who usually went to France for the summer couldn't go because of the war." They'd come here instead, shocking the local Portuguese fishing families with their notions of free love and Bolshevism, their wild parties, transforming the town with an influx of energy, creativity, and intellectualism. Eugene O'Neill lived out in the dunes and wrote his first play. Emma Goldman and John Reed talked politics and smoked cigarettes all night. Blanche Lazzell and Agnes Weinrich created the later-to-be-famous Provincetown white-line printing technique. Edna St. Vincent Millay pounded out poetry on an old typewriter in her garret digs; actors staged plays at the old Lewis Wharf; modernism as an art form developed from its roots at the Armory Show.

I didn't know any of that because I lived in town; I'll admit it: *Reds* is still one of my all-time favorite movies.

I imagined them sometimes, wraiths walking down Commercial Street, flitting in and out of the places that had housed their genius work, the Mary Heaton Vorse house, the John Dos Passos house—buildings I passed by every day, as the Race Point Inn is firmly entrenched in the gallery district of the East End.

It had to have been a wildly interesting time and place to be alive.

And among them, the founder of it all, the reason Greenwich Village had opted for Provincetown over the Cornish or East Hampton art colonies: Charles Hawthorne, who had opened the Cape Cod School of Art in 1899 and was the father of plein-air painting in the United States. "Painting," he said once, "is just like making an after-dinner speech. If you want to be remembered, say one thing and stop." I rather liked that thought, accustomed as I was to working with anxious wedding clients who needed to tell me everything about their history, plans, preferences, and pretty much the kitchen sink… on our first meeting. Economy of speech, whether spoken or on canvas, was something I'd come to appreciate.

My father, never particularly interested in history, said unhelpfully, "I just don't get it. Light is light, isn't it?"

Mirela looked as if she were going to pass out. "Light," she said severely, "is never just light. It is something… alive. Even artists who do not do representational work, artists like me, they know how to reflect this light." She touched her napkin to her lips, hesitating. Maybe in retrospect, that should have told me something. It wasn't particularly like Mirela to hesitate. "I meant to ask you—" she said to Ali and then stopped herself.

"What?"

She shook her head. "Never mind," she said. "It is not important."

I didn't think about that until much later when the talk at the PAAM was over, and my father was heading back to the inn to give my mother her nightly telephonic summary of his day, and the three of us were alone. We'd stopped at Spindler's for a nightcap, and Ali said, almost carelessly, "What was it you wanted to ask me about, Mirela?"

All the assurance she'd shown throughout the evening at the museum—when she was in her element—seemed to drain from her. She seemed, again, the hesitant Bulgarian art student who'd first come to town, never dreaming she had the talent to make her hobby into fame and fortune. "I just wonder," she said, more to her martini than to us, "how it is we make decisions when there can always be unintended consequences."

Ali and I exchanged a look. He said gently, "No decision is ever perfect."

"Sometimes," she said, still not looking at us, "it becomes a matter of determining who will get hurt, no?"

Weirder and weirder. "What are you talking about?" I demanded. "It would be a lot easier

to help you figure out your unintended consequences if you were more specific."

She smiled, finished her drink in a single gulp, and stood up. "Never mind," she said. "It is not important. I must go home. Erika will wonder what has happened to me."

Erika was Lily's current nanny. There had already been more than one. Anyone who could put up with my goddaughter was worth their weight in gold; what Erika wanted, Erika got. You really couldn't argue with that.

As Ali and I made our way back to my apartment, bright lights from the nightclubs and the restaurants spilling across the pave-ment as we were jostled by others walking around Commercial Street, pedicabs and bicycles still whizzing by, even at ten-thirty, I wondered if any of those early artists would recognize the town now. Sure, we have galler-ies and artists galore—the Fine Arts Work Center brings new visions in with their fellows every year; the Cape Cod School of Art itself has been resuscitated, and even our public buildings like town hall and the library are hung with Provincetown masterpieces—but there's something very… "commercial," I said to Ali. "Everything's gotten so commercial. It's all about the money now."

"That's a little unfair," he protested. "They have to make a living." Maybe he was thinking about Mirela's art, canvases that routinely sold for twenty or thirty or forty thousand dollars apiece. She was making a rather good living, yet even I couldn't accuse her of being in it for the money.

"Maybe," I said, still dissatisfied.

"Let it go," he recommended, slipping an arm around my shoulders and disappointing every gay guy on the street who'd been trying to catch his eye; Ali is, quite simply, a gorgeous man. Perceptive, too: he immediately went right to the heart of what I was really talking about. "Don't worry so much, Sydney. Mirela will tell us whatever it is when she's ready," he said.

"But she's afraid of hurting someone," I said. Mirela told me everything, and anything she didn't tell me, she told Ali—we were her closest friends.

I didn't like the idea she felt she had to keep something from us. "What does that mean, anyway? Who's she talking about? She hasn't seen Guy for over a year. Oh, wait—do you think there's someone else?" *And since when did you go around inquiring into the love lives of everyone around you, Riley? First Glenn, now Mirela?*

"I think," said Ali, "that you're taking all of this a little too personally."

"Maybe." I could feel the summer turning sour on me; those of us who live here call it Augustitis, when it's not yet time for the visitors to go home, but we're ready for some peace and quiet after serving their needs and whims all season. It was late September now, and generally, both the crowds and the Augustitis they engendered had dissipated by this time. But I still had that feeling, a sense of tiredness and impatience and a desire to do something, anything, to make the feeling go away. Glenn was acting strange; I was vaguely dissatisfied with my work; my father was in town; Mirela had a secret. None of it felt particularly good.

Or maybe the summer wasn't turning sour; maybe it was the martini I'd just finished.

Home brought its own set of challenges. If you think NYC apartments are tiny, then you have a hint of what it's like to rent in Provincetown. When captain's homes from the eighteenth century are turned into apartments and condos, they're not exactly spacious. My place—a glorified studio—had been small when it was just me and my cat Ibsen. Now, with Ali living here, it was getting a little claustrophobic.

Ali works out of the federal building in Boston, where he's in charge of a unit within the department for homeland security that deals with people trafficking. But he's on the road a great deal and is able to work from "home" a lot of the time—which we both interpret, now, as P'town, since he'd sold his well-appointed condo in Boston. About six months ago, we'd decided it was time to move up to a bigger apartment in town if we could find one, or possibly even to purchase a condo if we could—again—find one we could afford.

Both efforts had proved fruitless. Like many other coastal resort areas, Provincetown really hadn't thought through the implications of transforming a former fishing village into a playground for the wealthy, and real estate had gone over the top.

I wondered sometimes whether it was all a sign, a sign that maybe Ali and I weren't supposed to be together, or perhaps a sign we shouldn't be in Provincetown—I wasn't sure what it meant, only that it had to mean something. Hey, we all look for patterns; that was the pattern my brain was trying for. At the moment, anyway.

So in the meantime, we managed with my small place and the sofa that, in true Little Shop of Horrors form, threatened to swallow anyone who sat on it. I'd lost Ibsen the cat several times that way.

He was, needless to say, *Not Amused.*

"In any case," Ali was saying, "Mirela's a big girl; she can take care of herself. When she needs us, she'll let us know."

"I know," I said unhappily. I went through the motions of opening a can of cat food and fluffing it up—proper presentation being everything to Ibsen. I drank a whole glass of water down in one shot so the martini couldn't give me bad dreams—or, even worse, a hangover. I really should stick to wine.

Ali was meantime getting absorbed into the couch. "Your father wants us to meet him tomorrow," he said. "Any idea what that's about?"

I had no idea, really. "I have no idea," I said. "Apparently, no one tells me anything."

He whistled under his breath. "Mirela's really gotten under your skin, *cara*," he said. Ali's Lebanese, but he likes using Italian expressions; he thinks they make him sound sexy. (He's right, but I try not to let him know that.) He patted the sofa beside him. "Come on, leave the dishes. I'll do them later. You know things will look better in the morning. Meantime, *cara*, come over here."

I went.

3

My father was breakfasting at the inn when I arrived, and he wasn't alone. There was a woman with him, in her forties, with streaked brown hair tied into a careful-casual knot, wearing what I understood to be a trend called "coastal grandmother." Don't ask me; I'm not on TikTok. It has something to do with Diane Keaton in *Something's Gotta Give*. But this lady was definitely ready for a day at the seaside, the white linen pants with a perfect crease, the cotton sweater knotted oh-so-casually around her shoulders, and the striped blue and white shirt.

Everything about her screamed money.

If my father had decided at this late date to have an affair, he was certainly playing in the big leagues. Beside her, though, his grey hair looked distinguished, his glasses scholarly.

Maybe you do reflect the company you keep; my mother had assured me of that premise in no uncertain terms throughout my turbulent adolescence when she considered my friends to be of questionable morals.

If he was having an affair, he was making no secret of it. "Sydney! Come on over!"

I wondered what it would be like to have a stepmother within hailing distance of my own age. "Morning," I said vaguely to the table at large.

My father bent himself into that half-on-the-feet position men assume when they're trying to be polite. "Sydney, this is Caroline Harrison. Caroline, my daughter Sydney."

Caroline and I made vague greeting noises at each other, and, unasked, I took one of the empty chairs and looked around for a server. I had a feeling I was going to need the strongest coffee they had. Gallons of it. I had a martini-sized headache and wasn't really in the mood to meet with anyone or do anything.

"Your father," Caroline said smoothly, "was just telling me a little about the history of Provincetown."

"Was he now?" I looked at him, amused. My father, the history buff. Good thing I'd given him a quick tutorial the day before.

He caught the thought in the air—something he does with disconcerting regularity—and tossed it back to me. "Sydney's the real expert," he said easily. "Not to mention her friend Mirela."

"Mirela Dobreva?" She looked impressed. "I've seen her work in New York."

The coffee arrived without me asking for it. I do love working at the inn. "Are you interested in modern art, Caroline?" I asked politely. People who like seascapes don't generally go for what Mirela does.

Caroline smiled, exchanging a quick knowing glance with my father before sliding a card out of the small leather clutch-purse she had on the table. "You could say that," she said, handing me the card. "I'm an art broker."

She was right: there it was, sure enough, Caroline Harrison, art brokerage. "Are you here to see Mirela?" I asked. As far as I understood the process, Mirela's work was sold through galleries. I wasn't even sure what a broker *did*.

"Not at all," she said. "Although I'd be delighted to meet her. My agency deals primarily with nineteenth and early-to-mid-twentieth-century artists, though, of course, we can usually locate anything a client particularly wants."

I had a sudden vision of some high-stakes auction house like Christie's or Sotheby's and my parents sitting and waving cards. Couldn't quite make that one work. There had to be more to this. I looked at my father. "So, what, you're investing in nineteenth-century artists now?" I teased.

"Well, yes," he said.

I'd been joking. My father doesn't know anything about art. There was some decent art on the walls of their luxury home in New Hampshire, but all of it was inherited from my mother's side of the family. I'd be willing to bet my last dollar that my father, oblivious as ever to anything he doesn't find innately interesting, couldn't name a single piece. Plus, my father's idea of a highbrow evening is listening to classical music while he sips his single-malt and reads spy novels. "You're *what?*"

"Considering investing," he said calmly. I glanced at Caroline to see if she was in on some joke. She looked perfectly serious.

Okay, well, it's not as if he doesn't have the money. My father had been a gifted sales executive who, in addition to earning a six-to-seven-figure salary with outrageous incentive deals and commissions, had invested wisely and well. He and my mother live in minor opulence in a Stepford-wives neighborhood in southern New Hampshire. Not that you could tell anyone else lived nearby; landscaping and a general aloofness of the population took care of that. For all I knew, he could afford something from Sotheby's or Christie's. I just hadn't realized he had any interest in doing so.

"You're going to collect art?"

"Collect is a big word," said Caroline quickly. "We're just seeing what investments might make sense at this point."

"Because you don't know what to do with your money?" I didn't want to sound too sarcastic, though it probably came out that way. What I was feeling was some vague disorientation. Mirela, whose life had been pretty much an open book up until now, was stressing about unintended consequences (and when did she ever even learn that expression?) relating to some mysterious… something… and now my father was summoning art brokers when, as far as I knew, he'd always parked his money somewhere safe.

I didn't know that much about the art world, but I couldn't imagine it being safe.

"Art accrues value with time," said my father gently, apparently reading my mind. "And your mother and I want to make sure we're leaving you with good investments."

"Why? Are you sick? Is Ma sick?" Great: yet another anxiety.

"We're fine," he said. "Sydney, it's just an idea. Caroline happened to be in Boston, and it seemed a good opportunity, and she agreed to meet here." From the kitchen came the sound of something falling and shattering on the floor; I could only imagine what Angus, the pastry chef, was saying to whoever had dropped it.

"I had a couple of days off," Caroline put in quickly. "And as your parents were coming to the Cape anyway. . ."

It was, of course, perfectly normal, perfectly innocent, and I had to shake this mood threatening my sanity and, before long, would be threatening my relationships. I managed a perky smile. "Well, then, great. Do you have an artist in mind?" I turned to Caroline. "Is that where you start, with an artist?" I asked curiously.

"Generally, we start with establishing how much money a client wants to spend," she said dryly. "So as not to disappoint."

I wasn't going to ask how much my father was putting on the table, though I really, really wanted to. "Okay." I drank some coffee. "I was wondering how—"

Someone had come up from behind me. "Stephen Riley! Good to see you," said Glenn's voice.

My father leaned over slightly to shake my boss' hand. "Good to be back," he said. Glenn liked my father because he was one of the few individuals on the planet who could tame Adrienne the diva chef. Probably for other reasons, too, but the Adrienne one was a winner. "Join us," my father invited, gesturing to the one empty chair at the table. "This is Caroline Harrison. Glenn owns the Race Point Inn," he added to her.

"Pleasure," said Caroline.

To my surprise, Glenn accepted the invitation. Maybe he was easing out of the mood he'd been in. That would be good news. "Caroline is an art broker," my father informed him.

"Are you?" Glenn looked instantly interested, and that, in turn, interested me. I wouldn't have thought he could tell a Monet from a Modigliani. There was apparently no end to the surprises people around me were revealing. "Are you here looking at something in particular?"

"Just meeting with Stephen," said Caroline smoothly. "And enjoying a couple of days away from the city." She certainly was skilled, I thought, in answering the question she wanted to answer rather than the one actually asked. I'd heard more than one politician do that, too.

Glenn was nodding; he knew all about people escaping from the city. "Sorry your wife couldn't join you," he said to my father.

I wasn't. Not even a little bit.

"Family things," my father said easily. He couldn't have been missing her too much; she would have been relentlessly towing him from one museum to another. Come to think of it, my mother was far more likely to want to get involved in the art world than my father. Curiouser and curiouser, as Lewis Carroll would have said.

"So, what are you thinking of buying?" Glenn asked my father.

"Caroline specializes in late nineteenth and early twentieth-century artists," said my father. "So we were thinking—"

"Really?" The word fairly burst from Glenn. He was looking at Caroline. "How coincidental! I just recently bought a Charles Hawthorne!" he exclaimed.

"Did you?" Caroline and I said the words nearly in unison. I was feeling completely out of the loop. What was this, everyone investing in art, making art, talking about art, and I'd had no idea?

"Yes," Glenn was saying. "It was a lucky fluke, really. It's that feller who owns Mirela's gallery—one of his artists had some connection to some paintings that apparently no one even knew existed. They weren't part of anyone's official list of publications, I should say paintings—is that what you call it?"

"The *catalogue raisonné*," said Caroline, nodding.

"Apparently, a whole bunch of paintings didn't make it in," said Glenn comfortably. "They just appeared. Almost out of nowhere. One of those stories you hear about sometimes. Some old feller storing them in his attic or something, his nephew finding them all when the old man died. Actually, it wasn't an attic—can't remember just now. Really a stroke of luck. I said, why not get one for the inn? I thought the price was a little steep but not too bad when you consider—well, Provincetown, Hawthorne, you know?"

Caroline was smiling again. "I would love to see it," she said.

My father seemed pleased the conversation had shifted away from him. "Hawthorne," he said now. "Don't think I know him." He was looking at me as though I had somehow betrayed his trust by not offering a full biography, waiting to cue my usual travel guide routine. It wasn't happening; all I knew about Hawthorne was he'd set up a school here for doing plein-air painting, and people had come from all over to be part of it. Really the start of the official art colony. "He was a little more strait-laced than a lot of the bohemians," I said uncertainly. "Wasn't he?"

Caroline hadn't taken her gaze off Glenn. "He didn't care much for the wild parties," she admitted, "nor for abstract art. He was always a realist. He was in charge of the Provincetown Art Association and practically banned modernists from exhibiting there. Where is this painting?"

Not one to lose track of essentials, this Caroline, I thought. But I was curious, too. "I don't think I've seen it either," I said—again, a little hesitantly. The truth was I wouldn't know a Hawthorne painting if it were delivered to my front door. It was perfectly conceivable I'd already walked by it somewhere in the inn, and it never even registered.

But I wondered, too, why Mirela hadn't mentioned anything about Glenn buying a painting at her gallery. Most of the stuff they had on display was more Mirela's style, abstract and visceral. I really should go look up Hawthorne.

Glenn was delighted. "Come see it," he invited the table at large. "It's in my apartment now—haven't insured it yet, but as soon as I do, it'll go on display in the inn." A shadow crossing his voice there, something still not right, but no time to ask about it, as he was already shepherding us out of the dining-room and back to the small elevator that connected the first floor exclusively to his quarters.

And they were nice quarters indeed. Barry and Glenn had eschewed renting out the inn's penthouse (and making a small fortune, with its spectacular views of the harbor) and had made it their home—a beautiful airy living room, well-appointed kitchen, two bedrooms, even two bathrooms. And views, as I mentioned, to die for. I'd only ever been up there once before, when Barry was still alive, and he hosted some sort of costume party—I couldn't remember the occasion. The apartment was every bit as beautiful as I'd remembered.

The painting itself was a little awkward; he'd obviously taken a different piece down in order to display this one, and it looked a little out of place on the wall beside a couple of Mirela's paintings. If what Caroline had said was true, then old Charlie was probably turning over in his grave, being in such proximity to modern art.

I liked the painting a lot. It was painted from the perspective of someone standing on a wharf, looking down onto the deck of a fishing boat; the fish in the baskets and on the deck were iridescent. The fishermen were dressed in heavy oilcloths and bog boots; one had a wide-brimmed hat on, a wore a gray beard. Hawthorne had caught them just as they were getting ready to haul the fish up onto the pier, and while their expressions weren't very readable, what you could see clearly was the exhaustion in the sagging shoulders, the worry on their brows. He had captured perfectly, exactly, a moment in the fishing-village Provincetown still was when Hawthorne had lived here. I felt, absurdly, a lump in my throat.

Glenn looked like a proud father. "What do you think?" he said, beaming. "I never imagined owning anything like this."

My father looked suitably impressed. Carline leaned closer in, inspecting. "Very nice," she murmured. "Where did you say you bought this?"

"You see," Glenn said to my father, "it was a good deal, after all. Your art broker wants my source!"

"His name is Rhys Whitney," I said. "It's the Whitney Worthington Gallery." You don't get much more WASP-preppie sounding than that, and Rhys lived up to the name. He had a yacht. He wore loafers with no socks. The same casually knotted sweater around his shoulders as Caroline was wearing now. They would probably get along very nicely.

Mirela thought he was an idiot. I refrained from mentioning that part.

"I see," Caroline murmured, still inspecting the painting. The colors alone, I thought, were mesmerizing. If this was an example of Hawthorne's work, then I should probably look for more of it. Maybe I could afford a print on Etsy; they did reproductions.

Glenn glanced at his watch, and she caught the movement and straightened up. "It's a beautiful piece," she said. "But we shouldn't take any more of your time."

My father had an idea; I could see it forming in his face before he even opened his mouth. "Did you say this guy, this Whitney person, has others?" he asked Glenn. Turning to Caroline, he said, "I wouldn't mind something like this."

She smiled and patted his arm. "We'll find you something nice, Stephen," she said, but she said it abstractedly as though her mind were already somewhere else. As though, I thought, she had been doing sums in her head. "Where is this gallery?"

My father glanced at me. "On Commercial Street," I said. Almost everything in Provincetown is on Commercial Street, including the inn itself. "I can show you if you'd like."

"Maybe later," she said with that same distant attention. "Thank you."

We trooped back into the elevator and rode in silence down to the ground floor. "You probably have work to do," Glenn said to me as the doors opened. "I won't keep you any longer."

I can take a hint as quickly as the next girl. "Catch up with you later," I said to my father. "Nice to meet you," I said to Caroline. I didn't say anything to Glenn. What was he so uptight about, anyway? Mike had said it wasn't financial. The inn was thriving. Business was good and looked to remain so for the foreseeable future. It had to be personal.

I just hoped it wasn't personal—with me.

The guilty part of me was already assessing what I might have done wrong. But, seriously, how far wrong can you go when all you do is weddings and other events? I could get anything anyone had asked for: musicians, balloons, limousines. I could manage pagan weddings and Jewish weddings and quick let's-get-this-done-in-five-minutes weddings. I could do it all in my sleep.

I hadn't done anything wrong. I brought a steady stream of income to the inn. People came back for their anniversaries. People sent me flowers, for heaven's sake, and took me to dinner year after year when they returned to town.

What was *wrong?*

***

I inspected my cubbyhole. Nothing to do there. Mike wasn't anywhere in sight, which was unfortunate, as I could generally team up with him on some project or another when I didn't have anything on my docket. I always felt a little guilty pulling a salary on the days when there was absolutely nothing to do. Up until recently, I'd been able to fill in the time trying to keep up with social media for the inn, but last winter, we'd hired an expert to do the heavy lifting there for us, so I couldn't even take refuge online anymore except for doing the wedding-only posts he graciously permitted me to occasionally make.

The inn was ticking away nicely without any help from me. I shrugged and headed out.

Maybe if I couldn't solve the mystery of Glenn's mood swings, I could at least get some information for my father. After all, he had said something about this painting being an investment for my future…

It's true I was an only child, but things hadn't started out that way. When I was eight years old, my teenage sister Alexandra had been kidnapped, a victim of human trafficking, the very thing Ali now investigated and, hopefully, closed down. She and a couple of other girls had managed to escape, and she saved their lives—even though doing it cost Alexandra her own.

For years and years, we hadn't known what had happened to Alex, how she'd died, or where she might be buried until last year. I'd been seeing Ali for a while, and there was another kidnapping, this one here in P'town. I finally told him about Alex—and as my parents were both in town at the time, he was able to observe first-hand their pain and turmoil; without saying anything to me, he launched his own investigation and learned all the details of how and why my sister had died. I guess that's what people call closure. My parents were happy enough with it.

I'd have still preferred to have my sister back in real life, laughing and impetuous, beautiful, spinning around in her thrift-shop eclectic clothes, scarves flying, giggles falling like confetti around her. I couldn't imagine what she'd be up to by now. Living in Finland and getting high on the Northern Lights. Elected a senator in Oregon. Going around the world in a sailboat. Maybe even becoming an artist.

So now there was just me. There had been no children from the ghost; she died before she'd even had a whole lot of boyfriends. None from me, either; Ali and I were pretty sure that, whatever the future held, diapers weren't in it—being godparents to Mirela's daughter Lily had proven to be more than enough for both of us, though we'd never have told Mirela that.

Besides, I wasn't about to duplicate the past.

My family of origin hadn't exactly inspired warm Norman Rockwell images of family life. It wasn't abusive… it was just… well, the thing is, you never stop feeling it when a child dies. No family ever comes through that experience unscathed. Most parents of dead children divorce—there's just too much pain, too much grief, and too much guilt. More than enough blame to go around, even when no blame was warranted.

I had no idea how my parents had managed to hold their marriage together, and sometimes I wondered why they'd bothered; there was always that unspoken conflict between them. Driving in the car, my mother would remove her jacket because she was too warm; my father would respond by turning on the air conditioning, and she'd silently put the jacket back on because now she was too cold. They could go through several iterations of this without saying a word to each other.

I think she never forgave him for not being able to rescue Alexandra, but she never told him what the resentment was about, so he spent a great deal of time trying to make up to her for something that clearly baffled him.

I remember one summer the Harbor Stage Company in Wellfleet put on Bryony Lavery's play called Frozen. There's a mother in it, a woman whose daughter was taken by a pedo-phile and murdered, and the mother says, grieving, "she was my little girl." And the remaining daughter, the one who had the effrontery to stay alive, to keep living, says poignantly, "So was I, Mum."

So was I.

There was never a time when Alex wasn't present in my home, not ever. Never a time when my parents didn't worry and fear what might have happened to her. Never a time when my mother wouldn't suddenly burst into tears or get drunk and bitter on Christmas Eve.

As my father and I tried to decorate the Christmas tree, she'd be saying, "I can't enjoy the holiday without her. . ."

Never a time when Alex's elegantly framed photographs on the grand piano—there were never any of me there—weren't religiously dusted and sighed over. Never a time when I didn't hear the refrain, "if only your sister were here. . ."

Never a time when I didn't feel obscenely inadequate for not being her. She had become a legend in our minds; had she lived, the unspoken family folklore went, she would have been perfect. And if I'm truthful, it's one of the things that drove me away from church and the whole Catholic faith. God had clearly made a mistake and taken the wrong sister, and who can believe in a god who makes mistakes like that?

Sometimes I missed it. The way the liturgy wraps around you, warm and comforting, saying the same words that have been said for centuries around the world. Words that put you into this stream of humanity reaching for the spiritual. The candles, the incense, the chant. The magic of transformation. The sense of this being the world's deepest and most intimate act. There was a lot to miss.

But I'd only been inside a church sporadically as an adult; I just couldn't make that particular leap. St. Peter the Apostle church in P'town was beautiful, airy, and filled with brilliant stained-glass windows reflecting the town's fishing past, but I felt like a hypocrite any time I went there. An intruder. Someone who didn't belong.

It wasn't the church's fault. It wasn't the priests' fault—Father Mick had retired to be succeeded by Father Phil—and I think they'd have been happy to welcome me back into the fold. *Not yet*, a voice inside me said. *Maybe not ever*, I responded to the voice.

And so, in my immediate family, there was no one left but me. I'll confess, I've never given much thought to what I might inherit when my parents died—I've always been too wrapped up in my own life choices to worry a lot about theirs—but now it seemed there might be a Hawthorne included.

Hopefully, not for a very long time. I may complain about my parents—well, okay, complain about my *mother*—but that doesn't mean I want to hasten their demise. Just as I'm all they've got, they're all I've got.

Besides, I couldn't quite see a Hawthorne gracing the off-off-off-white wall above the Little Shop of Horrors sofa in my tiny apartment. It was a little too much for the imagination.

Ali had informed me he had to work all day, so I did the next thing that occurred to me and headed out to find Mirela. She wasn't at her studio painting—when will I learn to text someone and find out whether they're available before deciding to go find them?—and I knew the nanny was taking care of Lily, so Mirela was probably doing her stint at the gallery; in Provincetown, it's the custom for artists being represented to pick up a shift or two on the sales side as well. Collectors like it; they get to chat with the artist whose work they're (hopefully!) buying, and the artists get whatever it is artists pick up from their audience.

The Whitney Worthington Gallery is in the East End, only a few blocks away from the inn. Rhys represents his own work, Mirela's, another Bulgarian artist named Iskren Something-or-other, and is co-owner with Joshua Worthington, another WASP-y artist who does Daliesque representations of oysters. I kid you not: canvas after canvas after canvas of oysters. Just oysters. And people love it.

I'll never understand art.

But this was also where Glenn had gotten his Hawthorne, and it looked like Caroline had some interest in checking it out—*and* if she was getting one for my father, then it wouldn't hurt for me to check out the situation ahead of time, either.

Admit it, Riley: you're just really bored.

Mirela was alone in the gallery, sitting behind an elegant table (high-end galleries would never be so crass as to have a sales counter and point-of-sale machine, this is about Art with a capital A), scrolling through her phone. "Hello, sunshine," she said. "I do not remember you are coming to the gallery today." Mirela thinks "sunshine" is a term of endearment. I've never been able to disabuse her of that notion.

"Well, I didn't exactly make an appointment," I said. "Thought you might be glad to see me."

"Have you brought me chocolate?"

"No."

She shrugged. "Then how happy can I be to see you?" She sighed and tossed the phone down. "I believe I will divorce my daughter," she said.

"I don't think that's a thing," I said slowly. I was looking around, hoping to see a Hawthorne. In this gallery of primal colors (and the occasional primal scream), he'd stand out like a… well, I didn't know what. But something. Definitely something.

She saw me looking and arched her perfectly shaped eyebrows. "Are you interested in depictions of oysters?" she asked politely.

I shook my head. "Not particularly. Though if you had any *clams*, well, that would be another story."

"One mollusk," she said, "is just as bad as the next one."

"Not if you're another mollusk." I was staring at a large canvas, beautifully framed. The oysters in this one seemed to be floating on some sort of background. The sea, the air, who knew?

Mirela sighed. "Sydney. What is it you are here for?"

I pulled up another chair. "Yes, thank you, I think I will sit down," I said. "My father has decided he wants to buy art," I said.

She raised her eyebrows. "Something of mine?" she asked.

"You're a little too avant-garde for his tastes, I'm afraid." When she first came to town, Mirela painted fishing boats and sunsets over flooded marshes. Within two years, she was doing extraordinary abstracts that screamed, laughed, and wept. I don't like modern art very much. There's nothing about abstract expressionism that makes sense to me—I've seen Rothko's stuff, and, seriously?

Rectangles on rectangles?—but even I felt my pulse quicken when I looked at one of Mirela's pieces. They grab your heart and your soul and don't let you go.

In my own defense, I'm not the only person who doesn't get what avant-garde art is trying to tell me. Not very long ago, a curator in Germany discovered a Mondrian piece had been hanging upside-down for seventy-five years. None of the art critics who looked at it during those years knew the difference—in fact, they all pointed out to each other how clever was the "skyline" of New York City supposedly portrayed in the painting. (It's a collection of lines. Colorful lines, sure. Some are thicker than others, okay. But at the end of the day, it's still just lines.)

That particular story did afford me a moment or two of schadenfreude when I read about it in The Guardian; it helps dismiss the popularity and astronomical price tags of abstract art. But beyond the hilarity, there is another message about the nature of art itself. The Guardian had also informed me that when aesthetes gathered in Sotheby's in 2018 to see the auction of Girl With Balloon by Banksy, they were shocked to witness the piece self-destruct once it had been purchased—it included a built-in shredder, courtesy of the artist. The entire story—the collectors' reactions, the joke, the new astronomical price tag—was itself a powerful work of performance art.

It's a reminder, of course, that there's no right answer when it comes to art; it means something different not just for different people but also different times, depending on any century's given knowledge. Enduring works of art can be transformed—or possibly stay alive, even when they've been torn to pieces.

But my parents were both definitely in the figurative art camp. No Banksy for them. "He's hired an art broker," I said now to Mirela.

She nodded. "Someone to take his money," she said. "That is how it works. What is it he wants to buy?"

"Well, now, that's the thing," I said. "He didn't really know—I think he's paying her for educating him as much as he is for finding him something—and then Glenn came in and said he had a Charles Hawthorne painting, and he took us upstairs and showed it to us. And then, as soon as he saw it, my father decided he wants one, too." I paused. "Funny thing is, though, Glenn said the Hawthorne came from *here*. From the Whitney Worthington. But you guys don't do dead painters."

"At the rate my daughter is going, that will soon describe me," Mirela said. She caught my expression and relented. "Yes, all right, I know this piece. It is fishermen just in the harbor, yes? With the fish on the deck of the boat, all silver and shining?"

It was a decent enough description. I nodded.

She shrugged, picked up her phone again, frowned, and tossed it back onto the table. "Rhys always is looking for the next new thing," she said.

"You're kidding, right?" I said. "Are we talking about the same Charles Hawthorne? Hate to tell you this, Mirela, but he hasn't been a new thing since—oh, I don't know, 1920?"

"A new thing in *business*," she said firmly. "That is what is interesting to Rhys. The next new thing in selling art. In making money. And in—fame, fame in the art world. It is something very important to suddenly discover a cache of paintings by a famous artist." She paused. "Paintings nobody even knew existed," she added.

I finally caught the tone, then, belatedly. "Hang on," I said. "Is *this* that thing you were worried about? The unintended consequences thing?"

She was looking past me into the street. A male couple had paused outside the gallery and were looking at the oysters on display in the window, having what appeared to be an animated conversation about them. How do you have an animated conversation about a painting of oysters? "There is no reason to think there is anything wrong with that painting," she said obliquely.

"And the others?"

She looked back at me then, and I saw worry in her eyes. "What others?"

"You just said yourself there was a cache of paintings," I pointed out. "Is there anything wrong with the rest of them? I mean… are they all authentic?" That had to be the thing. I didn't know much about art, but I was finally starting to catch on, and it's true: once you slowed down to think about it, it did seem— well, *fortuitous*—to find a bunch of paintings by an artist who… "You don't think they're genuine," I said suddenly, accusing her.

She was back to looking at the street. Maybe she wanted to be sure we weren't overheard, ready to change the conversation should anyone come in. "I have no reason," she said carefully, "to believe they are not."

"Come on, Mirela, it's me," I said impatiently. "You're not in a court of law here, no-one else is listening. Tell me!"

She rounded on me. "Tell you what?" she demanded. "This has nothing to do with you. This is not one of your mystery investigations, Sydney."

"Don't you *want* to know?" I asked. I was feeling slightly hurt that she'd snapped at me like that. "Doesn't it matter if your gallery owner is selling questionable paintings? You can't be scared Rhys will close the shop and leave you high and dry? Seriously, Mirela, it's not like you don't have job security. The other galleries in town would *line up* to represent you! You're not married to this guy or to whatever it is you think he's doing for you. And if there really is something criminal going on here—"

"Stop." Her voice was low. "Stop now. You cannot do this. You know nothing about the art world. And this is not your business."

Both of which were true, obviously, but it was equally true that knowing nothing about a subject area and said subject area being none of my business had ever stood in my way in the past. "I'm not going to let my father buy something that's—a forgery," I said.

There: the word was finally out.

"And do you think *I* would?" she countered. "It is nothing, Sydney. It is a feeling I have, but it is nothing more than that. Rhys has provenance—provenance means there is a written record of where the paintings were, always, starting with Charles Hawthorne and finishing here. He is convinced they are genuine. And your father's assistant—"

"—art broker," I corrected. I was a little miffed she'd felt she had to define provenance to me. I may not know a lot about the art world, but I am in a general way pretty literate.

"Okay, yes, art broker, she will be sure to look into it also. She will earn the money your father pays her. You do not understand, Sydney: no one wants their reputation ruined. In this world, the reputation, it is everything. It would be the end of a gallery. It *has* been the end of a gallery."

"Okay, but—"

"Go and look it up," she said quickly. "Look up the Knoedler Gallery. See what happens there." She was hissing the sibilants, which meant she was upset.

"Why don't you give me the Reader's Digest version," I suggested.

She sighed impatiently. Mirela doesn't suffer fools gladly; I sometimes wonder why she puts up with me. "The Knoedler and Company gallery in New York City," she said. "The oldest, the most trusted, the most venerable, the most important gallery on the east coast. The director was approached by an individual who had access to a number of painters' work—Rothko, Pollack, I am not sure who else. The gallery sold the paintings on to art collectors. For eighty million dollars."

"They were all fakes?" This was fascinating.

"On one of the pieces," said Mirela scornfully, "the artist doing the paintings *misspelled* the real artist's name in the signature. That was what you would say is an insult in your face, I think. It was very arrogant, of course. They were sneering at the art world. They thought people would be stupid." She shrugged. "Perhaps they were right. They did trick a lot of people, important people, people who should have known better. People who overlooked the arrogance."

"It's hard to believe," I said.

"It ruined the gallery," she said. "After nearly two centuries in existence, it closed overnight. There was a sensational trial, but it ended with a settlement, so we do not know what the outcome might have been. But either way, the gallery was no more."

That had come out way too smoothly; she had too much information and knew too many details. I narrowed my eyes. "You've been looking this up," I said.

"I only want to have my own heart at peace," she said.

She wouldn't have taken the time to look it up if she hadn't been worried; heart at peace or not, Mirela doesn't believe in wasting time. Either something was badly wrong, or something had made her think it was.

"So you're saying what happened at this New York gallery couldn't happen here. You're saying Rhys wouldn't want to jeopardize the Whitney Worthington," I said. "He'd never pass on a fake—if he knew it *was* one."

She nodded. "And, Sydney, I do think he would know. Rhys is smarter than he seems to be. At least he is smart in his world, in the professional world. His father was an art dealer; this is in his blood. He was looking at paintings and learning from them when he was a child. He is himself an artist. He has a degree in art restoration. He would not be fooled by a signature." She sighed. "But it is a difficult thing, do you see? After everything that happened at the Knoedler, and some other galleries, and even Christie's auction house in London—because it sold a fake van Gogh to some Japanese investors, you probably know about that also—well, no one wishes to put their name to authenticate something at all questionable. Too many reputations are at stake for that."

"That's not true," I protested. "There's even a show on YouTube called… um… oh, right, that's it, Find Your Fortune, Fortune or Fake, I don't know, something like that? These two art experts are running around authenticating hidden treasures, stuff from people's attics or Great-Aunt Sarah, or even from eBay, pieces like that. And there are apparently a lot of them if you can believe the show. It's sort of a high-end artsy Antiques Roadshow." I only knew all this thanks to a bout with the flu the previous winter when I'd sat in bed with my laptop, and YouTube was my only entertainment. "They're constantly proving paintings or statues are genuine."

"That is *television*," Mirela said with an air of finality as though that settled it. "It is not the real world."

"Hmm." I was finding myself more and more interested, despite knowing next to nothing about art. I needed to go beyond Fake or Fortune—that was the name, Fake or Fortune—of course, that was for beginners. And while I may have acquired a certain local reputation as a solver of mysteries, they most often have involved, at some level or another, a corpse.

Maybe it would be fun to do something else. Become an art sleuth. Why not?

Mirela was looking at me. "Do not think what you are thinking," she said.

"I'm not thinking anything."

But of course I was.

4

I found Ali making sandwiches in the galley kitchen. "I knew you'd be back as soon as I got the food out," he said. "You must have food radar. Cheese and tomato?"

"Sure." I flopped down in the armchair, avoiding the sofa. I didn't have two hours to spend extricating myself from its clutches. "You're not going to believe how I spent my morning."

"Looking into art fraud?" He put the plate on the coffee table in front of me. "Chips?"

"Okay: either you've developed psychic abilities, or Mirela called you," I said.

He nodded, leaning over to shake Cape Cod Potato Chips from the bag onto my plate. "It was Mirela," he said, fetching his own sandwich and bringing over one of the kitchen chairs to sit on; we both tend to leave the sofa for slow, peaceful evenings. I may occasionally solve mysteries, but I'm half-convinced one of these days, I'll find a body trapped in the sofa's clutches, someone who died struggling to get out. "You have her worried," said Ali.

"I have *her* worried? I'm the one whose father might be buying a fake. In fact, I'm the one who works for the guy who maybe did buy a fake." I took a bite. It was perfect. Ali always puts exactly the right amount of mayonnaise on his sandwiches. And some sort of herb. He had to have been a short-order cook in a previous life.

"That's something of a jump at this stage, isn't it?" He took a bite of his sandwich, chewing as he reflected. "I don't know much about this Hawthorne guy, but isn't it possible this is just what Glenn said? Maybe it really is that simple. After all, you're always hearing of masterpieces being discovered in some obscure place, stuff that disappeared into private collections and then came to light later?"

"Maybe." I dabbed at my mouth with a napkin. I was liking the counterfeit theory more and more, though even I had to admit I had absolutely no evidence for believing it. Besides, I wasn't the one who was worried. Mirela was worried, and Mirela doesn't worry easily; she has a phlegmatic approach to life.

Maybe that was something you learned in Eastern Europe. "I think it's what Mirela was talking about yesterday, you know, when she wanted to ask you a question and then didn't."

He nodded. "Yeah, it is. She said so. She's concerned about the gallery. She thinks a lot of people could get hurt—that's what she meant by unintended consequences. She asked me to look into it in a professional capacity."

"*Can* you?"

He laughed. "Mirela seems to be laboring under the misconception that law enforcement is just one big happy family, a well-oiled machinery that communicates seamlessly together and cooperates fully," he said. "That would be the joke of the year if it weren't so unfortunate. But even if it were true, and it's not, but if it were, I still couldn't help her. This isn't exactly my department. It's not even my agency's department. We don't do anything that's vaguely *related* to art fraud." He caught my look. "Come on, Sydney. We're Immigration and Customs Enforcement, remember? Closest *we* have to something like that is the unit that returns pilfered artifacts to the countries we—the U.S., that is—um—stole them from. It's called the Cultural Property and Antiquities Investigations section. I do know someone there, but I haven't been able to get hold of him yet."

Whether or not he'd meant to do it, he'd effectively sidetracked my thoughts. I am the queen of rabbit holes. "Oh, right, aren't they the ones who returned all those artifacts Americans took out of Iraq after invading it?" I occasionally enjoy reminding Ali I'm not quite as patriotic America-can-do-no-wrong as he is.

He looked pained. "Yes," he admitted, "but they also track down forgeries on occasion."

I let him off the hook. "Tough job," I commented. "People who work there must have to spend all their time apologizing to other countries. Oh, sorry, we didn't mean to wander off with those priceless statues and tribal masks; they just got into our suitcases by accident. So, so sorry."

"What you want," said Ali, ignoring me and getting back to essentials, "is another mystery." There was the smallest glimmer of amusement in his eyes.

I rose to the bait, of course. "Wait, what? You don't think *I* should—"

"No. I don't think you should. That's the point. This isn't one of your sleuthing opportunities. I think you have a whole lot of nothing here. Nothing," he repeated frankly.

"No one has identified Glenn's painting as a fake or a copy. No one but you and Mirela, and her only vaguely, has raised any questions about the Whitney Worthington or about its owner." He shot me a quick look undergirded by amusement. "Well, except the fashion police would have a field day with Rhys, but that's not under federal jurisdiction. I'm straight, and even *I* know cravats aren't the thing anymore."

I didn't laugh. "But Mirela—"

"Mirela is worried. And maybe she should be worried, and maybe she's just blown something innocent out of proportion. It wouldn't be the first time; she's close to the gallery, she has her own issues, and she might be going off on a tangent. Remember that she hasn't offered any evidence, just a feeling. Either way, it's not your job to find out. There are people who do this sort of thing. Professionally." He stood up and took his plate over to the sink. "Not," he added, "people who had to look up Charles Webster Hawthorne's name on Wikipedia."

I made a face. "So what do I tell my father?"

He switched off the water and turned to face me, leaning back against the sink, drying his hands with the dishtowel before flipping it over his shoulder. "You tell your father nothing," he said. "He's hired a professional to teach him what he needs to know. He's done the right thing, and it's none of your business. Unless you think his expert is in cahoots with your mythical forger."

"You never know," I said defensively.

"You're bored," he said cheerfully. "You're not loving your job; you're looking for something exciting to do. "

"I don't *hate* my job," I objected halfheartedly. Well, maybe. Some days.

"Yeah, but you don't love it anymore, either. You know it, I know it, but that's between you and Glenn. And I'm happy to help you figure out what you want to do about your professional future if you'd like to have that conversation. But I promise you, the answer isn't to invent another mystery out of whole cloth."

"Or whole art canvas, as the case may be." I was even smiling a little.

"As the case may be." He winked.

My phone vibrated, and I scowled at it. "Text from my father," I said. "Dinner tonight." I looked up at Ali. "So maybe all shall be revealed," I said.

"Good place to start," said Ali with enthusiasm. He liked Adrienne the diva chef's creations as much as did my father.

I joined him at the sink and rinsed my plate. His laptop was open on the table, papers in piles around it. "Work okay?"

He shrugged. "Is it ever?"

"Can you talk about it?" He couldn't always. In fact, most of the time, he couldn't. He'd gone on undercover investigations when I hadn't even known what continent he was on. He didn't take the kind of business trip where you send postcards and from which you bring back presents.

He sighed. "Why not? It's not a particular secret anymore. It's a new-ish scam that's kind of romance-meets-cryptocurrency."

I raised my eyebrows. "Sounds like a promising if weird beginning," I said.

He ignored me. "Say some guy connects with you on WhatsApp, and you fall for him. You end up telling him a whole lot more than you should about yourself and your life, and especially your financial status. Then he gets you to invest in some new cryptocurrency platform he's been associated with, tells you he's made a lot of money there and wants to share with you, and you invest, and abracadabra, you make some money. You're both excited. So he gets you to invest again, and you lose a little money, but the next time you make some, and overall you're doing well. Plus, you're really liking the guy. You can see where this is going."

"I didn't know people still fell for that. It's a step up from the Nigerian prince, but. . ."

"He's better than they were," says Ali. "That was old-school. These people spent a lot of time researching and developing these scripts. They spent a lot of time studying the psychology of potential marks." The propane heater let out a series of loud bangs, which happened anytime the temperature in the room changed and the metal expanded or retracted. He waited until it was done before continuing. "So now you're in deep. You're starting to say you really want to meet him in real life because, like I said, you've fallen for him. And he needs one more investment, maybe a lot bigger one because this time it's an even better opportunity and he's already proven he can deliver the goods, and plus maybe his boss has said that after this he can take a nice long vacation."

"With me," I said, nodding.

"With you," Ali confirmed. "So maybe this one last big investment goes through, and it's a bust, or maybe he finds out your financial well is dry—anyway, something happens, and suddenly from one day to the next, you find out the platform's fraudulent, the guy you've fallen in love with never actually existed, and your money's all gone."

I was thinking about all these lonely people who hitched their wagon to a star that was burning way too bright. "Damn. The world's full of scams, isn't it? Fake paintings, cryptocurrency."

"You don't know about the fake paintings," he said, shaking his head. "I, on the other hand, do know about cryptocurrency."

A thought occurred to me. "But this isn't your beat either, is it?" When I first met Ali, he was investigating fake marriages for ICE, which meant that (in my book, anyway) he wasn't particularly one of the good guys. With all the bad things going on in the world, seriously, just leave the people who just want to get married alone. There are a lot worse reasons for marriage than merely obtaining a route to citizenship. I like to think it's my influence that got him to transfer into ICE's human trafficking division.

Though on the flip side, it's a lot more dangerous than checking up on green cards.

"We're cooperating," he said. He sounded tired. "The whole duped victim and online predator is as old as the internet, yeah. Older, in fact. But there's more to it than that, a lot more damaging to more people, actually, and that's where I come in."

"How? How did you get connected to cryptocurrency?" The truth was, I didn't have even the vaguest notion of what cryptocurrency was. I knew it had been in the news a lot, and some major versions of it had tanked, but that was about all. I have a hard enough time understanding my own checking account.

Ali got that voice, the one he gets when he's trying to distance himself from something terrible. I'd heard it a lot of times before, and I winced every time. "The industry's propped up by thousands of people trapped in forced labor and violence." He looked uneasily at the sofa and chose his same straight chair instead. "This is a situation where there's enough pain to go around. The victims aren't just on one side of the computer screen."

"What does that mean?"

"That fellow posing as your new excellent boyfriend? Chances are amazingly good he's been trafficked. People get lured into jobs, and some of them aren't even lured at all; some of them are recruited, which usually is a euphemism for being kidnapped. Generally, they're taken somewhere where they can be isolated, it's far from home, they don't know anybody, they're hungry, they haven't had any sleep—"

"I get the picture," I said. I really didn't want to.

"Okay," said Ali. "So now they're put to work. It's really no different from sex trafficking. Just a different commodity. The process is the same."

"Holy shit," I breathed. Every time I get a glimpse into Ali's murky world, I realize yet again how lucky I am. There but for the grace of God… a God I wasn't yet sure I believed in, because—again—if He were out there somewhere, He shouldn't have been allowing stuff like this to happen.

I took a deep breath and found to my surprise my hands were trembling slightly. "What are you doing about it?"

"Dealing with jurisdictional politics," he said shortly. "Traditionally, most of the call centers, these compounds, they're in Southeast Asia—Myanmar, Laos, Cambodia, countries with a lot of poverty and a lot of violence. ICE can advise, and we've been doing that, sending cyber experts over there—and there are a lot of good people on the other end, people setting up safe houses in places like Phnom Penh, getting these people out and keeping them safe, returning them home when they can, that kind of thing. It's not enough, but it's something. We're trying to get security services in these countries to take a little more interest, too, but they're all understaffed, and it's not as high a priority as some of the other stuff they're focusing on. I get that; believe me when I tell you some of that other stuff makes this pale by comparison. But it's spreading—and now we're starting to see it here, too." He shrugged. "In the US, they're often connected in some way to the cult scene, possibly some of the more out-there conspiracy groups, places that—again—have isolated compounds and guards and people watching all the time. We're liaising with the FBI about that."

That made sense: there was always communication between cult deprogrammers and the FBI and ICE. As it turns out, not everyone is totally on board with being part of the next Jonestown or Waco.

"We hate jurisdictional politics," I said.

"We hate jurisdictional politics," he agreed with a wan smile.

I pushed myself off the sink. "I'll leave you to it, then," I said. "Dinner's at six-thirty."

"I'll be there." Ali's never late for one of Adrienne the diva chef's meals. Nor, come to think of it, is anyone else.

Ever.

I put on a sweater—there was a reason the heater had been banging away— and went back to the inn, mostly on the premise that looking like I was working would both give me something to do and possibly assuage whatever beast was bothering Glenn. Though he'd seemed quite his old self when he was showing us the Hawthorne. Maybe art does have a soothing effect on people, after all.

I took the open door of Mike's office as an invitation and strolled in. "Aha," I said. "I have bearded the lion in its lair."

He looked up at me over the sheaf of invoices he'd been counting. "What?"

"I've always wanted to use that expression."

He was trying not to smile. "So happy I could make your dreams come true, Sydney," he said, his eyes back on the stack of papers.

I flopped down in one of the two client chairs facing his desk, uninvited. "Glenn bought a painting by Charles Hawthorne," I said.

"I know." He tossed the invoices down, clasped his hands behind his head, and leaned back in his chair. He was getting a five o'clock shadow at two in the afternoon but was still quite good-looking. I seem to have surrounded myself with handsome men. "About an hour ago, he had me order tickets for him to some gallery show next month in New York," he said.

"He's into *art* now?" I'd noticed this phenomenon before: once you start getting interested in something, it's all you see or hear for a while; it seems to be everywhere around you. Think of an elephant, and suddenly everyone's talking about elephants, or so it seems. Our brains create patterns, I reminded myself, where often there were none. But still...

Aside from everything else, it just didn't seem like Glenn's thing. Not that people shouldn't develop new interests, but this was way, way out of what I perceived as his comfort zone. Business, yes; nightclubs, sure; eating out, hell, yeah... but culture? Not so much. "So if he's traveling to see stuff, then this isn't just one painting he likes," I said slowly. "It's more than that. Is he looking to become a collector?"

And if so, why would that put him in such a bad mood? Hobbies are supposed to make you feel *better*, aren't they?

"Based on a little more information than we had this morning, I rather think," said Mike, his voice deliberately expressionless, "that he's collecting the collector."

"Oh." We looked at each other for a moment in total understanding. I knew we were both thinking of Barry, Glenn's longtime partner and the previous owner of the Race Point Inn—until he was murdered right here on the premises, a fact we tend not to share with our guests—and Glenn generously and in Barry's memory left his own life in Chicago behind and took up where his boyfriend had left off. He'd had some romantic liaisons over the past years, but nothing serious. No reason to think this one, or anyone, would be.

Except, perhaps, for the Hawthorne now hanging in the penthouse. However much he'd paid for it, the amount wasn't trivial. Maybe not in the Old Masters' league, but not from one of the tourist-oriented art shacks on the pier, either. And you don't spend that kind of money unless you're serious about something... or somebody.

"Okay," I said. "Come clean. Tell me."

"He's booked two trips to Amsterdam this fall," said Mike. "One's coming up in a few days, actually. But he's not staying at any hotels."

"Sounds promising. What else?"

"What am I, Glenn's social secretary?"

"You're Glenn's manager and right-hand-man," I said soothingly. "Besides, nothing happens at the Race Point you don't know about."

"Flattery," said Mike, "will get you everywhere. Okay. He gets up early to make phone calls. And I mean early. Like even before six."

Getting up early is not generally a hallmark of innkeepers in P'town. Not in the summer, anyway, when there's so much nightlife going on, guests coming in late, impromptu after-parties around the pool or in one of the bars. "Early phone calls," I said, considering the information. "Have you been listening in?"

He gave me a look. "Sweetie. You think *I'm* here at six o'clock in the morning?" he asked incredulously. "I'm not even at the *gym* at six o'clock in the morning." He shook his head. "Gloria told me." Gloria was the breakfast and brunch equivalent of a maître d'; she and Martin shared lunch duties, and dinner was all his.

"Okay, then, what did she say? Who's he calling?"

"She doesn't eavesdrop," he said. "At least, not intentionally."

"How disappointing."

He flashed me a smile. "Isn't it? But she did get a name. André."

"André," I said pensively. "French?"

Mike shrugged. "I did ask around after we talked," he admitted. "But really, you know as much as I know."

"I doubt that," I said. "But your money's on a new boyfriend, isn't it? So you're probably right. Someone named André who lives in Amsterdam and is involved in the art world." I twisted a strand of my hair around a finger. "Still, it's no reason to be in such a foul mood. Even the bartenders have noticed."

"Are you kidding?" said Mike. The bartenders are always the *first* to notice. They're our canaries in the coal mine. And, anyway, there's more. The *on-dit* around the bazaars is that he's been taking classes at the PAAM and going on The Stroll." Friday nights, from five to ten o'clock in-season, all the galleries throw open their doors. They do opening receptions. They offer wine and canapés. They sell a lot of art. "And when I went into his office an hour ago, I noticed—well, I suppose I hadn't been paying attention before, you know how it is—anyway, I noticed he's been collecting books. Big books, expensive, and all about art, from publishers like Phaidon and Tate and Thames & Hudson." He paused. "It's as if he's giving himself an education. And one really can't imagine him going to those lengths for anyone who isn't a serious interest."

I nodded. "Enter the mysterious André. Good work, detective," I said.

"We aim to please."

We fell silent for a moment, the lighthearted banter dissolving slowly in the air between us. I swallowed. "If he's seeing this guy, and we're not, then it's not likely to involve the inn, is it?" I asked. "I mean, if it were going to affect us, we'd have met this André guy, right? He'd be around; he'd come stay here and hang out. Right?" I paused. "Or maybe Glenn's just going to sell the inn like we were afraid he'd do last time and go live in Europe." I suddenly felt like I couldn't breathe. I might be bored with my work, but that was a far cry from the thought of losing the Race Point. Damn this André, anyway.

"You are the only person I know who can go from zero to one hundred on the anxiety scale in seconds flat," Mike said. "Jumping to conclusions in a single bound."

"And you're not? Tell me you aren't worried about the future!" It was indeed worrisome, mostly because of the recent corporate presence in town. Inns were moving from the "labor of love" category into the "how much money can we make for our shareholders" category, and it was scary. Even a venerable tourist bar had been snapped up by some LLC;

when a well-known guesthouse was sold to another corporation, the koi in the pond outside—venerable in their own right—had all suddenly died.

"I'm worried about the future, sure," Mike said now. "But not ours. Not the Race Point. We have a good team here. We have the town's only Michelin-rated restaurant. Even you bring in a lot of trade, Sydney, in your own little way."

"Thanks ever so much."

"You're welcome. The point is, Glenn knows all that. He wouldn't sell out. Remember, we went through this before? He said he'd always be honest with us."

"That was then," I said darkly. "This is now."

"Stop it," Mike said. "Whatever is happening is going to happen whether you know about it or not. There's nothing you can do. Glenn has a right to a life and a right to be happy with someone if that's what he wants. And a right to tell us about it or not tell us about it."

I didn't say anything; I was thinking absolutely unworthy thoughts. *Sure*, I prodded myself. *Glenn has a right to happiness as long as it doesn't interfere with mine. Nice sentiments, Riley. Very caring, you are.* "I wish everything didn't have to change," I finally said. I sounded small. I was feeling small. *Breathe, Riley. Just breathe.*

"Well," said Mike, "here's an idea: whatever changes are in the pipeline, it's maybe time you and I got to know a little about art. To keep up with things." He sighed. "You know, this could just be a—a hobby kind of thing for a while. An enthusiasm. And maybe Glenn's just looking to fill the inn with art, which wouldn't actually be such a bad idea." A bird landed outside the window and complained noisily about something, then flew away, up over the lamppost. "Something will reveal itself eventually. It always does."

"That's very Zen of you."

He looked a little surprised. "Well, not Zen." There was a long pause. He cleared his throat. "Catholic, actually. I've been going— I've gone back to Mass. After all these years." He was watching me, waiting for a reaction; he knew I'd grown up Catholic, too.

Now *there* was a topic I wasn't willing to re-open anytime in the near future. I had my own feelings about how lapsed a Catholic I might have become. "Whatever," I said fatuously.

He nodded as though my response had confirmed something, and leafed idly through his appointment book. "Best thing we can do is wait and see."

"Well, turns out I've got nothing but time," I said. "Speaking of which, do you have anything for me to do?"

He glanced up. "Weddings?"

"Scheduled, arranged, planned, and close to execution," I said. "Also, the fiftieth birthday thing next week with two hundred people. Also, the retirement party for Elise over at the bank. I've okayed the design of the new pamphlets. I've kept up with my blog posts and done my wedding social media every day, religiously. Point is, I'm dedicated. I'm also going out of my mind here, Mike. You've got to help me out."

"Your boyfriend's here; your father's in town," said Mike. "Sounds like the perfect time to ease up a little. Just enjoy. You've earned it."

"We all have." It had been a killer season, though not in the way that would have interested Sydney Riley, wedding planner, and sleuth-dealing-with-downtime. Just busy as hell, the streets thronged with tourists, the inns and restaurants and clubs filled to the brim. Just the usual summer madness, not the adventures I occasionally found here.

The truth was, I hadn't set out to be Provincetown's answer to Miss Marple… or Jessica Fletcher… or any of the single ladies out there solving startling crimes in deceptively small and quaint villages. My crime-stopper career had, in fact, all started with Barry, my erstwhile boss and devoted friend, the fine summer day I'd gone for an early-morning swim and found his body floating in the inn's pool.

Granted, that experience (which I still occasionally re-live in my dreams when other monsters take a night off) wouldn't have set most people off on a career of detection—it probably would have sent *most* people running off to their therapists, come to think of it, since I'd actually physically brushed up against his corpse, but you have to understand: I adored Barry.

I'd met him when I was at my most vulnerable, very soon after my then-husband announced pretty much out of the blue he'd found someone he wanted to be with instead of me. I hadn't seen that one coming, though I'd later done more than one drunken postmortem on the marriage and realized I could have known if I'd known what to look for.

But how could I have known what to look for when I didn't know I should be looking for anything? I'd thought we were happy.

I was scared and hurt and felt like the floor had just fallen out of my life, and walked into the lobby of the Race Point Inn completely by accident, though Barry always maintained it wasn't accidental at all; it was *Meant To Be.* Some hidden compass in my psyche had pointed me toward P'town. It's how most of us arrived here, to tell the truth—the washashores, as they call us, people who came here from somewhere else for a whole host of reasons we might not even have been all that aware of… and never left.

You don't end up in Provincetown accidentally. It calls to you—its summer splendor and its winter starkness, its history and its present and its future, and for some of us, there's no way to let go. We have to be here.

Within a month, I had adopted a cat — Ibsen—and moved lock, stock, and barrel (or at least whatever I could fit in my Honda, known forevermore as the Little Green Car) to the Cape. Barry had found me a tiny place to live, hired me as a wedding planner and events coordinator even though I'd never done anything of the sort before, and generally helped me rebuild my life—except I wasn't really rebuilding anything.

I was re-creating myself from scratch. We're kind of famous for enabling people to do that here in Provincetown. Some people, especially in the Bad Old Days of the AIDS epidemic, have come here to die; but many more came here to be reborn. To find something they'd thought was lost. To find home, even.

My mother thought the whole wedding planning stuff was excellent—she's constitutionally unable to imagine any kind of happiness outside of walks down the aisle and had started trying to set me up with potential suitors when the ink wasn't even yet dry on my divorce papers.

And then I met Ali, a second-generation Lebanese Muslim who worked in law enforcement, who hadn't exactly measured up in her eyes—she referred to him as "that man" and clearly hoped he'd go away—but time passed, and then, of course, he gave her closure around my sister Alexandra, and suddenly he became a real person to her. She's never apologized to either of us, naturally; that would be asking a little too much. But she was generally more sympathetic and had, thank God, stopped telling me about every eligible male in what felt like the whole of New England but was actually only any suddenly single offspring of other inhabitants of her social circles.

And she had a *lot* of social circles.

After I helped solve Barry's murder, it seemed somehow any crime committed in town ended up having some connection to me—even to the point of my literally tripping over a body one cold December evening a few years back. And let's face it, I loved what I did at the inn, and I loved my town, but the truth was my brain wasn't fully engaged until I discovered that curiosity and persistence really solve crimes—and that I had plenty of each.

Or maybe I was just a dead-body magnet. That's what Julie, my friend in the police department, seemed to believe. Ali thought I was at the very least practicing to become one myself—well, okay, there had been a few scary moments over the years, but I had generally managed to avoid death, usually with a lot of help from my friends. The Beatles would have been proud.

My phone vibrated in my pocket, and I frowned at the display. "My mother," I groaned.

"Take it," Mike advised. "Best thing could've happened. It'll distract you. Close the door on your way out."

"That a hint?"

"It's a requirement."

Outside his office, I swiped the phone. "Hey, Ma."

She wasted no time with pleasantries. "Sydney! Thank God you answered! Can you please tell me what on earth your father thinks he's doing?"

Breathe, Riley. I always feel like a panic attack is seconds away when I'm talking with my mother. *Just breathe.* I let a couple of beats go by before I answered. "I don't know. What do *you* think he thinks he's doing?"

"Don't take a tone with me, Sydney Riley. You know I hate it when you take a tone."

"I'm not taking a tone, Ma." Of course, I was taking a tone.

"Of course you are," she snapped. "I don't have time for this. Your aunt can barely spare me, and there are far too many things to do here." She made it sound like she was boiling water and applying compresses, a regular Florence Nightingale. I knew better. My aunt lives in a large house on six acres and employs half the town—cleaning ladies, a part-time gardener, someone who came in and cooked. Based on past experience, my mother hadn't broken so much as a fingernail, much less a sweat, since she'd been there.

I sighed. "He's thinking about investing in art," I said.

"Don't be silly. We've never talked about *art.*" She said it in the same way she'd have said, *we've never talked about sadomasochism.* "And, besides, if he were serious, he'd be in Zurich or Paris, not Provincetown."

"We're the oldest continuous art colony in North America, Ma," I said, immediately on the defensive. She does that to me a lot. And when I get on the defensive, I start sounding like a tour director. "Jackson Pollock was here. And—um—Robert Motherwell. And a whole lot of others." Whose names I couldn't immediately bring to mind.

"Your father knows better than to bring any of *that* sort of thing into our house," she said dismissively. Mirela had once given my parents one of her smaller abstract works for Christmas. It would probably have sold for ten thousand dollars. My mother had banished it to my father's study.

"I think he's keeping an open mind," I said. *You could try that, too.* But I didn't say it.

"Well, I think it's ridiculous. And that art person, that woman—"

"Caroline," I supplied.

"Yes, well, whatever her name is, I hope she doesn't talk him into buying anything we'll all regret. There *is* such a thing as buyer's remorse, you know."

Well, yeah, but just generally not occurring *before* one makes the purchase. Still, it was somehow charming, I thought, that while my mother was excoriating my father over a woman, she didn't for an instant think there was a chance he was behaving improperly. Like I said, I don't know what their magic marriage formula is; but however they managed it, it certainly never fails to impress me.

She wasn't finished. "You know how your father can be."

Mostly, "how my father can be" translated into him letting her do all the talking, savoring the newspaper and a glass of good Scotch, and once in a blue moon digging his heels in over something my mother would remind him of for the following six months. "I just think he's getting interested in art," I said mildly. "It's good to have a new hobby, Ma. It keeps you young."

"Hmpf," she said, or something close to it. "I'm counting on you to keep an eye on him, Sydney. Don't let him do anything impulsive."

I was being dismissed; it felt like a good time to salute. "I'll do my best," I promised insincerely.

"You do that. Oh, and tell him to answer his telephone once in a while. I'm on a schedule here; I can't keep calling."

"Okay." I could ask about my aunt but decided that was a can of worms for another time. "Bye, Ma."

"You remember, Sydney."

"I will. Bye."

At least she had given me an idea. It was time to see what exactly was happening with my father. And Caroline.

And maybe even a Hawthorne.

5

They didn't come back until dinnertime.

I had no idea where anyone was. Well, Ali presumably spent the afternoon working. Mirela called from the gallery and reported that she hadn't seen either my father or Caroline and that she was going home to spend time with her daughter.

I found a little paperwork and managed to look busy. Most of the afternoon, however, I spent diving down various rabbit holes to learn something about art fraud.

It was an impressively big business indeed—and had been for some time. Probably the cave painters at Lascaux had had someone tracing over their bison to reproduce the images in the next cave over.

Michelangelo, I learned, had been a forger early on. "It's fascinating," I told Mike when he had the misfortune of stopping by my cubby-hole. "Some of these great artists, they couldn't sell under their own names. They weren't known in the art world, which was just as snobbish then as it is now. And, well, they had to eat, right?"

"Michelangelo? The Sistine Chapel guy?"

"Don't pretend. I know you went to art school."

"Long, long ago, on a planet far away," he intoned. "Go on, what did Michelangelo forge?"

"Well, apparently, ancient Greek and Roman statuary was all the rage," I said. "So this young, unknown artist whose work nobody cared about schemed with a crooked art dealer to create a statue that looked just like the artifacts. Then he broke it up a little and buried it in the dealer's vegetable garden. The dealer dug it up—what a find!—and sold it as an ancient Roman original. And it worked. They even did it a whole bunch of times, probably made a fair bit of cash, got him set up for his career." I shrugged. "Or, at the very least, kept him reasonably well-fed. People loved it." I smiled. "Even better, the joke lives on. Imagine you're some rich guy now, and you're kind of proud of this slightly broken Roman statue you have over by your koi pond, and you probably paid a couple thousand dollars for this wonderful antique. Somewhere out there, there are guys like that, guys who have Michelangelo's work without knowing what it is, without knowing that broken old statue is probably worth hundreds of thousands of dollars instead!"

"We always like it," said Mike, nodding, "when the joke's on the rich guy."

"Don't we just?" I started laughing and then caught his quick glance over at Reception, casual, just Mike keeping an eye on the place even when he was in conversation. Mike was such a great manager. *What if…*

I stopped that thought in midflight. "Then there's David Bowie," I said.

"David *Bowie* was an art forger? This I don't believe." It has to be said: Mike can tell you every one of Bowie's songs on every one of his albums and the stories behind each of them. Mike owns the vinyl. He used to travel to see Bowie in person. He's a volunteer DJ with a Bowie-centric show over at WOMR community radio every other week. He's insane.

"Not exactly, but maybe one step better," I said. "Listen to this: he goes to this party—"

"When?"

"I don't know, do I? 1998, 2000, who knows. That's not the point. The point is he goes to this party holding a book. He announces it's the biography of this famous, fairly recently deceased artist called Nat Tate. He even reads a couple of sections out of the book to the other guests."

"Sounds like the life of the party," said Mike. "David *Bowie* did this? I've never gone to a party where someone read chapters from a book. Not exactly Disco Inferno, was it?"

"Shut up and listen," I said. "It gets better."

"We can only hope."

"So Bowie's there, and he keeps talking about this artist, how much he loves the guy's work and can't believe how under-appreciated this painter is. He says Tate actually played an important role in the development of art in the twentieth century."

Mike was nodding. "Someone made a mockup of the book," he guessed.

"More than that. Bowie had started something. Gallerists the world over began to scramble to find work by Tate, so they could snap something up for themselves. The art world is so attuned to the next big thing, and everyone wants to get out in front... a whole bunch of gallery owners and dealers started saying they'd, in fact, always admired Tate's work. Some people said they'd met him and that he'd been this incredible influence on their art appreciation—that they learned all this stuff from him."

"I'm going to guess there was no Tate?"

"Spot-on," I said. "Bowie finally was done playing with them and must have loved admitting that Tate was a figment of his imagination. He'd written this biography—along with Gore Vidal, can you imagine? And the guy who did Picasso's biography, I've forgotten his name—to prove a point about the celebrity status of famous artists and the whirlwind of money and fame that can surround them when someone influential says they're important."

Mike was appreciative. "Must have laughed himself silly," he said. "I'll have to look into that. I can talk about it on my next Bowie show." He thought about it for a moment. "Still, it's a lot of work just for a practical joke, isn't it? Writing a whole book?"

"That's nothing," I said. "These places, these people—the money involved is stupefying. Hundreds of millions of dollars. Writing a book is nothing; art forgers spend hours and hours perfecting materials, perfecting styles, and getting everything right: they have to because technology is so advanced. I don't know how anyone can get away with it now, but apparently, they do."

"But they do it for money," he said. "Bowie did it to make fun of them."

I laughed. "You don't think the forgers don't enjoy that, too? Everyone wants to poke fun at the establishment, any establishment, especially one as old and stuffy as the art establishment. Imagine being a painter who never quite made it to the upper echelons and then watching the same people who rejected your work paying millions of dollars for it when it's got someone else's name on it? Imagine how—I don't know, *superior* to them all you'd feel. Like Michelangelo, back in the day."

"Yeah, I can imagine."

I leaned back; my chair creaked dangerously. Maybe I could spend some of my downtime this week or next week, or any week looking for a new chair. "On top of everything else, there's a fantasy behind it, too," I said. "What if you had the daring and the talent to produce a fake work of art *so drop-dead authentic* that no one could tell it was fake? There's an audacity to that, a kind of grand illusion. Bowie understood that completely, and so do the really great forgers. On some level, I'd think art lovers would be outraged, but on another level, they might want to applaud."

"I would," Mike said. "It's all this game of whoever has the most toys wins, isn't it?"

"Especially," I said, "if the toy is a Picasso or a Rembrandt."

One of the Kevins wandered over. "Something going on in the kitchen," he said.

Mike straightened up. "What?"

The kid shrugged. "Don't know. But you could hear Adrienne hollering."

We all knew whatever disaster was going on would keep going on until it got fixed. Adrienne the diva chef was fantastic at what she did—*and* was also the most short-fused individual I'd ever met. I tended to avoid her at all costs. "I'll come," said Mike. "Wish me luck," he added over his shoulder to me. "We who are about to die salute you."

"Don't forget your armor!" I called back and watched him go. Even preparing to face the dragon, going straight into the dragon's lair, Mike was calm, unruffled, and courteous. He was one hell of a manager. I hoped he was going to stay one forever.

And, damn it, we *had* been down this road before.

It seems there's a certain level of precariousness we in Provincetown have learned to live with, but it's scary. I wasn't immune to the fear: I rented. And my apartment might be small, and it might have the disadvantage of being located over a dance club (which made for a whole lot of Lady Gaga at midnight when I was trying to get to sleep), but sooner or later, my old Portuguese landlord was going to decide to sell up and head back to the Azores, as he'd been threatening to do for years.

What would happen if Glenn sold the inn? Where would Mike go? There were other high-end inns and hotels in town, though none that really could compare with the Race Point. We had a pool, we had several bars and dining areas, we had a spa, we had a formal tea service (not to be confused with Tea Dance, down the street at the Boatslip, which was anything but formal), we had a Michelin-rated restaurant… we had Adrienne the diva chef. If Mike wanted to run another place like this, he'd have to leave town, go to Boston, or even farther afield. And that was a personal problem, as he was—finally—living with a guy he really liked; he wasn't even quite so irritated anymore when I teased him about getting a wedding together for the two of them. His boyfriend was one of the local veterinarians. Where could they go together? Or would they just break up?

Where would I go, come to that?

I was projecting way too much. Glenn being cranky did not necessarily translate into Glenn selling the inn. It could be a lot of other things. It could be—

"Oh, God!" I said out loud. The Kevin behind Reception turned to look at me. "What's the matter?"

I had to take my hand away from my mouth to answer. "Nothing." It came out as an unconvincing croak. I had it. Glenn was dying.

It had to be his health. What else could have upset him so much? Perhaps he was dying, and the trips he had scheduled were for some sort of esoteric medical treatment. Maybe the mysterious André was a Last Fling or even a doctor who was treating him. Why on earth hadn't we thought of that?

No. I couldn't stand it if Glenn died. I couldn't lose him, too, not after losing Barry. Losing Glenn would be the last straw.

Which, of course, once again brought it all back around to me. Sometimes I just can't get out of my own way.

At one level, it was none of my business. At another level, I was more determined than ever to find the truth.

***

Ali appeared around cocktail time, which was sweet of him: he always respects the ritual, if not the alcohol. "You look tired," I observed as he kissed my cheek and sat next to me at the bar.

"That usually means you look old," he said.

"You don't look old." In fact, he looked rather luscious. Yeah, there were shadows under his eyes, but he had his designer stubble thing going and hadn't combed his hair; he looked like someone from a boy band ten years later.

"Well, what would you prefer?" I asked. "I could say, hi, honey, how was your day, but you're probably not supposed to talk about it in public. So… you look tired. My expression of sympathy and connectedness." I signaled to the Kevin behind the bar. "Have a drink."

"Grapefruit juice," Ali said to the bartender. Back in Beirut, where he was born, Muslims had been westernized to the point of occasionally imbibing alcohol; but Lebanon had changed since its civil wars. Still, I also remembered he'd never had any in his life. A commitment to a religion he never even thought about.

"So what's new on the Hawthorne front?" he asked, probably knowing it would serve as a terrific red herring should I be tempted to delve more into his day and what additional horrors he'd uncovered therein.

It worked, of course. "Nothing to report," I said. "But tomorrow's Friday."

"Yes, it is," he agreed.

"And that's Gallery Stroll night."

"Uh-huh."

"Well, it wouldn't hurt, would it, to stop in at Mirela's gallery? Ask Rhys if he has any more new Hawthornes?"

Ali's eyebrows went up, and he whistled under his breath. I've always wished I could do that. "*New* Hawthornes?" he repeated. "You wouldn't have already made your mind up, would you, *cara*?"

I shrugged. Even inventing a mystery had to be better than dealing with some of the grim potential realities I'd been thinking about. "It just would be interesting," I said.

He smiled as he sipped his juice, not looking at me. "What?" I demanded. "It's not impossible."

"Of course not, *cara*, but it's highly im-probable, too. Do you know the hoops you'd have to jump through to get a fake painting authenticated?"

"I thought it wasn't your department."

"It isn't my department, but I've been looking into it. Technology is not the forger's friend. They do x-rays. They test the age of the canvas. They look to see whether the chemical makeup of a certain shade of paint was available at the time the painting was supposed to have been done. They look for a definite paper trail from the artist down to the current owner. You know how hard it would be to make *all* that happen? How precisely would the planets have to be lined up? And then explain why no-one ever heard of this particular painting? And all that on top of having an incredibly killer talent to imitate—no, *replicate*—the artist's work in the first place?" He shook his head. "It's a romantic enough notion, *cara*, but I just don't see it. Besides, aren't most forgers interested in bigger names? Wasn't that multi-multi-million dollar painting the Saudi prince bought thought to be a fake? That's where the payoff might be worth the effort."

Not, of course, that I'd want to be that particular hapless forger once MBS got hold of him. "On the other hand," I said, "maybe staying with an artist who's a little more under the radar would be helpful. I mean, Hawthorne may be super-famous here, but he's no van Gogh or Rembrandt or Monet. None of his paintings are going through authentication at Christie's or Sotheby's or anyplace like that." I took a breath; I was becoming more and more interested in my own manufactured mystery. "*And* I think Caroline knows more than she's letting on."

"What makes you think that?"

"When she looked at Glenn's painting, she seemed to be—almost purring."

"Leaving aside the improbability of that as a physical feat," said Ali, "couldn't that indicate a connoisseur's pleasure at seeing a fabulous painting?"

"She asked where it came from and seemed surprised it even existed."

He sighed. "Again, *cara*, so what? It's her field. Of course, she's excited by a new discovery."

"So maybe it's just a feeling," I said stubbornly. The Kevin behind the bar poured another glass of Côtes du Rhône and slid it across to me, unasked. I have them pretty well trained. I took an initial sip. "Okay, so maybe I'm looking for drama where there's no drama. Either way, it's interesting, though, isn't it? If nothing else, I'd love to hear the story of how these paintings got lost and found again. That would be worth the price of admission right there."

"So we're going on the Gallery Stroll," Ali concluded.

"We're going on the Gallery Stroll," I confirmed.

The headwaiter, Martin, appeared from behind us. "I thought I'd find you here," he said. "Hey, Ali, how are you?"

"Good, good," said Ali, half-turning on his barstool to shake Martin's hand.

"Here for the weekend?"

"Something like that." We hadn't yet told everybody Ali was living in Provincetown. Besides, he was still in Boston. A lot.

Martin nodded and turned to me. "Your father and his guest are ready to be seated," he said. "Did you want to come join them?"

Of course we did.

***

Naturally, me being me, I couldn't resist bringing it up again.

I was playing with my paella, half-listening to my father and Caroline talking about art, with Ali making the occasional interested comment. I waited for a pause in the conversation. "So, did you go see the Hawthornes?" I asked finally.

Everyone looked a little startled., and I realized what a non sequitur it had been. "Just wondering," I said semi-apologetically. "Since Glenn seems to love his so much."

"We did," my father said. "Just stunning, really, though I'm not sure your mother would like them. They're kind of dark, aren't they?"

"He painted people, not fields of flowers," said Caroline. She sounded a little exasperated. I had a feeling it was not the first time today they'd had this conversation.

"Your mother likes flowers," my father said to me. Actually, I'd have thought flowers would be her least-favorite subjects since she had an unerring tendency to kill plants as soon as she brought them into the house; but maybe he hadn't liked the paintings or their price tags and was just looking for an easy out. "So what were these paintings of?" I asked.

"One of them was of people, but their faces were blurry," he said.

"Mudheads," said Caroline.

"Mudheads?" I asked. I wasn't sure I'd understood her correctly.

She took a sip of the excellent Châteauneuf-du-Pape, and thought about it for a moment. "Charles Hawthorne, as you probably know, founded the Cape Cod School of Art," she said.

I'd only learned that recently, but I kept quiet; there was just the smallest overtone of condescension in her voice I didn't like. Maybe if she schooled us, she could charge my father a fatter consultant's fee.

"And he introduced the concept of plein-air painting to Provincetown," she was saying, oblivious to my thoughts. "Students were to paint from live models in the bright sunlight on the beach. They were instructed to only paint the broad patterns of light and shade and not get caught up in the details. This way, they were quickly taught two fundamentals of modern painting." She held up one finger. "First, the impact of a painting is in the broad shapes, not the details, and second"—she held up another finger—"the sunlight effect is achieved through the juxtaposition of these large color areas against each other. So you get Mudheads, where the person's features are irrelevant. The viewer is free to insert any thought or feeling there they want."

"I like paintings that say what they're trying to say," said my father, a little peevishly. "I don't need to guess at it. There's too much of that already in life. Art's for relaxation, anyway, isn't it?"

"Not everyone would agree with you," said Ali, making a valiant effort to enter the conversation. "Some people like to feel challenged by a work of art."

"On their living-room wall?" My father looked unconvinced.

Caroline made a dismissive gesture. "It doesn't matter," she said, her voice soothing. "We'll find something else for you, Stephen. Never mind."

I had been thinking and wasn't sure I liked my thoughts. "Provincetown," I said, "doesn't seem like the best place to do that." Everyone stared at me. I grabbed a swallow from my wineglass before I started. "I'm just wondering why you're looking in Provincetown at all," I said. *That's you, Riley: the crazy lady at the table.* "I mean, if you want to buy fine art, there are other places that could give you a wider choice, aren't there? Boston or New York—or Chicago? Why come to Provincetown?"

Okay, now I was sure: Caroline definitely didn't like me. I saw a flash of annoyance in her eyes before she spoke. "Your father particularly wanted a Provincetown artist," she said sweetly, "because his daughter lives here, and it would be a way of feeling closer to her."

Damn. I took another gulp of a beautiful wine that should never be gulped. So much for claiming any moral high ground here.

"There are certainly any number of artists to choose from in P'town," put in Ali in an attempt to deflect the growing tension. "If you don't like Charles Hawthorne, there's a lot more. Do you have someone else in mind? We're doing the Gallery Stroll tomorrow evening. Maybe you could, too. It's a great opportunity to talk to the artists and get a feel for their work."

I was still thinking, a reckless endeavor given Caroline's quick mind. "In the meantime, tell us about the Hawthornes," I suggested. "Even if you don't want to buy one, it's an extraordinary event, really. I wonder why it wasn't in the paper. Did you get to talk to Rhys? Is he putting on a big show around them? Where did he say he'd found them?"

"Extraordinary, really," said my father. He took a last bite of his *filet mignon au beurre blanc* and sighed in satisfaction. "That woman knows what she's doing."

I assumed he was talking about Adrienne the diva chef, but it was unclear. "What's extraordinary?" I asked.

"The story," said my father. "Apparently, they're renovating a house over on Pearl Street." I exchanged looks with Ali; renovations, in P'town, usually means destroying what is there and put in something both upscale and ordinary in its place. You wouldn't think architects could manage that, but they often did. "And these canvases were there, right in the wall, boarded up inside it, just wrapped in paper. Apparently, they used them as insulation. Extraordinary," he said again.

Not so extraordinary, though I rather hoped my father wouldn't make the connection. Ali and I looked at each other again, both of us probably remembering a time a few years back when other artifacts had been discovered walled up over on Pleasant Street—and a skeleton along with them. People put all sorts of things in walls for all sorts of reasons. Just ask Edgar Allan Poe.

"But how can you be sure they're authentic?" I said instead.

Caroline answered. "There are a number of ways," she said. "When someone wishes to authenticate a work, they use forensic methods, as you've probably seen on television, checking the kind of paint used, whether the artist had access to them, and so on. And the canvas itself is tested, of course. But there are other things. The frame usually tells a tale, though in this case, the frames were somewhat damaged."

"What does the frame tell you?" I was interested in spite of myself.

"Galleries and auction houses mark the frames," she said. "They've been doing that for centuries. So part of the detective work is matching up the markings on the frame with the artist's whereabouts or those of the painting. And then, of course, there's the paperwork." She sighed. "Well-known painters with a body of work often have a catalogue raisonné, I think we talked about this before—it's a book put together by an expert on the artist which lists all the extant works by that artist. So it helps if a painting is in the relevant catalogue raisonné."

Ali was interested, too. "Are these listed in Charles Hawthorne's catalogue?" he asked.

"He doesn't have one," said Caroline. "I've been looking into it. Possibly because he wasn't considered important enough? His work was represented by a gallery on Newbury Street in Boston, I think—or maybe the family moved his work since then? I seem to have heard something about that, part of a different conversation, though right now, I can't remember. In any case, that's not an option here. But there are so many other factors—the way an artist holds his brush, the use of color—in Hawthorne's case, the sense of shapes underlying everything; he was very attuned to shapes. He told his students to put the shapes in first."

The waiter came and took away our dishes. "That was delicious," Ali told him. "Please thank the chef for us." Adrienne would accept compliments only as her due, but I found myself smiling and looking rather fondly at my boyfriend. He's kind even when his kindness isn't appreciated.

My father looked like he was considering going to sleep.

"Here's a question," I said. "What if—" I caught Ali's eye, saw the infinitesimal shake of his head, but continued anyway, because that's what I do, "What if someone set out to fake a Charles Hawthorne?"

Caroline was unperturbed. "It's always a possibility, though naturally, the artist would have to be very good," she said. "But that's true for any forgery, isn't it?"

"Good *and* lucky," I said, and she laughed. "I don't know about the luck," she said. "It's more like being initiated into a cult or some secret society. You know, the first rule of Fight Club… There's such a spectacular contradiction at the heart of art forgery. And really, no one wants to talk about it. And I mean no one. Forgeries that pretend to be paintings by timeless artists or are misidentified as being by a given artist? Right now, they're hanging in museums or hidden away in private collections all over the world. No one knows how many, but my guess, and it's a conservative guess, is we're looking at twenty percent—imagine that—twenty percent of all art on display wasn't painted by the artist whose name is on the frame."

I was staring at her. "Twenty percent?" I think I was squeaking.

She shrugged. "It doesn't really matter. Because no one wants to be told they have a fake, so it's all hush-hush. No one talks about Fight Club. Anyway, whatever the percentage, there are more of them than anyone knows, and they're all out there hiding in plain sight."

"So why don't we hear more about it?" I asked, fascinated in spite of myself. "There have to be people out there, professionals, curators, people like that, people looking to set the record straight, aren't there? Some sort of art police?"

"Not as much as you'd think," she said. "You've probably heard of companies—big companies, major corporations—that quietly fire someone who's been stealing from them for years, but they don't bring any legal proceedings against them because it would advertise the company's security weaknesses? Well, that goes by about five hundredfold in the art world, where reputation is everything. Who wants to be known as the gallery that bought a fake Degas? The collector with a series of Rembrandt sketches... done in the twentieth century? No one wants to be duped, and especially no one wants to be *known* to have been duped. There's a lot of pride, a lot of one-upmanship. Collectors and museums are all about pride and reputation."

She paused and took a sip of wine. "Of that twenty percent, I'd guess at least five or six percent are known, absolutely known, to be fakes by someone—someone who isn't about to lose their job or their status by talking about it."

"But that's just wrong!" My father; a man of moral absolutes. "It's cheating. Every time someone looks at that painting and thinks it's a Degas—isn't that the one you mentioned? Every time someone looks at it, they're be-ing—what's the word I want? Deprived? Deceived? Hoaxed, maybe. The painting people are seeing isn't the painting they think it is!"

He must have been outraged. For my father, that was a speech of massive proportions. Not to mention a major dip into the thesaurus.

Caroline acknowledged him with a nod. "For sure, when a case of forgery does come to light, it tends to be greeted with very public moral outrage. The act of imitating a famous artist's work—and, especially, profiting off it?

That's seen either as a sleazy, low-life con or a major crime. In fact, it's both."

"Sydney and I were talking about some people—artists—wanting to embarrass the powers that be in the art world. Maybe to get back at the critics who'd dissed their work. If I were going to forge a painting," said Ali unexpectedly, "I'd put some subversive detail in, discreetly so it wasn't obvious, just to be able to thumb my nose at the establishment later when it came to light."

"Like what?" asked my father.

"Oh, I don't know. Like the pigs and the Beatles someone put in a fake painting on that episode of *Midsomer Murders*."

"You watch *Midsomer Murders*?" I was astonished.

"I did when we were first dating," Ali said. "You'd made it clear to me that if I was going to hang out with you, I needed to get more skilled at detecting."

Caroline was looking baffled. "What are you talking about?"

"Sydney," Ali told her, "has a hobby."

"Stop it," I said.

"She's an amateur sleuth," said my father unexpectedly. "You think they're only in books or on TV, but my daughter really is one." He sounded proud in spite of himself.

"What kind of sleuthing?"

I sighed. "It's not really that big a thing," I said. "Just sometimes—"

"The town's detective chief says she trips over dead bodies," said Ali. He had evidently decided this was a less-fraught conversational trail. I wasn't sure I agreed.

But the truth was that maybe it *was* just a hobby. Maybe I really was making something up here. I was bored, and I'd found a field I didn't know much about, and it had piqued my interest, and maybe all that had happened was I'd made up a story to go along with my curiosity and alleviate my boredom.

On the other hand, Mirela was worried about the "unintended consequences" of something she thought was happening at the Whitney Worthington. And as far as I could tell, the only thing she could be worried about that was new was Rhys's discovery of several unknown paintings by someone he didn't even represent—someone who wasn't even generally to be found in a gallery but rather gracing the walls of museums. How had that hapless person renovating their house known what the paintings were worth? How had they chosen Rhys, someone who spent far more time in New York than he ever did in P'town? It didn't seem an obvious choice.

It might just be a line of inquiry, however.

I smiled at Caroline and said, "It's really just a hobby. Not nearly as interesting as what you do. At the end of the day, I'm just the wedding planner."

I could feel my father's eyes on me, appraising and perhaps just a little shocked. But I knew how to deal with that. "What," I asked the table at large, "is for dessert?"

6

The next day was Erika, the nanny's day off, so Mirela had Lily in tow.

Ali was working from home again—he'd come back to the apartment from dinner at the inn with some sort of revitalized energy about his case and had been deep in discussion on Zoom when I left the apartment the next morning, so I told her to meet me at the inn. The summer crowds had thinned out, and the pool wasn't filled with men in Speedos, much to my relief. I've never been a big in-your-face kind of person about anything, and Province-town sometimes went a little too far in the let-it-all-hang-out direction.

We sat at a table near the tiki bar and watched Lily playing with some sort of educational toy my father had brought her; it looked like something you'd need a doctorate to decode, but Lily was managing pretty well. "So," I said to Mirela, "my father was at your gallery yesterday."

"With his assistant," she said, nodding.

"Art broker," I corrected. I looked at her curiously. "You don't like Caroline," I said. When she didn't answer, I added, "It's okay. Neither do I."

"I do not think she is dishonest," said Mirela slowly.

"But?"

She shook her head. "There is something I do not understand there," she said. "And what I do not understand, I fear."

"And so sayeth we all," I murmured. I was convinced fear was the major motivator for everything bad that happened on the world stage. It started wars. It covered up genocides. I wasn't sure exactly how knowing that helped me live my life in any meaningful way, but it certainly explained a lot of what I read in the news.

We watched Lily for a few minutes in silence, and then I said, a little diffidently, "The Hawthornes?"

"Yes, what about them?" Her voice was sharp.

I took a deep breath. "Are they real?"

"And I am now an art appraiser, me?"

"You're someone who's worried," I said. "Come on, Mirela, I won't hold you to it. Have you seen the paintings?"

She hesitated before answering. "I have not seen all of them," she said. "But some things are wrong."

"Such as?"

She sniffed. "Milo Griffin," she said. "I do not trust him."

Lily was trying to get her attention. "Ice cream!"

"Not now," said Mirela.

"Who's Milo Griffin?" I asked.

"Ice cream!" It was a wail of agony; clearly this was a matter of life and death.

"The more you scream, the longer you will have nothing," said Mirela firmly. She seemed to be better than me at blocking out the cries.

"Ice cream!"

"She really does have more of a vocabulary than that," Mirela said to me.

"I have no doubt," I agreed. "Who's Milo Griffin?"

She looked surprised. "He is an artist," she said. She had to speak loudly to be heard over her daughter's meltdown. "He is usually living in Provincetown, somewhere in the West End, I think. Or often he is in Paris. He is represented by my gallery. You must know him, sunshine. I thought you knew everybody."

There was a particularly loud scream. "I don't know Milo Griffin," I said. The only thing I really knew right at that moment was that I was never, ever, ever having a child. I looked at my goddaughter in some dismay. "I don't suppose we could just get her an—"

"No," interrupted Mirela. She looked slightly shocked. "She must learn she cannot obtain anything by screeching."

"Is there anything you can give her to stop—"

Mirela said something that sounded like "oh, *procolnet*," which I took to be an expletive, as she scooped Lily up and held her tightly on her lap. "That will do," she said severely, and to my astonishment, Lily stopped. Was there a button Mirela had pushed on the child's back? I would have to learn how to do that.

I cleared my throat. "Milo?" I asked again.

"What do you want me to tell you? His life history? He is an abstract expressionist."

I tried for humor. "Oh, well, *that* must be why I don't know him."

I should have known better. Mirela is my closest friend, she is a lovely, smart, and talented person, but somehow when they were handing out a sense of humor in her native

Bulgaria, she'd gotten skipped over. "You know other artists who create abstract paintings," she said severely.

"What does he look like?"

Lily was struggling to get down off Mirela's lap, and Mirela was having none of it. "Oh, what do I know? He is ordinary. He looks like anyone else out on the street."

When you considered what a lot of men out on Provincetown's streets looked like, the statement encompassed multitudes. "He wears high heels and a Superman cape?"

"You are not funny," she informed me.

"*You* are not descriptive," I responded. "What, Mirela? I want to recognize him at the Stop & Shop."

"I have never seen him at the Stop & Shop," she said pensively. "Perhaps that is odd."

It wasn't a tangent I wanted to pursue. "Where's his studio?"

She gave me a look. "You do not interrupt anyone's work," she said.

"I wasn't going to drop in on him, for heaven's sake," I said. "Just want to—you know, *situate* him." It's not entirely off the wall; I know a woman who lives on Tasha Hill, and whenever I drive by, I keep an eye out for her. Just to wave to.

Am I really the only person who does that?

"I do not know where he works," she said. "And I cannot say even if I did." Okay, now I got it: that was code, for sure. In Provincetown, land of unaffordable real estate, many condos designated as studios are surreptitiously lived in. And artists, it seemed, stuck together, even if it was clear from Mirela's tone that Milo wasn't high on her list of Most Admired People.

There are some things you just don't do.

I sighed. Maybe I needed another hobby, like cross-stitching or playing the flute, something I could pick up and put down at will. Sleuthing didn't just involve solving a mystery; it also involved *finding* a mystery, and as hard as I was trying, this one just wasn't cooperating.

Someday I'll learn not to be too prescient.

I stood up and stretched. "I don't know about you," I said, "but I'm going to go look at his work."

"At whose work?"

"Milo Griffin," I said.

"You have seen it many times," she said, shaking her head. "You have been to the gallery. You have sat behind the desk at the gallery."

True enough: in the wintertime, I occasionally had a side gig on decent weekends opening up a gallery for an absent owner—no doubt at that snowy moment enjoying the sun in Palm Springs or Key West—to see if a few sales might trickle in. Of course, my usual sales patter involved thrusting postcards or pamphlets into potential clients' hands. I don't actually know much about art, even less about the Worthington Whitney's usual penchant for abstraction.

"That doesn't mean I could pick out his work," I said as diplomatically as I could manage. "See you later, Mirela. Bye, Lily."

Lily looked like she was about to start in on her second act. I fled.

***

There was an argument going on.

Rhys Whitney, all five feet seven of him, was blocking the doorway. I heard him before I actually got to the door due to it being open and his voice being loud. If it had been high season, he'd have attracted a small crowd of onlookers. As it was, people seemed to be quickening their steps to get by. Smart people. "And I don't want you around until then!"

Fortunately, the gallery windows were large and sweeping and with only small pieces in front, so you could see into the room. What I saw was a guy who'd apparently acquired his wardrobe from a fire sale at Pirates of the Caribbean: a wine-colored velvet jacket with a ruffle at the cuffs and boots worn over his pants. His hair wasn't in locks, but it well might have been; it was long and dark and cascaded in curls around his shoulders. Small Van Dyck beard. Something flash in his ears. Gorgeous eyes. (Well, you have to notice these things, don't you?)

If this was the mysterious Milo, then he was certainly dressing the part. And I had for *sure* never seen him at the Stop & Shop.

He caught sight of me over Rhys's shoulder and made some sort of gesture that must have meant something to the other man. Rhys turned to see who it was and, recognizing me, immediately scowled.

I have that effect on some people.

"We're just closing," he said. "Mirela isn't here."

"Oh, hi, Rhys," I said cheerfully. "That's okay; I wasn't looking for her."

"Then what are you here for?" Always pleasant, that was Rhys.

"To look at art," I said, spreading my hands in an I-have-absolutely-nothing-to-hide gesture. "That's what you do here, right? Sell art?"

He let out an exasperated sigh. "We're just locking up," he said. "The door was supposed to be closed."

Difficult when you're standing in it. I kept my innocent, cheerful look and said, past him, "Hi! I'm Sydney Riley. I don't think we've—"

"That's enough," said Rhys. He turned back to the pirate. "I'll let you know about the others," he said and then lowered his voice, which meant only half of the town could hear him. "And don't fuck with me this time, Milo."

"Oh!" I said brightly. "You must be Milo Griffin! Mirela's been talking about you… I was trying to figure where I'd seen you before." It wasn't just at the Stop & Shop that I couldn't place him; I was fairly certain I'd never seen this man anywhere. Outfits like that tend to stick in your mind.

He seemed, if anything, amused. "And did you?"

"Sorry? Did I what?"

"Figure out where it was you saw me." The smile was nice, too.

"That's enough," said Rhys. "The gallery is closed."

"Really?" I countered. "Just before a Friday Stroll? What'd you do, Rhys, sell your whole inventory? 'Cause that's the only reason I can think of you'd be closing during a Stroll. Gosh, most of the galleries put out wine and cheese!"

Milo said, "Rhys seems to think he does better with—private sales." There was a dangerous undertone in his voice.

"Mirela might not agree," I said, trying my hand at being threatening. I'm not very good at it; this attempt was clearly no exception.

"Mirela is my business," said Rhys. "And I really think—"

"Then I'll be off," said Milo, stepping forward and pretty much forcing Rhys out of the doorway. With me still standing on the other side, he had a moment of finding his feet and deciding where to move them. Milo ended up on the steps beside me. "So," he said, as though Rhys didn't exist. "The fascinating Sydney Riley. Perhaps we can do the Stroll together now."

"Absolutely," I said.

I didn't look back. I didn't have to; I could feel Rhys glaring at me, his gaze targeting a spot right between my shoulder blades. But maybe—just maybe—there was a little disquiet there, too.

Time to do some serious sleuthing, I decided. "It's funny," I said as Milo and I fell into step on the sidewalk, "but you don't look like an abstract expressionist."

He laughed. "I see you don't believe in the lubricating qualities of small talk," he said.

I shrugged. "Life is short."

"So it is. Well, Sydney Riley, the truth is my work doesn't fit in with any school of art," he said. "I do work for Rhys because it sells—not as well as I'd like it to, but it does provide the pittance one needs to live."

Not in P'town and Paris, I thought. Life in that rarefied air requires a smidge more than a pittance. "So, what style is your favorite?" And wouldn't it be lovely if he were to say Hawthorne? Mudheads?

"You misunderstand," said Milo. He stopped abruptly on the sidewalk, presumably to make his point more strongly. "I refuse to be ruthlessly faithful to the original conception of art because the subtext is as important as the subject matter."

"Huh?" I'd followed that thought for a moment, but then it jumped on a bus and left me behind. "I'm sorry?"

"Any style can be imitated," Milo said. We paused in front of the Packard Gallery. "Mastering a technique, in fact mastering many techniques, helps artists learn the sheer bourgeois nature of most forms of expression," he went on. "And then they must make a choice.

To settle for the conventions of one's age, or to refuse to be fettered by them."

"Um… okay," I said. "Does that mean all artists can imitate other artists?"

"Few are good enough," he said. "I think we should say no to the Packard Gallery tonight. What do you think?"

"Whatever works for you." This had somehow morphed into a shared activity, and I didn't understand his aversion to one of the town's most venerable galleries, but okay. "So you're saying you could copy any artist's style?"

He lifted a shoulder. "In China, it is its own art form," he said.

"Copying?"

"Being part of the vision from the inside."

Is that what they're calling it? "I—um—recently met an art broker," I said. "We talked about—well, stuff like that. She said twenty percent of the art in museums and private collections are forgeries, and some people even know which ones some of them are. What's the difference between that and the copying you're talking about? Is it just the signature?

The luscious brown eyes were devouring me, though not in the way I might have fantasized. "Who is that?"

I shrugged. "Just an art broker," I said. "Staying at the inn where I work. She said—"

"Who is she?"

An annoying coastal grandmother, I wanted to say. "Caroline Harrison," I said, not sure if I should be telling him her name or not, but it was too late. "I don't know if you've heard of her—"

"Oh, yes," he said surprisingly. "Caroline and I go way back. We may be described as having—what do you say—a history?"

I hate it when people whose first (and usually only) language is English pretend otherwise in order to seem more exotic, more international, though come to think of it, international was exactly what Milo Griffin was. Still, the dark eyes were fast losing their appeal. "I don't know," I said, "What would *you* say?"

"I would say," said Milo smoothly, a hand suddenly under my elbow, "this has been a delightful conversation, but I have more important things to do."

That's you put in your place, Riley. "Okay, but…"

He dropped his hand and gave me a half-bow. "We will talk again, Sydney Riley," he said. "You can be sure of that."

I retraced my steps, passing in front of the Whitney Worthington. Rhys had been right: it was closed.

***

When I got back to the inn, the crowd was just starting to disperse.

"What's happened?" I hadn't heard sirens from down the street, but there were two Provincetown cruisers sitting on Commercial Street outside the front entrance, lights flashing, and a guy was just shutting the back door of the fire department's ambulance; this time, I did hear the siren start wailing as it pulled away.

"Someone over there saw it," a short woman dressed in pastels said, gesturing. "I got here too late." She sounded disappointed.

"Saw what?" But she was already talking with her companion about who had seen something first, and I moved as smoothly as I could through the knot of people. The rush of the season might be over, but schadenfreude is always a big draw. No one can resist an accident.

But I stopped being polite when I caught sight of a familiar face in front of the crowd. My father, standing alone in the street. I pushed through more assertively and grabbed his arm. "Are you okay?"

He looked a little dazed. "Yes," he said. "I'm not hurt." He sounded like he was in shock. He glanced at me as though not really recognizing me. As though he wasn't really there. The word *disassociation* came to mind. "What happened?" I demanded again.

He was still looking at the street as though it might have some answers. "It was sudden—" he said and broke off as one of the cops approached him. "You were with Ms. Harrison?" he asked.

"Yes, yes," my father said. He wasn't really focusing, and I suddenly got it. "Caroline? Is Caroline hurt, Dad?"

"Excuse me," said the cop. I didn't know who he was, which was unusual in Provincetown—mostly, we know all the police, at least by sight. Some of us even a little more than that. Then again, he looked young enough to be a recent academy graduate. Hell, he looked young enough to be a recent *middle school* graduate. "You are?"

"I'm Sydney Riley," I said. "I work at the inn." I made a vague gesture behind me. "This is my father." I turned back to him. "Are you all right?"

"There was plenty of space," he said vaguely.

"He's in shock," I said to the cop. "Can we take this inside? Get him a glass of water?" I gestured at the inn behind us.

He glanced around and, apparently seeing nothing to contradict the idea, nodded. "Okay," he said.

Sitting down, my father didn't look any less dazed. "It just came up on the sidewalk," he said. "We were walking down to the gallery—"

The cop was taking notes. "Which gallery is that?"

My father looked at me a little helplessly. "The Whitney Worthington?" I suggested. "Where Mirela shows her work?"

My father nodded. "Meeting the owner," he said.

Rhys hadn't told me that. Was he trying to avoid them? Was that why he was so anxious to close? I'd assumed it had something to do with Milo, but perhaps not.

The cop didn't care about that. "And you got a look at the car?" he asked.

"She was hit by a *car*?" I echoed. "*Here*?"

The cop spared me a glance. But there was a good reason to be surprised. Commercial Street is, for most of the season, a traffic accident just waiting to happen. It's one-way for much of its length, but that only applies to motor vehicles; bicycles can—and do—whiz both ways at alarming rates, cutting in and out of traffic without a glance or a care. And the relatively new motorized e-scooters were supposed to go only one way, but with no actual enforcement of that rule, chaos inevitably ensues. Add to that the masses of visitors who subscribe to the belief Commercial Street is a pedestrian walkway, and you have cars and trucks driving, pedicabs (with the drivers looking at their phones rather than the traffic) zooming one way, bicycles zooming both ways, and people, their children, and their dogs stepping wherever they want whenever they want, without looking in any direction at all… and you have, as I said, an accident waiting to happen. Provincetown hasn't yet learned to enforce traffic rules, so the free-for-all was ongoing.

And those accidents do happen. Quite a few of them. But they rarely result in anyone being transported to the hospital; because of the sheer numbers of people and vehicles, no one can manage that kind of speed.

Yet now, apparently, someone had.

The cop cleared his throat, and my father's eyes came back to him. "An SUV," he said. "Big. New."

I caught the eye of the Kevin behind the desk at Reception. "Can you get us a glass of water?" I asked. What my father really needed was a brandy, but I couldn't see the cop agreeing to that. The moment he left, though… "How about the license plate? Did you see that?"

My father looked at him as though he were deranged. "There wasn't time," he said. "Just turned, and there it was, coming up on the sidewalk. All I could see was this massive grille coming at us. Caroline was walking a little ahead of me on the sidewalk—I always walk on the sidewalk in Provincetown, Sydney, you know that."

I did. In a town notorious for visitors walking in the middle of the street, my father was an exception.

He was still talking. "We were discussing a painting. . ." His voice trailed off. He wouldn't buy anything now, I realized. He wouldn't want anything hanging in his house that would remind him of this. Too much association with… "How is Caroline?" I asked the cop suddenly. "You guys transported her. Is she going to be okay?"

He gave me a look. His handbook probably said he was the one asking the questions. Tough. I was, after all, P'town's Miss Marple. "Come on, her health isn't a state secret, surely," I said.

He didn't like that. That's the first thing they teach at the academy, I'm convinced of it: leave your sense of humor right here, folks;

you won't be needing it again. "Are you a relative of hers?" he asked.

"No," I said. "As I just told you, I'm a relative of *his.*" I indicated my father. "And it would go a long way to making him feel better if you told him how she's doing."

"I don't have that information." And I wouldn't give it to you if I did, his expression and tone united to say.

I sighed. This kid wasn't going to last long in Provincetown, where most of the cops know most of the townies and, in general, treat them like human beings.

The Kevin from Reception was at my elbow with a glass of water, ice clinking. I helped my father with it; his hands were trembling.

As well they might. I couldn't imagine how I'd feel if my companion had suddenly been hit—and, apparently, by a driver who didn't wait around to see how she had fared. That grille my father had seen looming behind them must have come very close to him indeed.

I've seen drivers do all sorts of mad things on Commercial Street. Even go up on the sidewalk, usually because they're texting and driving, sometimes because they're impaired and driving—we are a town, after all, with five liquor stores and six adult-use cannabis dispensaries. But the street had to have been pretty quiet when this happened, or else the "run" part of the hit-and-run wouldn't have been very successful.

And the driver had gone up on the sidewalk.

I took a deep breath. "Listen," I said to the cop, "he's staying right here, at the Race Point. You can find him anytime. As you can see, he's in shock. He might remember more later." *Go away,* I thought. For heaven's sake, I'd watched enough mystery shows to know that, sometimes, all that people had to do was say, "this isn't a good time," and the cops would just leave them alone. Like that ever happened in real life.

Ah, fiction.

He could take a hint, at least. Or else he felt the same way about me as I was feeling about him. He stood up, pulled a business card from his wallet, and offered it to my father. "Call if you remember anything," he said.

My father just looked blankly at the card, and the cop sighed with some unnecessary ostentation and put it down on the table. Maybe he felt like he wasn't getting the respect he deserved. I just wanted him to leave.

He did, finally, and Mike appeared suddenly with a glass of amber liquid for my father. "Here, Stephen, drink this," he said and looked at me. "Did he say anything about Caroline? She's going to be all right, isn't she?"

He sounded more anxious than if we were discussing a mere guest. I frowned. "You know her?"

He looked bemused. "I've known her for years," he said. "We were at school together back in the days when I thought I had some talent for art." He paused. "I introduced her to your dad, actually, so really I'm the one responsible for her being here."

"I didn't know." I turned back toward my father. "I'm sure she'll be okay," I said, not sure who I was speaking to—my father, Mike, or myself. "Do you want to go up to your room and rest? I can—"

"I'm not an invalid," he said irritably.

"No, but you've had a shock," I said.

He drank the booze down fast and held the empty glass toward Mike. "Do not tell your mother," he said to me.

"No problem," I responded. That was one conversation I certainly didn't want to have.

"If she knew, she'd feel she had to come here," he said.

"We don't want that," I said in fervent agreement. In this, at least, my father and I were as one.

7

We were, apparently, staying in for dinner.

"Well," Ali said when I called him, "what does your father want to do? He's the one who's just had a shock."

"He's talked Martin into doing room service," I said. The Race Point Inn doesn't generally do room service. "He's going to have an early night. Where do you want to go?"

"Actually," he said, "let's eat in. I went to the Stop & Shop."

I raised my eyebrows, even though he couldn't see me. "Really? Does that mean you're cooking?"

"In view of your usual attempts at cuisine, that's a safe plan, don't you think?"

"I'm not a terrible cook," I protested. (I am a terrible cook.)

"Of course, you're not," said Ali soothingly. There are reasons I love this man. "I was just in the mood for Lebanese food."

"They have falafel at The Canteen," I pointed out.

"And it's very nice," he said. "But they don't have *farrouj meshwi.*"

He had me there. Chicken in garlic sauce, warm flatbread, and a tabbouleh salad; I could already taste the dinner in my mind. "All right," I said. "I'm in."

"Of course you are, *cara*," he said. "What time are you home?"

"I'll check on my father and then get out of here," I promised. "If I call the hospital, will they tell me how Caroline is doing? I'd love to be able to tell him she's okay."

"Probably not unless you're family," he said. "Let him rest; tomorrow you may be able to find out more. I'm opening your wine now."

It wasn't until I was making my way down Commercial Street toward my apartment that one of his words registered with me. Ali had said, "home." Not "here" or "back" or any of those things. *What time are you home?* I had a sudden intense warm feeling in my stomach. I liked that word in his mouth.

It was a reminder that we really were building something together. After all, Ali had just sold his elegant condo in Boston, the one that was never ever broken into because, until recently, his sister was the police commissioner. It was a lot bigger and nicer than my tiny place on Carver Street. But he'd sold it, and now when he wasn't away on some assignment, he was with me in Provincetown. Which was both delightful and—also more and more—claustrophobic.

I shrugged it off like I could afford to move anywhere else, even if rentals were available. Which they're not.

The apartment smelled divine, making me wonder why we didn't do this every night. The small table was set, and true to his promise, a glass of Cotes du Rhone was breathing nicely on the coffee table in front of the Little Shop of Horrors sofa. I gave in and allowed it to envelop me, and Ibsen immediately jumped up and started purring. I sipped the wine and relaxed into the twin embraces of my furniture and my cat. "This is perfect."

Ali was putting dishes on the table. "How's your father?"

"Shaken, not stirred." I took another sip. Liquid rubies. "He'll be all right. I think he'll be all right, anyway. But it was so weird, Ali. He says the SUV went right up onto the sidewalk."

"Distracted driver?"

I hesitated. "My father thinks it was intentional."

Ali shrugged. "It probably feels that way," he acknowledged. "But you know as well as I do our brains often assign meaning to random events. Did he say he thinks it was meant for him? Is that what this is about?"

"Not even. They were together, yeah, but he'd stopped, they were right outside the inn, and you know how Martin posts the restaurant specials on that board? He'd stopped to see what Adrienne was up to tonight. And Caroline had walked on ahead—not far, but far enough. He thinks it was aiming at her."

"Come eat," Ali said, tossing the dishtowel casually over his shoulder like a Lebanese—and far more handsome—Gordon Ramsey. "The police will follow up," he added. "Best to leave any worries about it to them."

I'd managed to extract myself from the sofa on the second try and gave him a look as I slid onto the bench in front of the table. "You know my history of leaving police matters to the police."

"Don't I just." He put a steaming plate in front of me. "*Bon appétit, cara.*"

"You're so sexy when you mix languages."

He laughed and sat across from me, sipping his sparkling water. "So," he said.

"Riveting start to a conversation." The only times Ali did that was when he was about to tell me something I wasn't going to want to hear. "I should have known this meal was a bribe."

"Is it working?"

"Depends on what you say next." I touched my napkin to my lips and took another sip of wine. I had a feeling I was going to need something in my bloodstream besides blood.

"This assignment I'm on. . ."

"The crypto-traffickers," I said, nodding.

He made a face. "Not quite, but you're close. We can't touch any of the outfits operating out of Southeast Asia; we don't have jurisdiction," he said.

"Good. Then we won't be going to Thailand."

"But," he said, staying infuriatingly on track, "I think I told you it's moved here, too."

Another sip of wine. "Uh-huh."

"So this last while, for a couple of weeks, I've been working undercover. Posing as one of the possible marks."

"You can do undercover remotely? How twenty-first century of you."

"Are you going to listen to this or not?"

I'd have liked to opt for "not." I knew why he hadn't told me the whole story before. Ali knows I hate undercover. I hate it with a passion. It's dangerous, and it's scary—one remark, one foot wrong, and you can end up dead—and every time Ali did it, I was a nervous wreck. Never mind that over the past few years, I'd been in danger a whole lot more regularly than my boyfriend; I still wanted to throw up whenever I heard that word.

Still, "remote undercover" sounded a lot more manageable. I sighed. "Tell me."

He'd been eating. Now he swallowed, took a drink, and wiped his mouth. Not good signs; he was preparing what he was about to say. "I probably wouldn't mention it, even, except that I may be veering over into your traffic lane."

I stared at him. "You're planning a wedding?"

"Funny girl," he said. He should have seen that one coming. "You remember, I told you a lot of the operations are involved in acquiring cryptocurrency, right?"

"Right." I had no idea where this was going.

"One of the things people spend crypto on is high-end art," he said. "Remember, one of crypto's basic attractions is it's perceived as being outside the law—because it's online, it's international, isn't attached to any government or bank."

"The perfect currency for bad guys," I said, nodding. "I got that."

"Here in the States, the IRS is trying to go after people who don't report their crypto. But, like I said, not really my wheelhouse."

Enough with the mixed metaphors. We'd been driving along in separate lanes, now we were at sea, moving around a wheelhouse. "But it's about to be in mine?"

"Well, like I said, art. Which is the only thing you've been talking about for a while."

I made a face. "Not true," I protested half-heartedly.

"No, you've also been talking about how worried you are about Glenn," he acknowledged. "But let's get back to art. To forgeries. If I understand it correctly, crypto might be the best thing to hit the art world since your Michelangelo started doing his fake Roman statues." He sighed. "Okay. Your friend Caroline says forgeries make up about twenty percent of the art in museums and collections worldwide today, right? Well, turns out she's way conservative in her estimate. There's an outfit in Switzerland, in the Geneva Freeport—which is this ultra-secure facility where they store a million or so artworks and routinely verify paintings—and their head honcho says between seventy and ninety percent of what he sees is either forged or misattributed."

"What is there left to believe in life?" I asked lightly and drank some more wine.

"Ultimately, a lot of people think blockchain's going to reduce those figures dramatically," Ali said. "Because there's—"

"Wait," I interrupted, holding up a hand. Like most sentient beings, I'd heard of blockchain. Also, like most sentient beings, I had no idea what it really referred to. "Blockchain?"

"Crypto is the currency," Ali said. "Blockchain is the technology. It's kind of like a distributed ledger that links records together." He shook his head. "It doesn't matter, really. It's just my boss seems to think we could wait this one out because it's the blockchain that's going to solve the issue of art fraud. Look: verifying the authenticity and provenance of a piece of art can cost thousands of dollars; those guys at the Freeport charge up to twenty thousand to do it. Blockchain uses a distributed authentication protocol to verify transactions and discourage fakes."

I poured some more wine. I felt like I was back in school, in some required class I wasn't doing terribly well in. I have regular *nightmares* about that class. And now, here it was in my living-room. "If you tell me you're going to Geneva—"

"I'm not going to Geneva," said Ali. "My guys—that is, the people who've brought this scam to the States—have new scripts to pull in their marks, and one of what they're offering is some pretty great art at some pretty ridiculous prices. Claiming they'll be verified, the provenance accounted for, all that. They're really looking for people like your dad, but on a bigger scale."

"They'll never get my father," I predicted. "He's allergic to computers."

"*Like* your father. The point being," said Ali patiently, "I've set myself up as a mark. I've been investing gradually. New to the world. Just testing the waters, you know? I know I particularly like Provincetown artists, but that's all I know. And I don't feel like jumping in for a Grand Master… I want to start small."

"With a Hawthorne."

"With a Hawthorne," he agreed, nodding. "But I've already indicated if everything goes well, I'm really interested in eventually moving up. To another artist who lived and worked at least part of the time in P'town. And Jackson Pollack's one of the most popular artists to be faked." He paused. "From their point of view. I'm pretty much perfect."

"Wait," I said. "You're doing that from here? What if they get the IP address? What if—"

"Calm down," said Ali. "First of all, we've got a VPN; they're not picking up any IP address. We do know what we're doing, *cara*. But secondly, remember the person on the other end of the screen? She's a victim, too. She's been trafficked. She needs help a lot more than the rich guys getting fleeced. That's where my sympathies lie. I'm not too concerned about a millionaire losing a million or two."

"She?"

He shrugged. "I'm just guessing here. Could be a guy pretending. But I'm male, and chances are they have a woman trying to catch my eye."

"A trafficked woman."

He nodded. "I'm telling you this—well, I probably should've told you a couple of days ago, but we got the setup, and by then, I grabbed onto the whole Hawthorne thing you're doing. It's unusual—and that's what makes it seem genuine. And probably it won't affect you in any way, *cara*. I just wanted you to know since I'm doing it here."

"And involving our town."

He lifted his eyebrows. "I hardly think anyone's going to be checking me, or Hawthorne, or where we are physically. This is all done at a distance. Their world is online. Ginger probably doesn't even know where Provincetown is."

"Pretty name."

He made a face. "Not a real one," he said.

"There was a Ginger on Gilligan's Island," I said. "A movie star. She was beautiful."

"*Cara*, you are much too young to have watched that show."

I shrugged. "For a while in middle school, we thought we were cool by being uncool. You know, trying to show we despised conventions, we were so much more profound than all that? We used to watch all those reruns. Gilligan's Island, I Dream of Jeannie…"

"Far be it from me to halt this stroll down Memory Lane," said Ali, "but Ibsen is throwing up."

⁊⌇⌇⌇⁊

We woke up to grim news.

Mike was clearly still at the gym when he called my mobile; I could hear the clank and thud of weights being moved around. "Have you heard?"

"Heard what?" I propped myself up on one elbow and peered fuzzily at the clock, which peered fuzzily back. "Cripes, Mike, it's six-thirty."

"She died," he said.

"Who died?"

"Your father's art guide. Caroline Harrison."

I sat all the way up. Beside me, Ali stirred and turned over. I moved an ineffectual inch away so as not to disturb him. "She's *dead*? I thought—"

"Yeah, we all did. Listen, Sydney, can you get over to the inn? I'm on my way as soon as I shower. It happened right in front of us, she was a guest staying here, and I'd like to make sure we handle this—thoughtfully."

"And get good PR," I said.

"You have a twisted mind," said Mike. "Okay, yes, it won't hurt us to get in front of it. And for sure, all the news stories will be associating our name with the accident."

"If it *was* an accident," I said. A shiver ran up my spine; my mother would have said someone had walked over my grave. Since I planned to be cremated, I wasn't sure the expression worked anymore; but the shiver was real. "My father thinks it was deliberate. Oh! My father—"

"Another reason for you to get over there," said Mike. "He could probably use your support, and maybe—"

A thought had occurred to me; I didn't even notice I was interrupting him. "Wait, Mike—what about Glenn? He needs to—"

"Glenn's not going to be able to handle it. He's having a hard time keeping up with things as it is," said Mike sharply. He let out a gust of air. "He fired Jordan last night."

Jordan was, presumably, one of the Kevins at the inn. "What did he do?"

"Jordan? Not the point. I was probably going to fire him anyway. But there's a process for these things. I'm the one who's supposed to make those decisions. . .and Glenn's always respected that; he's always followed the procedure. Now, not so much. And it's not just around staffing issues, either."

"What is happening to him?" I whispered. "Mike, there's something really wrong."

"I know, I know. Just get over there, will you? We'll handle this together."

"Yeah, okay." I clicked off and sat for a moment, gathering my thoughts, which at six-thirty in the morning tend to be wooly at best. Caroline dead? If the accident hadn't been an accident—as my father seemed to believe, and he was the least fanciful person I knew—then who had done it? And why?

Had my "mystery" finally caught up to a murder? Had it… caused one?

I prodded Ali's shoulder. It was time to disturb him, after all.

8

The television in the breakfast room at the inn was talking about the weather. "It looks as if this is going to intensify over the next twenty-four to forty-eight hours," some disembodied voice was saying. "If it does, Nora, we can watch for the Cape and Islands to be hardest hit. Some people there are already boarding up, just in case."

The first nor'easter of the season and its timing couldn't have been much worse. I grabbed a coffee and a sweet roll and headed back to my cubbyhole, where Mike was waiting. He knew I wouldn't be coherent before coffee.

"Well," he was saying, "it may still be just what it looks like—a hit-and-run, sure, but an accident."

"You don't believe that," I said.

"I don't believe that," he agreed. "But who'd want her dead?"

That was a good question. Neither of us knew enough about her for any reasonable theories to take hold. Mike had known her back in school; I'd known her for the last three days.

My cubbyhole behind Reception was crowded even when no one was in it, and with two of us there, we couldn't speak much above whispers if we didn't want everyone in the front lobby to overhear our conversation. The police were apparently sending someone to talk with my father—who was still upstairs in his room—and with us; we'd been instructed to not leave the building. The wheels of justice were slowly grinding into motion.

My mother was just going to *love* this.

A slim woman in her forties had approached the desk. "Excuse me," she said to the Kevin who was there, "I'm looking for Mr. Michael Madison?"

The kid half-turned to get our attention; that's all there was room for. "Mike?"

"Yeah." He pushed himself up off my desk and stepped over to the counter. "Can I help you?"

She looked faintly familiar to me. "I hope so," she said. "I'm—my name is Jane Pfeiffer. I'm—I was—Caroline Harrison's sister."

That was the familiar bit, the curve of her mouth, the gray-green eyes under the groomed eyebrows, the haircut that screamed Newbury Street. Another coastal grandmother type.

On the other hand, her name sounded a little like a pharmaceutical company.

Mike shook her hand gravely. "I'm so sorry for your loss,"

"Yes." She had her sister's impatience, too, I saw. "I wanted—is there somewhere we can go? To talk?"

"Of course," he said, flashing me a look. "Come back to my office. Sydney? This is Caroline's sister. Can you get us some coffee?" He looked away quickly; he didn't usually treat me like a 1960s secretary. Most likely, he didn't want the Kevin at the desk overhearing anything—and bringing in the coffee would give me an excellent excuse to stay and participate in the conversation.

Never ever, I reminded myself, underestimate Mike.

Coffee brewed, tray prepared—Gloria even added a vase with a couple of dahlias in it; she thinks of everything—and I was back in his office, hoping I hadn't missed too much. "Ah,

Sydney," said Mike as I opened the door. "Thank you. Jane, this is Sydney Riley. It's her father who was employing your sister. He was with her when it happened. Sydney, this is Jane Pfeiffer."

She didn't look much more pleased to see me than Caroline had; maybe there was something about me that just rubbed the whole family the wrong way. "I'm so sorry about the accident," I said. "My father will be devastated. He liked your sister a lot."

Jane was accepting a cup of coffee poured for her by Mike. "She was very good at her job," she said obliquely.

There didn't seem to be an answer to that, so I retreated to the back of the room, leaning my bottom against a credenza and trying to appear invisible. Mike didn't even glance my way. "Unfortunately," he was saying, "there's not much we can do to help you. As I understand it, your sister's—your sister will have to have an autopsy."

"A car hit her," she said tonelessly. "I don't expect anyone's going to suspect yellow fever."

My interest perked up. Ooooh, sarcasm? I liked her better already.

"If the driver is apprehended and charged, the district attorney's office will need to have a legal cause of death," said Mike soothingly. He wasn't being especially erudite about the process; most of us at the Race Point Inn knew that kind of thing, largely thanks to my extra-curricular activities.

Jane made a gesture of impatience. "I need to know what she was doing," she said.

Mike glanced at me but answered easily enough. "I believe she was walking along the sidewalk—" he began, but she cut him off. "In Provincetown," she said. "What she was doing in Provincetown."

He was patience itself. "Sydney's father, Stephen Riley, hired Caroline to help him acquire some pieces of art by Provincetown artists," he said. "They looked into one artist called Charles Hawthorne, who's quite well-known around here. I think he decided against Hawthorne, though, right, Sydney?" There was a glint in his eye that said, clearly, *restrain yourself.*

As if I ever could.

"Yes," I said. "He thought the work was too dark. But Caroline was still interested in viewing some of Hawthorne's paintings that have become—well, recently available. She looked at one of them and said something about recognizing the brushstrokes."

"Recognizing the brushstrokes? Is that what you said?"

I nodded helpfully. "Well, it makes sense, doesn't it? He was working within the time she's an expert at." My thoughts were running away with any grammar I had left. Besides, shouldn't we be talking about her sister? "Are you an art expert as well, Ms. Pfeiffer?"

"Caroline and I had a similar upbringing," she said drily. She certainly wasn't overindulging in expressions of grief. Sisters, I thought, probably have as many issues and conflicts as did mothers and daughters. Alexandra and I hadn't, but I was only eight when she disappeared. I had no idea whether we'd have become friends by now or not. I'd like to think we might have managed it.

"Would you like to see her room? Maybe pick up her belongings?" Mike asked. "And I can get you something to eat if you're hungry."

"I'm not hungry." It was brusque, dismissive. "And I want to see these paintings."

Mike and I both gaped at her. There are certain situations where you just have no response; this was one of them. Grief takes different forms, I reminded myself. But—you want to see the paintings before you see your sister's body?

On the other hand, if Jane was interested, then maybe my theory about nefarious forgeries still held. Maybe she and Caroline had communicated. Maybe she knew something we didn't; maybe Caroline had passed her some thought, some wisdom, some facts mysteriously, a heartbeat running through shared bloodlines, common DNA.

Or even, more prosaically, through the telephone.

"We can arrange that," I said. "But one of them is in—private hands. I'll have to see how the owner feels about it. The others are in a gallery locally." Or so I thought; Rhys had them, but where he'd stored them was anyone's guess.

"There's a nor'easter coming," said Mike, always the practical voice in any crowd. "I think the storm track is set to really hit in a couple of days, but that could change. Are you thinking of staying? It might be a good idea. I can get you settled here, and Sydney will find out about viewing the painting. And anything else around your sister's death we can help with, of course—"

"I'd like to see her," said Jane. Maybe she'd noticed our surprise at her first reaction; in any case, her voice now was gentler. "When is the autopsy taking place, do you know?"

"What I'm going to do," said Mike, "is put you in touch with Julie Agassi. She's the head of the detective unit here in Provincetown. She can tell you what you need to know—about the incident and about your sister." He pulled out his phone. "Give me your number, and I'll text hers to you."

Jane complied, but she looked like her mind was somewhere else. "Thanks," she said. "Got it. And, yes, I think I will stay for a few days at least."

"Even without any weather on the way, that's the right decision," Mike said approvingly. He gestured toward the front desk. "Mark out there will take care of checking you in, getting your things up to your room. We can put your car in the underground garage—it'll be safest there once the storm hits, with the wind we're expecting."

"We're expecting winds?" I asked. I never look at the weather forecasts. I like to say I enjoy being surprised, but the truth is I'm lazy.

"We're always expecting winds; it's the Cape," said Mike. He wasn't looking at me.

Jane turned to me. "And I'd like to see your father," she said.

It seemed the police did, too; she wasn't going to have to wait long to speak to Julie. While we'd been in the office, two police cars had pulled up in front of the inn. I felt a sudden rush of a protective feeling. My father was still in his room, no doubt still in shock.

He didn't need another cross-examination. He also really didn't need to be talking to the recently bereaved. "Okay," I said. "After you check in, maybe. I haven't spoken to him yet today myself."

Julie had two uniformed officers with her, and she wasn't best pleased to see me. "For heaven's sake, I might have known," she said. Exasperated. "Sydney Riley."

"Hi, Julie." Sometimes I think we're friends, and sometimes I think she'd be just as happy if I moved to Siberia. "I work here, remember?"

She narrowed her eyes. "It was your father with her," she said.

"Yep."

"If it's not one Riley, it's another."

"Yep." Rather than stay on this course of conversation, which could lead nowhere I really wanted to go, I made introductions. "Lieutenant Julie Agassi, this is—um—Jane Pfeiffer. She's Caroline Harrison's sister."

"Thank you," Julie said. "Ms. Pfeiffer. My condolences. I hope you don't mind; we'd like to have a word."

Jane nodded. She didn't look much happier about seeing Julie than Julie had looked about seeing me.

I said, "You can talk in the lounge, through here. It's private." The smallish sitting room had seen many discussions and conferences from some of my previous dabbling in mysteries. Might as well add one to the list, particularly if things at the inn were falling apart, Glenn was sick or dying, or just plain fed up. I was starting to look at every room, every piece of furniture, with premature nostalgia.

I think Julie's plan had been to take Jane down to the brand-new police station that had been such a divisive issue in town; everyone was pretty intent on demonstrating how necessary it had been to build it, and I was sure there was ample room there for "helping the police with their inquiries"; but if I could keep her out of it, that was all to the better. If I could sit in on the conversation, better still.

Curiosity may have killed the cat, but it kept my life interesting.

Julie's eye met mine, and she relented. "Just a brief conversation," she said. "If you're staying in town, we may need to speak with you again at the station."

Jane nodded. "Of course." Most people, when given that menacing line from individuals wearing uniforms, would look nervous, uncertain, even frightened. Hell, I knew Julie, and *I* still could feel intimidated when she went into that mode. Her voice grew louder, her words more clipped. Officialese.

Jane, on the other hand, could have been accepting an invitation to tea. She looked at me. "Which way?"

I got them settled in and asked if anyone needed anything and then, as inconspicuously as possible, perched on the edge of the occasional table beside the door. I'd arranged it so Julie's back was to me. Maybe she wouldn't notice. Not much chance of that, of course; the second thing they teach at the Academy, after *lose your sense of humor*, is *notice everything*.

I was slightly surprised she didn't tell me to close the door on my way out.

"Your sister was Caroline Harrison." It wasn't a question.

Jane looked, if anything, amused. "Yes," she said. "She was an art broker. She lived at five-fifteen Starr Street, Brooklyn." As though she'd been through this drill before.

Julie merely nodded. "And when was the last time you spoke?"

Jane hesitated. "Last weekend, I think," she said. "I had some time off unexpectedly and was considering visiting her, but she said she was going to be out of town."

"Is that all?"

"All what?"

"All you talked about?"

Jane gave an exaggerated sigh. "We talked about art, detective. That's all anyone in our family ever does: talk about art."

"Any art in particular?"

Jane was looking at Julie as though reassessing something. It wasn't a complimentary look. "Yes," she said calmly. "We talked about pieces stolen from the Isabella Stewart Gardner Museum."

That startled Julie. Me, too, come to that. The Gardner heist had been last *century*, for heaven's sake. I remember; I'd been living in Boston at the time. Though just a child, of course. "Excuse me. Do you have information about the theft?" she asked.

I remembered, somewhere in the murky I-read-that-once section of my brain, that one of the suspected thieves had lived on the Cape.

Jane drew in a long breath and released it slowly. She'd already lost interest in the conversation. "It's a game," she said. "We both have an interest in the case. We talk about any progress being made. Caroline was convinced the pieces will never be recovered. She thinks they're gone forever. I have a little more faith in law enforcement." The way she was looking at Julie implied she might be rethinking that opinion.

Julie seemed unaffected. "Would you say your sister had any enemies, anyone who would wish her harm?"

"Are you saying this wasn't an accident?"

Julie looked up from her notebook. "I'm asking if you know of anyone who would wish to harm your sister," she said blandly.

"I don't know," said Jane. "There are professional conflicts, of course; everyone's got those. Jealousies. Enough to consider killing someone? I wouldn't have thought so."

"No one comes to mind?"

She sighed again. "No. And certainly no one who'd bother coming all the way to the end of the earth—sorry, but that's what this town feels like—to do it. Easier to catch her in the city, I'd have thought."

Julie shifted in her seat. "You're taking this very calmly," she observed.

"Would you prefer hysterics?" Jane shook her head. "My sister and I were never very close," she said. "Art, talking about art, that's the only thing we had in common, the only thing we really ever talked about. Our family life was—dysfunctional; I guess that's what they call it now. For a lot of reasons that have no relevance here, we didn't exactly develop strong bonds. That said, of course, I am grieving. Of course, I will miss her. But I don't see exactly why I'm being asked to justify anything. As far as I know, my sister was killed in a car accident last night."

"And you live in—Washington, DC? Do I have that right?" Julie knew she had it right; she doesn't ask questions when she doesn't already know the answer. "You arrived in Provincetown very quickly."

"I was in Boston," said Jane. "It's only an hour's flight," she added, her voice verging on condescending. She and Julie had not hit it off; they were circling each other like wild animals. Not many people want to take Julie Agassi on; I was looking at Jane in a new light. Sarcasm and courage. My kind of girl.

Julie decided to let that drop. She cleared her throat. "The vehicle that hit your sister was reported stolen the day before yesterday," she said.

Jane looked at her calmly. "Oh, yes?"

"It was reported stolen by Rhys Whitney," she said. And waited.

I wanted to jump up and down and wave my hand in the air. *Wait—Rhys' car was used to strike a pedestrian who maybe coincidentally was interested in certain new acquisitions to his gallery? Even in a small town like this, that has to be pushing coincidence a little too far...*

My role here, I reminded myself firmly, was of fly on the wall. Or spider under the table, as Mirela would say. I wondered what she was going to make of this news. Rhys as murderer?

If Jane recognized the name, she wasn't giving that away. "Oh, yes?" she said again.

Julie had had enough. She snapped her notebook shut decisively. "That's all for now," she said, standing up.

"When can I see my sister?" asked Jane.

"We'll contact you," said Julie. She turned around and caught sight of me. "Sydney, go away," she said.

I went away.

***

The sky was darkening to the east. One moment it looked like there was no way the sun wouldn't keep shining indefinitely; the next, there was a bank of dark clouds miles offshore, looking for all the world like a mountain range above the bay. The storm was offering us its calling card. The barometer was dropping and giving me a headache.

Glenn was nowhere to be seen, but my father had managed to get some coffee and a copy of the *Cape Cod Times* and was sitting on the uncomfortable settee in the lobby reading.

I sat down next to him. "How're you doing?"

He gave me a bruised look; I'd never before been aware of my father's fragility, his vulnerability. "I can't get her out of my mind," he said.

I reached over and took his hand. "I can imagine."

"She was here because of me," he said. "If I hadn't hired her, she'd still be safe in Boston."

"In New York, surely? She lived in Brooklyn," I said.

"No, she was in Boston," he said. "We were going to look at some work there, there was an auction at one of the Newbury Street galleries, but then I said I wanted a Provincetown artist—and to visit my daughter, too, of course."

"Of course." I squeezed his hand. But I was also thinking fast. Jane said she and Caroline had spoken a week ago, but Caroline had been in Boston, and Jane had just said she'd been in Boston when she got the call about her sister. What were the chances they hadn't seen each other when they were in the same city at the same time?

And did that mean anything? Was it even connected to the SUV that—

Rhys. Rhys' SUV. Stolen, he said. Someone joyriding? But if you stole a car, you wouldn't exactly still be driving it out in the open in a small town two days later, would you? Jane hadn't been wrong in saying we were at the end of the world: Land's End, they call it here, sitting at the tip of the Cape. Next stop, Portugal.

And only one road out of town. If you're driving, you're on Route Six. No other options. There's a story that once, back in the day, a couple of guys held up one of the banks in town and made their escape—on bicycles. Down Route Six. Not the brightest and the best of bank robbers, for sure, but a particularly Provincetown kind of story.

So why hadn't they just taken the SUV and hit the road and hoped they could beat the stolen vehicle updates and make it to the bridge connecting us to the mainland before the cops were on to them? Why would you wait around with a stolen vehicle in the town where you'd stolen it?

Unless, of course, it hadn't been stolen at all.

"Caroline's sister is here," I said. "She's staying at the inn for a few days. I don't know if you feel comfortable—"

He pulled his hand away from mine and looked at me with panic in his eyes. "I don't think—" he started, then stopped and cleared his throat. "Does she blame me?" he asked.

"Of course not." I reached over and took the newspaper from him, folded it, and put it on the coffee table in front of us. "It was an accident. You were at the wrong place at the wrong time." He started to say something, and I interrupted roughly. "Listen to me. I'm *glad* you stopped to read that menu! I'm *glad* you're okay. I couldn't stand losing you. I'm sorry about Caroline, but I'm grateful beyond words that it wasn't you that got hit."

I couldn't imagine how he was feeling. My father is uncomfortable with the expression of emotion, any emotion, at the best of times, and this certainly wasn't the best of times. He nodded and cleared his throat again. "I saw the police were here," he said.

"They were," I confirmed. "They may want to talk to you again, see if you've remembered anything further. Turns out the SUV that hit Caroline was stolen. So it really was just chance, you know, that this happened."

Well, maybe. I was beginning to think the mystery I'd started fabricating had become alarmingly true, that my ideas had somehow manifested in real life. It wasn't a particularly happy thought.

Had my reaction to my own boredom *made* something happen?

9

As usual, my mother's timing was impeccable and not in a good way. I noticed when I picked up the phone that I'd somehow missed two of her calls. She wasn't going to be best pleased about it.

"So you *are* still alive."

"Ma," I said in a desperate effort to stem the tide of recriminations I knew was coming, "I can't talk right now."

"Of course, you can talk right now; what do you think you're doing? Tell me why your father isn't answering his telephone. It has to do with that woman, doesn't it? What's she gotten him to buy?"

I sighed. "It's about Caroline, in a way," I said. "She's dead."

That silenced her. Extraordinary. I didn't think I'd ever experienced my mother speechless. I rather liked it.

Finally, she recovered. "Is that true, or is it what he told you to tell me?"

"It's true, Ma. She was killed in a hit-and-run on Commercial Street. Dad was with her; that's why he's not doing so well."

Her voice soared an octave. "He's hurt?"

"No, no, nothing like that," I said quickly. "Just feeling—well, all the things you'd feel. She wouldn't have been there if he hadn't hired her, you know, that kind of thing."

"That's nonsense," my mother said roundly. "I shall tell him so. Does that mean he's going home? Because I need to stay here a few more days, there won't be anyone there to take care of him."

My mother's presence or absence wouldn't have made a difference in anyone taking care of my father: she believed in frozen dinners on the nights when the housekeeper didn't cook for them, and they had two cleaners who came in four days a week. "I don't think he's in any state to travel anyway, Ma. He's pretty devastated."

"I knew this wouldn't end well. I told him that. If he insists on buying art, there is no need to hire an assistant. We could have gone to Paris or someplace more appropriate. He just went off with this idea on his own. It's quite inexplicable."

Except listening to you makes it understandable as hell. "I think he thought it could be fun. Learning something new," I said. She made some sort of noise, and I continued, "And he was really having fun with it. In fact, he and my boss have both been interested in art, well, this particular artist. . ."

My voice trailed off. Was there a connection there? Something tying together Glenn's new obsession with art, his trips to Amsterdam, and the death of the art broker? And come to think of it, wasn't it a coincidence my father had gotten interested in collecting at the same time as Glenn?

Breathe, Riley, I cautioned myself. On every police show I'd ever watched, at some point, one of the detectives would say to another, "I don't believe in coincidences." Like saying *I don't believe in science*, and we've all seen how far *that* got humanity. Coincidences exist. This could very well be one.

Or not.

"Sydney? Are you still there?"

I roused myself. "I'm here, Ma."

"Where is your father now?"

"He's here. Um, at the inn."

She sighed. "Maybe I should go there, too. Provide him with some moral support." Right: my mother's offer of moral support was roughly akin to what might be on offer from an alligator. A hungry one.

"Ma, you just said Aunt Germaine needs you."

"But your father may need me more." My mother, the martyr. "Sometimes people have to make hard choices to do the right thing."

"He's fine here, Ma." There may have been a note of panic in my voice; if there was one thing we absolutely didn't need right now, it was my mother. "He just needs some peace and quiet. Besides, there's a big storm coming soon. You don't want to be traveling. And the police may want to talk to him again."

"Did they catch him?"

"Who?" My mind didn't always leap in tandem with my mother's. Or even in the same direction.

"The driver, of course." She sounded impatient. "Are you even listening to me? You need to pay attention, Sydney. I've always said you didn't pay attention. Even when you were a little girl, you'd be daydreaming instead of—"

I cut her off. I had to. "They haven't arrested anybody yet, Ma. I'm sure they will."

"It's not as if they could have gone far." There it was again, clear even to my mother. It made no sense. Something was very wrong indeed about that SUV.

I hoped Julie was questioning Rhys.

I cleared my throat. "I'm sure the investigation will turn something up," I said, trying to make my voice more convincing than my thoughts. "And I'll ask Dad to call you."

"He doesn't *have* to call." The martyr was back; what was I thinking? She was never far away. "He has a lot on his mind, and I have my hands full here. Just tell him to answer one of my calls once in a while; that's all I ask."

"Okay, Ma."

"I don't ask much."

"Okay, Ma."

"Are you taking a tone with me, Sydney Riley?"

I was nearing the end of the third decade of my life, and my mother still acted, sometimes, as though I were five years old. "I'm not taking a tone," I said soothingly. "It's noisy here, is all. I have to go, Ma. I'll give him the message."

"What message?"

Seriously? Breathe, Riley; just breathe. "That you called. That he should talk to you."

"Oh, that. Well, of course. And make sure he's not eating too much red meat, and as for drinking. . ."

"I have to go, Ma." And that time, I really did.

My father had disappeared. So had Mike and Jane. Glenn was still, as far as I could tell, missing in action. Ali was working. That pretty much left only one person for me to be with, and she wasn't going to like it, but I really, really needed to talk. To make things start making sense. My head felt like it was about to explode.

I was right. About her not wanting to see me. "Sunshine, do you no longer have a job to go to?" Mirela wanted to know.

"Why's the gallery closed?" I'd stopped by the gallery first, then checked out her studio, thinking she might have started a new piece—Mirela feels oddly inspired by the potential of violent weather.

I finally tracked her down to—of all places—my apartment. The bonus was Ali was clearly taking a break to chat with her, and the more, the merrier, I decided.

She shrugged lightly. "Rhys is going to put boards on the windows," she said, "because of the storm. Perhaps he is getting ready for that now."

"On a Saturday in September? The storm isn't even close yet." People who come to Provincetown in the fall aren't interested in beaches and bonfires; they're here to stroll around town, look at the cafés and galleries, and spend some money. Closing on a Saturday—even with a nor'easter on the way—wouldn't be considered a good business practice.

And Rhys had always struck me as being a better businessman than he was an artist. "Is the storm going to be that bad?" I asked.

Ali answered. "Gale force wind gusts, and there's a high tide that's going to be a lot higher."

"You've been reading the news again," I said accusingly.

"Just anticipating the question, ma'am," he said, winking.

"Stop it, both of you!" Mirela's voice was sharp.

There was a short silence.

"Mirela," said Ali, "asked me to get in touch with someone in arts and antiquities at Homeland Security. It's—well, it's possible she may be on to something. I have a call in to the FBI."

I wasn't sure which had me more curious: that Mirela was really pushing this thing (in which case, it couldn't all be in my head, could it?) or that Ali had been willing to help in his official capacity. "Someone answers the phone at the FBI on a Saturday?" I asked.

"Someone always answers the phone at the FBI," said Ali. "It's just getting the right person *to* the phone that's the tricky part."

"And did you? Get the right person to the phone?"

"Well, right-adjacent, anyway," said Ali. "They're interested, said they'll look into sending a special agent from the art crime team over. But that won't be for a while."

"Because it's the weekend."

"Because it's the weekend, and there's a storm on the way. In another ten or twelve hours, nobody's going to be flying in or out of here."

I looked at Mirela. "So. You going to tell me, or are we playing twenty questions?"

"Sunshine, I do not know this game. But whatever it is, I am not playing."

Ali said, "Rhys has installed a state-of-the-art storage facility in the basement of the gallery. And Mirela doesn't have the key, but she—"

Mirela cut across his sentence with a sniff. "It was a ridiculous lock," she said with disdain.

I was fascinated. "What's in it?"

"Firstly, sunshine, he should not have the money to build this, even with a cheap ridiculous lock," she said. "And he never told me he was making something new downstairs. Not to me did he say it, and not to Iskren, who I know from many years in Plovdiv, and he is a very strange artist but an honest man. If he says he did not know, he did not know. I think Iskren and me, we are what is called collateral damage."

"Tied in with the unintended consequences," I agreed. Mirela had clearly been doing some reading. Enriching her vocabulary. "What about Milo?"

"I would ask Milo also, though I do not trust him as I trust Iskren," she said. "But Milo is not around. And Rhys is not around."

"Okay," I said. "I have news, too. Brace yourselves. Turns out the SUV in the hit-and-run? The one that killed Caroline? It's Rhys'. He claims it was stolen two days ago."

Mirela was shaking her head. "Rhys drives a sports car," she said. "A convertible. This is not the same vehicle."

Ali said, "Two days ago? And it's still in town?"

"In this thought, we are as one," I told him. "Why run the risk of keeping it in town?

Why didn't the police find it before? And why did someone want an art broker dead?"

"I think I know," said Mirela. We both turned to look at her. She was sitting at the table, rolling a glass around and around on top of it. If I didn't know better, I'd have said she was nervous. "In this room, this room with controlled moisture and light and heat, there are more paintings I have not seen before. In flat files, most of them, these are special drawers to keep paintings safe. But these are not our paintings. These are not paintings the gallery represents." She took a deep breath. "One of them was *Storm on the Sea of Galilee*. A boat—and Christ—in the rough water."

I shook my head. "Sorry? What's that?"

"It is a painting by Rembrandt van Rijk," she said.

Ali said, "Last seen at the Isabella Stewart Gardner Museum in 1990."

Oh.

No one said anything for a moment. There was nothing, really, one could reasonably say. Exclaiming fatuously about one of the world's most important art heists was useless.

Finally, I cleared my throat. "It *could* be a copy," I said at last.

"It has to be a copy," said Ali. "She didn't see any other pieces from the Gardner. But she did see a number of artists that probably shouldn't be there. That definitely aren't in Rhys' class." He glanced at Mirela. "No offense," he added.

"I do not take offense," she said. "I am not Rembrandt, me." She said it reverently, acolyte to master.

"So what does it all mean?" I demanded. "Let's lay it out. We have three paintings showing up at the gallery that are either newly discovered works by Charles Hawthorne or forgeries made to look like he did them. We have Glenn buying one of them and then going off the deep end."

"What does that mean?" asked Mirela. Ali was looking at me with interest, too.

"Glenn's been weird. Well, you saw the other day. He's yelling at people, and he never yells at people. He's making mysterious trips to Amsterdam, he's suddenly becoming an art expert, and he keeps disappearing."

"Into the swimming pool?" Mirela sounded slightly incredulous.

"Wait, what?" Then I realized. "It's an expression, Mirela. Going off the deep end means going a little crazy."

"And it's happened since he bought the Hawthorne?" asked Ali.

Mirela stopped twirling the glass. "It is not a magical painting," she said sharply. "It did not bring with it a curse on his life."

"No, of course not, but don't you see, it's all just too coincidental?" Okay, so I don't agree with the old I-don't-believe-in-coincidences chestnut, but even I have my limits. "All about art."

"All about that gallery," said Ali.

"So then enter my father and Caroline Harrison, and she's teaching him tons of stuff about art appreciation and collecting and all that jazz, and she goes to see the magical Hawthorne, and immediately she's under its spell, too. She demands to see the others. My father backs off—he wasn't too crazy about the mudheads—but she is acting like a bloodhound that's found a scent and's following it. And then *she* gets killed in a weird black swan event, and the driver escapes, and the vehicle turns out to belong to none other than Rhys. Who," I added with one last big intake of breath, "just happens to have in his basement a stack of stolen artwork, or forged artwork, take your pick, that may be worth millions."

"Black swan?" asked Mirela.

"It's a bird," said Ali.

"I am aware of that," she said. "I am not aware of an idiom in which it causes an accident."

"Once-in-a-lifetime event," I amended. "Focus, Mirela. Which do you think it is?"

"Which what?"

"Are the paintings you saw in the basement stolen? Or are they forgeries?"

She shook her head. "I do not know. Is it the real Rembrandt? The real Vermeer? The real Pissarro? If they were, he might have a better lock on the door."

"Did you look them up? The paintings you saw? Are they all stolen, like the one from the Gardner?"

Ali pulled his laptop over and hit a couple of keys. "Some are; the Rembrandt's obviously been on the top of the FBI's most-wanted art list. The van Gogh—it's a small piece called Poppy Flowers—was in a Cairo museum when it was stolen. Twice, actually."

"What d'you mean?"

"Stolen sometime in the 1970s. Somebody tried to sell it in Kuwait ten years later, and it was returned to the museum. Then stolen again in 2010."

"And they say lightning doesn't strike twice," I commented.

"More likely, the museum has crap securi-ty," said Ali practically. "The Monet—it's a study of Charing Cross Bridge—shouldn't be there at all. Or anywhere. It was lifted from a Dutch museum by a couple of people who met on Tinder, and the police found them, but the guy's mother saw the cops coming and burned the paintings."

"I'm imagining their Tinder profiles," I said. "Hobbies include romantic music, long walks on the beach, and art heists."

Ali ignored me. "So, yeah, some of the paintings are known, they're in the artists' catalogues raisonné, and they're probably still floating around somewhere on the black market."

"The Monet is gone," said Mirela sadly.

"Makes you wonder why it was there in the first place," said Ali.

"What about the rest of the paintings?" I asked. "Or is that all there was?"

Mirela was scrolling on her phone. "There are eight more," she said. "They are all in styles—"

"Wait. You took pictures?"

"Of course, I took pictures, sunshine. How else would I remember what is there?"

I was imagining Mirela snapping photos with her iPhone and Rhys coming unexpectedly down the stairs and catching her before sealing her in forever with the paintings. He might even have gotten a more serious lock she couldn't pick. "You took a risk," I said.

"That's what I told her," said Ali.

"If you would let me speak," she said, "I will tell you some are in styles that are consistent with the work of Monet, Pissarro, and Vermeer. And also some lesser-known artists. And before you ask, no, I am not an art critic. I also took the photographs so we could look them up."

I nodded. "Good idea. So for some of them, Rhys can say, look, this is the lost painting. And ask for a finder's fee, as they belonged to museums. But for the others, what's the play? He says he found them. Isn't it exciting, these works no one even knew existed? Is that it?"

"If they're good enough," said Ali. "If he could prove provenance."

"So maybe he's working on that. But how did he get them in the first place? Is Rhys that good an artist?"

"No," Mirela said. "Rhys could not do it. He does not have discipline. Or the talent, no; but it is mostly about the discipline. It is very difficult to copy a painter's style. To stay within their lines. The vision of the other artist, it must be taken into the heart. Rhys could never do that."

"All right," I said. "Then who?"

"Before you get too carried away," said Ali, "remember that this forger—if there is a forger—could be anywhere. Anywhere in the United States, anywhere in the world."

"I do not think so," said Mirela slowly. "Why would anyone bring the paintings to Provincetown? To a place right by the ocean where it is so humid he has to have a room built especially for them? That does not work." She shook her head. "Me, I think it is Milo."

"Milo? He's good enough?"

She balanced her hand in a *so-so* gesture. "I think so, yes. Well, sometimes. He is a man in love with his own talent, but that does not mean he is wrong. It does not mean he is not a first-class artist. It is surprising to him that he has not been recognized on the world stage, that his work is not at Sotheby's or Christie's, selling for millions of dollars." She hesitated. "In this, perhaps, he is right. I do not know, me, why he is not famous. The art world is a strange place."

"And that," said Ali, "is a pretty good starting-place for becoming a forger, isn't it? Someone with massive talent who isn't being given his due. The copies may bring in money, but they'll also bring in the immense satisfaction of having duped the very same people who rejected you."

"Caroline said something similar," I said. "Remember, Ali? You were there. She said the art of forgery is a subversive act. Embarrassing the experts, getting back at the critics."

"That," said Mirela, "describes Milo perfectly. He would want it to be known—after the sale has gone through, and he can laugh at the world. See what I did? How wonderful am I?"

"Okay," I said. "So… what if we're right? Milo's doing the paintings, and Rhys is figuring out how to fake provenance. How do they sell the paintings when they're ready? Who do they tell the story to?"

"I think this is where Hawthorne comes in," said Ali. "No, wait, *cara*, hear me out. I don't think they've done it before. Or maybe I mean haven't done it yet. Think about it. Rhys has limited name recognition in the industry. What's he going to do, throw a couple of Old Masters in his display window? Go through one of those TV reality shows?" He shook his head. "What if they decided to start small, with a decent, well-known artist but one with only a moderate reputation on the world stage. Try out the story. See where the weaknesses are."

"This is really happening, isn't it?" I said, suddenly feeling very small. "This isn't just me making things up."

"The question is," said Ali, "how it ties in to the one person in this town who might figure it out—remember, you said Caroline recognized the brushstrokes on Glenn's Hawthorne—so how it ties in to that one person getting killed by Rhys' stolen vehicle."

"Which is still MIA," I said in frustration, then caught sight of the art deco clock on the wall that had been Ali's only contribution so far to home décor. "Damn, I have to go. I don't want to leave my father alone."

"We will solve your mystery, sunshine," said Mirela. "Always, these things come together in the end for you, do they not?"

"Um—yeah, I guess." What I was thinking was that, in general, when things "came together," it was only because whoever I was supposed to be pursuing had started pursuing me, and not in a good way. I was hoping this time might be an exception.

She stood up. "And I will go, too," she said. "Kid Zhivkov will be getting up from her nap."

"Do one thing for me, Mirela," said Ali.

"Yes, of course. What is it?"

"Stay out of that basement. In fact, stay away from the gallery."

"Of course," she said again, pushing her hand into her pocket so we wouldn't see her crossed fingers. Except that I did.

I should have paid attention. Story of my life.

10

I walked around for a while.

My father was a big boy and could survive an hour longer without me by his side, and I needed time to think. And I've always done my best thinking when I'm moving, whether walking or driving.

The sky was still roiling with dark clouds way out over the water, but none of it had touched the town yet, and in fact, there was that gorgeous bright sunlight you sometimes get when there are dark clouds in the background. Someone should paint this.

Hell, it was Provincetown: someone undoubtedly had. Multiple someones.

The Race Point Inn was in the East End of town, so just to prolong my solitude, I headed west. Past the ever-changing shops, places that came and went along with the fashions they sold; past Spiritus Pizza, which will never leave, one of the few constants that brought all parts of the community together for a slice or an espresso milkshake at two o'clock in the afternoon—or in the morning. Past the Brasswood Inn, where they sometimes give concerts on Monday nights; past the cannabis shop and the Boatslip, where they hold Tea Dance throughout the season; past Coffey Men, Scott rearranging his window displays and grinning at me from behind a mannequin; past Joe Coffee (which the owners insist on styling as joe coffee) and Arcadia with its gorgeous fair-trade scarves, waving to Jay through the open door as I passed. I stopped at the Coast Guard station, where Commercial Street takes a turn to follow the harbor, and sat down on the bench and watched people walk by, which is, of course, Provincetown's premier entertainment.

Was I really going to leave? Was that going to be a thing?

If so, where? Back to Boston and Cambridge, where I'd spent most of my life? And do what? I was a wedding planner in a small town where I knew everyone and could find the most difficult and weird things, where I knew whom to ask. There were dozens like me in any urban area. And the point was, wasn't it, that I really didn't want to keep doing my *job*, not that I was tired of P'town per se?

So what then? Stay in town like so many others who piece together income from waiting tables and walking dogs, selling retail, and driving cabs? Was that what I wanted? It seemed a rich enough existence… for someone in their twenties, which I hadn't been for some time.

The truth was, I didn't want a job; I wanted a career. Something that challenged me, filled me with anticipation, and enriched my life. And I was woefully unprepared for almost anything. Back to school, then? To study what?

The thought of leaving had my stomach lurching; if I left, for sure, I could never come back. Never ever afford a place to live; never ever find work I enjoyed. The price you pay for living where other people come for vacation. And did I really want to leave?

No: I didn't. There were sunsets at Herring Cove, cycling down Commercial Street in the early mornings for a pastry from the Portuguese Bakery, sitting on the benches in front of Town Hall and watching the steady stream of people from all over the world. Sitting on a hot afternoon under the lattice at Suzanne's Garden and drinking in the lushness of the flowers. Walking down the street in the evenings with the lights spilling out over the pavement and the various bits of music of all sorts drifting out into the air. Hiking in the dunes and around Beech Forest. Taking a sail with my friend Thea in a small 19-foot rental from Flyer's. Even the whale watches had a plaintive appeal anytime I considered the option of leaving, tugging me back where I belonged.

That was it, of course, the feeling my place was here. I had myself become a town personality. Everyone knew the Race Point, everyone knew we did the best events in town (no need for false modesty: this was the truth), and everyone knew who was responsible for them.

And then there was "The Hobby." The fact that, as Julie Agassi frequently mourned, there wasn't a violent unexplained death on the Outer Cape I didn't end up becoming part of—investigating (which she referred to as meddling) and often solving (which she referred to as luck). For heaven's sake, they even called me Provincetown's answer to Miss Marple. When that happens, you become distinct from your own self; you become the role they've cast you in—or, to be fair, in which you've cast yourself. Did I want to be a role?

If you leave, you can't come back.

And none of this took into account the person who'd become so much a part of who I was that I couldn't see my way clear to imagining any kind of life without him. Ali Hassim. The son of sophisticated Lebanese immigrants who'd fled Beirut during the civil war when everything changed. A Muslim whose sister wore a hijab but who didn't pray or practice. A man whose work weighed him down with a hundred layers of pain, with thousands of voices crying out, who managed to see the cruelty and sheer unfairness he encountered every day and do what he could to change it.

He hadn't chosen Provincetown; he'd chosen *me*. For the first time, I really thought about what that had meant for Ali. In choosing me, he'd chosen Provincetown by default. Was that what I'd intended? Was it even fair?

Yeah, sure, we'd spent time together at his place in Boston before he sold it; we'd traveled together, spent dreary winter days toasting muffins over fires in the Cotswolds—because I could only take vacations in the off-season, and we both liked England—we'd seen bits and pieces of what life was like "over the bridge" that connected Land's End to the rest of the continent… but this was where I lived all the time, and he lived when he wasn't traveling, and what did it say to him if after asking him to change his world around to accommodate me, I said, no, this isn't enough?

I wasn't exactly liking the self-portrait emerging here. And this little corner of Commercial Street wasn't offering up any answers.

***

The first person I saw back at the inn was Glenn.

"Where have you been?" he growled.

"I went for a walk."

"I couldn't find you." He sounded more peevish than angry.

I sighed; my contract does not stipulate being on the premises twenty-four hours a day, but that wasn't what this was about. "You should call me," I said, feeling a little helpless. Obviously, his mood hadn't improved significantly. Anxiety Girl inside me fluttered and immediately went back to worrying he had some terminal illness.

"Well, I'm busy now," he said. "But if you can spare the time, I'd like a word with you later."

Great. Nothing like having a meeting you don't want to have in the first place hanging over your head. "What's it about?"

"If I had time to talk now, I'd take the time to talk now." He was scowling. "No weddings today?"

"No weddings today," I confirmed.

"Hmm. Okay. See me later."

I headed straight into Mike's office. "He's dying, isn't he?"

"What?" He looked up from his computer monitor, startled.

"Glenn. He has some kind of terminal illness. He wants to meet with me later."

Mike sighed. "He doesn't have a terminal illness," he said, his eyes going back to the monitor.

"You don't know that." I sat down in his client chair, uninvited.

"Sydney. Listen. You loved Barry, and you lost him. Now you love Glenn, and you don't want to lose him. I get all that. But people do things for all sorts of reasons, and you can't go reading your own fears into their actions." He glanced up. "Well, it being you, *you* can, but it's not a great idea. You're stressing yourself out. More importantly, you're starting to stress *me* out."

"I know." I stared out his window onto Commercial Street.

Mike relented. "He probably wants to tell you what he just told me. He's moved up his

Amsterdam trip. And—well, I should let him tell you, but—"

"Tell me!"

He shrugged. "We had it right. He wants to start spending more time with André. Who is Dutch, by the way, not French. And who is an artist. And who teaches art in the Netherlands."

"He told you all that?"

"He did. Just a while ago."

"Then, if everything is so hunky-dory, why's he being so irritable?"

Mike smiled and leaned back in his chair. "Because he feels guilty about us. Specifically, you and me. Thinks he's abandoning us."

"But—"

"So it would be a good thing if you could reassure him when he talks to you about it. Nothing's going to change all that much. He's not actually moving to Amsterdam, you know; he just wants to spend more time there. Be a little more hands-off with the inn."

"He never had to be that hands-on," I protested. "He always had us to run the place. Well, us and Martin. And Adrienne the diva chef." Actually, when it came down to it, a pretty good team.

"Yeah, well, maybe he felt he owed it to Barry to keep the place the same as it was.

Maybe this means he's finally getting over Barry."

"And this André—"

"—is none of our business," Mike finished. "Okay? Let your little bird fly away when he needs to, Mama."

I giggled. "Hardly *little*. Which is what I was going to ask. . ."

"Get out of my office," Mike said, leaning back over the desk, his eyes going to the monitor again. "And yeah, André's a bear."

"All I wanted to know."

I tracked my father down to the bar we would probably have called the "Little Bar," except the Atlantic House already had one called that, and no one can compete with them—it's where they say Tennessee Williams wrote The Glass Menagerie. But *our* "little bar" is lovely and cozy, with just five tables, lots of brass and polished mahogany, and stained glass over the bar itself.

My father was sitting at the bar, and sitting next to him was—inevitably, it seemed—Jane Pfeiffer.

I kissed my father's cheek and hopped up on an empty barstool. "How are you feeling?" I asked him.

"I'm fine," he said, and he really did look like a different person from the night before.

"Did you hear anything more about this storm that's supposed to be coming?" Jane asked me. "Will we lose electricity?"

"The inn has a generator," I answered absently. "Besides, it's still offshore. I think we're looking at another ten hours before we really start feeling it." That was a wild guess but probably as accurate as anything else.

One of the Kevins came over. "Coffee or wine?" They all know my tastes. I'm never sure if that's a good or bad thing.

"Coffee, thanks." It was what the others were drinking… and a little early in the day for wine, even for me.

"Your mother is worried," my father informed me, picking up his iPhone as if for demonstration purposes. "She seems to think if she were here, it wouldn't be so bad."

"Sounds like Ma." The bartender set the coffee in front of me, and I immediately took a sip and scalded my mouth. "Um," I said, putting it back down again, "if it's not too indelicate, what are you going to do now?" The question was, really, for either of them. If I'd been my father, I'd have wasted no time in getting out of Dodge.

"Your father still has some interest in starting a collection," said Jane. "I've encouraged him to think more about it. It can be a very fulfilling occupation."

"I see," I said, though I really didn't. If I had the odd twenty or thirty thousand lying around, I'd probably—heresy of heresies—replace my Honda, known affectionately as the Little Green Car. It was developing rust spots that might become an issue at the next annual inspection.

Still, that's me. We all spend our money in different ways, with different dreams for how it will make our lives better—and different regrets when it doesn't. "Do you collect?" I asked her.

"Oh, no," she said, but she was smiling. "I spend a great deal of my time traveling, so I don't really have the time to collect—well, and no time to enjoy the collection, either, I suppose. But I grew up in a home filled with great art, and it's made all the difference in my life. To be exposed to that kind of beauty, to understand—intuitively, through images—the grandeur and possibilities of the human spirit… well, I wouldn't have traded that for anything."

I tried the coffee again. Better. "Where did you and Caroline grow up? Or were you too far apart in age to be together?" I'd have guessed Caroline to be somewhat older, but what did I know; I still think I look like I'm in my twenties.

I'm the only one who thinks so, but it's my story, and I'm sticking to it.

"We lived in Boston," Jane was saying. "In one of the brownstones in Back Bay, not far from the Public Gardens. It was—a fairytale house, I guess I'd say, in so many ways. Secret passages—well, one, anyway, and a disused back staircase that had been built for the servants to use. I used to sit on that staircase, invisible, and eavesdrop on grown-ups' conversations." She was smiling, and there was a light in her eyes, a lightness in her voice. Good memories. "And art," she said. "Paintings everywhere, on every space on the walls, tapestries, statues, sculptures in the back garden. My father drilled us on them. We'd have to periodically do a tour of one of the rooms, reciting who'd done which painting, when and where it was created, what it said about the artist's style, that sort of thing." The smile had faded.

"What did—does—your father do?" I asked curiously. Probably independently wealthy if this magical house was anything to go by. I knew what Back Bay was like, and I'd be willing to bet it was at least three-quarters inherited money. People who made my wealthy parents look destitute.

"He's retired," she said. "He was—oh, still is, I suppose, though not officially—an art historian. He has an opinion on nearly every Great Master. He writes books. Occasionally teaches a seminar—he's professor emeritus at Harvard and Montserrat, gives well-attended lectures, has undergraduates fawning all over him." She wasn't looking at us anymore; there was some undercurrent in her voice that sounded raw and painful.

I cleared my throat. "And—um—your mother?"

A slight shrug. "She was one of his students, originally, but… well, she went on to have an artistic career of her own. She's a glassblower. She went abroad to study with Tagliapietra and never came back; now, she lives in Italy. She comes to the States from time to time to offer a master class or two."

"That must be hard," I said. "Not to see her very often." And, I thought, to take a backseat to her art and her mentor. "How old were you when your parents separated?"

A light shrug as though ridding herself of the memory. "We were young," she said. "In elementary school, both of us. My father never considered glass an art form, though, to be honest, I've come to believe that's just him wanting to get back at her and make his ego feel okay about her leaving. She was supposed to spend her life adoring him, and instead, she built up an adoring following of her own. The pupil surpassing the master. He couldn't have that. She ended up with a bigger name than he had." She paused. "Neither of us was ever allowed to work in glass."

The one thing I did know about those brownstones on Commonwealth Avenue was how dark they were, windows of old thick glass, trees growing up outside; I suppressed a shiver, imagining growing up in a dark house with an angry exacting father. It didn't really matter what priceless art pieces were on the wall. I was starting to feel sorry for her.

"I'm sorry," I said, a little inadequately. Sydney Riley, probing all your family secrets while you wait. "It sounds like a tough way to grow up."

Jane shrugged and managed a smile. "Never mind," she said, almost cheerfully. "It gave us both a good education, and a career in art is a beautiful thing, and I wouldn't have changed that part of things for the world. But tell me about yourself. Provincetown must be an exciting place to live, with all this creativity going on around you."

"It has its moments," I conceded. "It still attracts creative people for sure, but they're not the starving-artist type, not anymore. Back in the sixties and seventies, you could come here and crash on someone's couch and paint all day and talk about artsy things all night."

My father was looking at me a little quizzically. I had no idea where any of this was going, but I had a feeling Jane Pfeiffer held at least one key to figuring it out, and this conversation was as good as any other. If I really paid attention. "I live in a tiny studio over a nightclub, and most of the time, my boyfriend's there, too, when he can work from home. It's crowded, for sure, but we're lucky to have it at all."

She nodded sympathetically. "What does your boyfriend do?" she asked, nodding again as the bartender picked up the coffee pot and tilted it toward her inquiringly. She held up her cup and watched him fill it.

"He's in law enforcement," I said.

Jane's cup went back down with a loud clatter and spraying coffee. "Really? Oh, sorry, Stephen—" this to my father, who'd gotten splashed. "Um—sorry, so clumsy sometimes. Um, what branch does he work in? Your boyfriend, I mean?"

"Department of Homeland Security," I said, watching her. What was *that* about? "He's in Immigration and Customs Enforcement, but he works in the human trafficking division."

Jane seemed to have recovered her composure. "I see. That couldn't be easy," she said. "For either of you."

"It's horrible," I agreed.

"How do you work on that sort of thing from home?" my father wanted to know. "I didn't know police could work from home."

I sighed. It wasn't *exactly* a secret, but. . . "Right now, he's undercover, but it's online," I said. "I mean, the people he's tracking, they're online. So he can do it from anywhere, really."

"Online?" Her interest had sharpened; I would almost feel the air crackle between us. "Tell me—um, can you tell us more?"

I didn't see why not; it's not as though these two were involved. "There's a scam that's been going on," I said. "I mean, it's an old scam but updated. Someone lures someone else in through an app, usually romantically. They get the person, the victim, to trust them, maybe even to fall in love with them. Then they start making suggestions, getting the other person to invest in stuff—cryptocurrency, mainly, though I think there are other things." I couldn't remember, really; it seemed like that conversation had taken place a long time ago. And it didn't seem the moment to bring up the art part of the scam. It hadn't even sounded like Ali was completely sure about that.

Jane was nodding. "And the first few transactions go extremely well," she said. "The investor gets some nice little returns on some modest investments. And their trust builds. The scammer plays it out as long as they can, making sure they have the other person well and truly hooked. And then they come up with one big investment, tell the mark to put all their money into it, and the person loses everything, and the scammer vanishes."

My father was staring at her. "You sound like this has happened to you," he said.

Jane shook her head. "Not personally," she said and then turned back to me. "Go on," she urged. "There must be more to it here if ICE is involved."

"Well, the problem isn't what they're doing to the person being fleeced," I said. I didn't think I'd ever used the word *fleeced* in conversation before. "I mean, yeah, that's a problem, but the point is the people who are luring the wealthy victims. A whole lot of them are trafficked.

"Good Lord!" My father was staring at me. "I didn't know this."

I shrugged. "Ali doesn't talk a lot about his work," I said. "For obvious reasons."

"And now he's posing as one of the marks?" Jane asked.

I nodded. "I don't know how it all works," I said. "I mean, actually, I don't know anything about it—how he gets them to open up to him, how he'll arrest them, I don't even know where they are."

"Probably offshore," commented my father, who had clearly decided it was time to join the conversation.

"Some are," I agreed. "He said a lot of the sites are in southeast Asia. But they're here, too. In the United States, I mean."

"The crypto angle is interesting," said Jane, finally drinking her coffee. "There's a lot of crypto tied up with high-end art, too. I wouldn't be surprised if there was some overlap there with what your boyfriend—Ali, is that his name?—is doing. Art holds value better than any currency." She paused. "I'd like you to introduce me to him—if you don't mind."

"Maybe." I wasn't sure what else to say and had no idea what to make of her sharpened interest—either in the trafficking or in my boyfriend. "Anyway, it gets a little cramped when he's there, and I'm there."

"And the cat," said my father, who dislikes cats.

"And the cat," I added, smiling. "At least I know I won't be collecting any art; even if I could afford it, there'd be no place for it to go!"

"Sydney's friend Mirela gave Sydney a canvas," my father said to Jane. "I think it's behind your couch, isn't it?"

"It just doesn't fit anywhere," I said, a little defensively. "Mirela is a local artist," I said to Jane. "She does—"

"Mirela Dobreva," she said, nodding. "Oh, I know. I've seen her work. She did a show last year in DC. She's very gifted."

"Not exactly the same as the Old Masters," I said. "She started out doing fishing boats, you know, for the local tourists. They sold, but then she kind of came into her own, and now she does completely different stuff. She's intuitive. She says she channels things. Sometimes the results are quite scary." I remembered, not that long ago when a fishing-boat sank with people on board. Mirela didn't know anything about it, yet she spent a night in her studio doing frenzied abstract paintings of people dying. She really was absorbing. . . something.

Jane's focus was drifting. "Where does she show?" she asked, a little absently.

"I wouldn't mind going to see—if it's true there's time before the weather gets worse out there—"

"The gallery's closed," I said. "No one really knows why; there are still plenty of people in town. But Rhys closed—and he's nowhere around to—"

"Rhys *Whitney?*" The sharpened attention was back with a click I could almost hear. "She's with Rhys Whitney?"

"Not exactly *with*," I said, a little uncomfortably. "He represents her, and she shows at his gallery, but I don't think she even really likes—"

"I should have known that," Jane said, almost to herself. "Should have remembered he has a place here." She looked up at me. "Tell me, Sydney—is Milo Griffin part of that group?"

I nodded. "You know Milo." I tried to make it halfway between a statement and a question. It ended up sounding like a squeak.

"Oh, I know Milo," she said, and even my father looked startled at the bitterness in her voice. She caught his look. "The art world is small," she said to him. "We've all at least heard of each other. Most of us have worked together, have shared space, or have been to the same openings. And Milo—when he first came to the States, he studied in Boston. It's very much a small town in many ways. We all knew each other."

I couldn't remember Caroline mentioning that. "Were you friends?" I asked cautiously.

"Friends?" The bitterness would have been apparent even to Ibsen had he been there to hear it. "Oh, so much more than friends." She sighed. "I'm sorry. I don't mean to be melodramatic. But Milo Griffin's the reason Caroline and I—he's why there were problems between us. The estrangement. All over a man—how trite and how sad."

I personally couldn't imagine having a crush on Milo but to each their own. "You were both in love with him?" I asked.

My father stirred uncomfortably. "Sydney, it's none—"

Jane held up a hand. "It's all right, Stephen," she said, and she suddenly sounded tired. "It's not her fault. I'm the one who brought it up. Yes, I was head over heels for Milo, and for a while there, I thought he was with me, too. Now that I've come to know him better—well, there are probably a hundred other women who thought that at one time or another. Turns out Milo isn't the kind of guy who limits his options. Not with women, not with paintings, not in life."

There was a brief silence. She shrugged. "But there it is. Naïve in love, I guess. Even when it was starting to dawn on me not all his stories made sense, when I was starting to hear that little voice that warns you away from the edge—even then, I believed what I wanted to believe, and I believed in us. As a couple, I mean. I thought there wasn't anything that couldn't be sorted. I thought… well, I kept thinking that, kept listening to him lie about where he was and what he was doing until he met the one person he couldn't keep hidden from me."

"Caroline," I said.

A twisted smile. "First, we were in competition for our father's affection and recognition, and then we were in competition for Milo's. And both times, she won. Maybe he saw something in her that reflected something in him, you know? Caroline was a person eternally on the edge of getting her life together. Maybe Milo is, too."

There was a moment of silence, stretching out taut and tight around us, spinning out her words until they seemed to echo around us. Caroline and Milo? Here in Provincetown? Wasn't that stretching credibility a bit too far?

Jane homed in on it, of course. I was beginning to respect her mind. "Stephen," she said, "tell me something. Was it your idea to come to Provincetown in search of something to start your collection?"

"Well, yes," he said, but he sounded doubtful. "That is to say, Sydney's here, and we know the town. My wife and I come down here often, and so when Caroline suggested thinking about collecting someone local… Oh," he said, understanding dawning. "I wasn't telling Caroline about Provincetown, was I?"

Jane was nodding. "She talked you into it," she said, "without you realizing it. Not your fault; it's not the first time she's persuaded someone to do something they end up thinking is their own idea. She can persuade anyone to do anything, whether it's in their best interests or not. She's very good at that sort of thing." She stopped. "She *was* very good at it," she amended.

I still wasn't seeing a whole lot of grief. I was starting to understand why.

"You think she wanted to start things up with Milo again?" I asked. "I mean, I know he's been in Paris the last few years." Who had told me that? Mirela? Rhys? "Surely she could have done that without this whole—"

I stopped. Partly because of what I was seeing in Jane's face, but partly, too, because my own racing thoughts were finally catching up with me. And I wondered if I shouldn't have been able to perhaps piece it together earlier.

Caroline and Milo, not my father—much less me—had been the reason they'd come to Provincetown. There had been meticulous planning involved. Something happening here was bigger than just a reunion, just the chance to see an old flame; Caroline could have done that at any time, without ever involving my father—every summer, our normal population of three thousand people swells to sixty thousand. No one needs a reason to come to Provincetown.

I've mentioned it before, but you don't just happen to find yourself in P'town. We're at Land's End: beyond lay the treacherous sandbars that had earned the Outer Cape its nickname—the graveyard of the Atlantic. You get here, and there's nowhere else to go. And it attracts the kind of people who find themselves in other dead ends, the kind of people who are running from something.

People come here to paint pictures in the famous Cape light; they come to party with the gay community; they come to be alone. But no one needs a reason or at least a reason they'd have to try and make plausible to others. No one asks you why you're here; they know. You heard Provincetown calling your name. At some deep unexplored level of your being, you *belong.*

So the thought of Caroline using my father as a beard of sorts just didn't make sense. She could have dropped in, hunted Milo down, said whatever it was she felt she had to say to him, case closed. Whatever reason she wanted to be here and see Milo, I couldn't believe it was just about looking up an old flame.

Especially when you end up being killed. By a vehicle owned by the aforementioned old flame's professional colleague.

Okay, so I was seriously rethinking that whole "there is no such thing as a coincidence" idea. Maybe there isn't.

I took a long, deep, steadying breath. "Jane," I said, "why did Caroline want to see Milo? And why are you here—I mean, I know you came when you heard about Caroline's accident, but why are you really here?"

She narrowed her eyes. "My sister—"

"It's more than that," I said briskly. "You say you hadn't seen her recently, only talked on the phone last weekend, but you were both in Boston just now before coming to P'town, and

I can't believe you didn't see each other. And I also can't believe this is just about helping my father acquire a painting or about chasing down an old boyfriend. There are things going on at the Whitney Worthington, and Rhys and Milo are in it up to their ears, and I want to know what you know about that."

She looked a little bemused. "And why are you interested?" she countered.

"Because my best friend is involved, whether she wants to be or not," I said. "If there's a scandal around the gallery, she's going to bear the consequences." Well, her and the mysterious Iskren, who I'd yet to meet even after five years. And the other partner, the one who painted oysters, oysters, and more oysters. "People get hurt," I said. "I don't want my friend being your collateral damage."

Jane sipped her coffee. "There's always collateral damage," she said softly.

"Fine. Do whatever you like. As long as the collateral damage doesn't involve Mirela."

"Sydney—" My father put a restraining hand on my arm. "Jane's trying to help—"

"Jane's here for her own reasons," I said sharply and turned back to her. "Just tell me you didn't plan this in Boston when you and Caroline were both there last week. Maybe realizing Milo's in Provincetown, maybe figure out which of you he might still like, and I'll tell you one thing, if this is all some kind of family drama, then I'll be—"

"Oh, stop," she said, waving her hand in front of my eyes. "Don't be absurd. There's no family drama now. My sister is dead, remember?"

Silence. Oh, damn. Not exactly sensitive. *Breathe, Riley.* "I'm sorry," I finally managed to say in what my own sister, Alexandra, used to call my Tiny Mouse Voice. This business of talking about sisters—especially dead ones— was starting to make me a little crazy.

My father, who has spent a lifetime making it a point to neither hear nor understand emotional conflict when it erupts around him, said calmly, "Maybe we can have something a little stronger than coffee."

I was seething but didn't know where to go with any of this. The bartender, a different one of the Kevins, responded with alacrity. "Scotch," said my father. "Jane? Sydney?"

"Nothing," I said. I hadn't taken my eyes off her.

"Grey Goose, straight up," Jane said. Her gaze hadn't wavered, either.

My father made a sort of Star Trek Jean-Luc Picard "make it so" gesture and didn't say anything. I wasn't surprised; I'd see him back off from too many arguments, turn away from slammed doors, and pretend he couldn't hear raised voices. He'd run a mile to keep away from messy emotional outbursts or fraught conversations. He was a master at not seeing what he didn't want to see, at not hearing what he didn't want to hear.

Of course, pouring Grey Goose over the situation wasn't exactly going to make things less flammable, either.

I took a deep breath. "Is it true? Did Caroline come to P'town because Milo was here?"

For a moment, I didn't think she was going to answer. She waited until her glass was in front of her and my father had been served, and then she downed the whole thing in one gulp. Impressive. I'd have been choking my stomach lining up after that. "Yes," she said. "I think probably so. Of course, she's not here to ask, is she?"

I wasn't falling for the guilt trip twice. "And do you think she knew what he's been doing?"

She looked at me impassively. "I have no idea," she said. "What is it you think he's been doing?"

Okay. Maybe we'd been skirting the subject for too long. Maybe I should just put my cards on the table.

Maybe I should have had that drink.

"I think Milo's been forging paintings, and Rhys has been selling them as originals," I said. "And I think you've known that all along."

11

I found it extremely disconcerting that Jane's response was to smile. Damn it, I'd been rather proud of figuring that out. Looking forward to her surprise.

"Well," she said and then paused, turning away to catch the bartender's eye and raise her glass for a second round. She waited until he'd given her a refill before continuing. "They said you were clever."

"Who said?" Of course, they were right; credit where credit's due.

"Around," she said vaguely. This time she sipped the vodka. "Actually, Glenn told me," she said.

"You know Glenn?" She'd been in town, what, five minutes?

She didn't bother answering. "The problem is," she said slowly, as though thinking something through, "Rhys thinks he can control it, and he can't. It's gotten way past the point of him controlling anything."

"Wait," I said. "You know something's going on? With the Hawthornes?"

"Oh, is it Hawthornes this time?" She was politeness itself. "Oh, of course. Charles Hawthorne. The Cape Cod School of Art. Plein-air painting. Yeah, that makes sense."

My father said admiringly, "You know a lot about Provincetown painters."

"The Hawthornes are for practice," Jane said briskly. "Of course, I'm not saying Hawthorne wasn't a great painter, mind you: of course he was. But he's not getting the same scrutiny as if we were dealing with a Cézanne, or a Matisse, or something. So it's a safe place to see if one's techniques work."

"Techniques for painting or techniques for selling?"

She nodded, approving. "Yes," she said. "Exactly. Rhys Whitney for the authentication and the sales, and Milo Griffin for the work. Though it's hard to imagine Milo could produce enough paintings to make it worthwhile. Not at Hawthorne prices."

"Tell me two things," I said. I really, really wished I'd gotten that drink. "Who are you, and what are you doing here, really?"

She nodded again and finished off the Grey Goose. She reached into the purse on the bar next to her, and I wondered for a moment if things were about to get even more exciting, but it was a small leather folder she pulled out with a badge and an identification card inside.

"FBI," said my father, impressed.

"You could have said that from the start," I complained.

"Not always a good idea," said Jane. "You have time for another drink?"

"Absolutely," I said fervently. This time when the Kevin returned, I made sure I got my order in first.

Jane waited until I'd had a swallow of wine before continuing. "We've had an art crime team in place since 2004," she said. "We started out dealing primarily with theft—paintings, statues, even odd things like a Stradivarius that's still missing, still on the list if you can believe that. But these days, the largest part of our portfolio is related to fraud." She sighed. "I live in DC, but I've been working out of the Boston office—and, by the way, your boyfriend's sister has been very helpful to us in a number of cases."

"You knew who he was all along!" I exclaimed. No one likes being kept in the dark, and I was starting to get seriously irritated with this woman. Impressed, yeah, but irritated, too.

Jane downed another shot of Grey Goose, caught her breath, and put the glass back on the bar. "I tried to talk Caroline out of coming down here," she said. "I may have once dated Milo Griffin, but these days I'm rather clear-headed about some of his enterprises. Caroline was—well, let's just say she saw it differently."

"How?" I asked cautiously.

"Major blind spot," said Jane. "She was an otherwise intelligent woman who never got over Milo and never believed anything bad of him. It happens. She always thought they'd broken up for one reason or another—and the reasons changed over time—but that eventually, he'd come to his senses and go back to her. At least I was never quite that naïve. She told me she was coming down to the Cape—she'd heard he was back from Paris, don't ask me how, it's pretty clear she was cyberstalking him—and she just needed an excuse to come here."

Beside me, my father stirred. No one likes to be duped. Typically, though, he didn't say anything.

"What was she *thinking*?" I asked. "Seriously, she thought if she just showed up, Milo would fall for her all over again?"

Jane sighed. "You liked her, didn't you?" she asked.

"She seemed quite respectable," said my father.

"Not quite a ringing endorsement," I commented.

"She wasn't the world's nicest person," said Jane. "I loved Caroline, but she wasn't always easy to love. She could be… ruthless, I suppose, is the word I want. She knew about him doing the copies. She thought if she could prove it, she'd have something to hold over him. A reason for him to pay attention to her again."

"That's a step beyond stalking, isn't it?" I said. "Wait, though—she didn't seem to know Glenn had a Hawthorne, and when we went up to the penthouse, and she got a look at it, she said—"

"—she recognized the brushstrokes," finished my father.

Jane was nodding. "Which may or may not have been true," she said. "I don't know that she could have known Milo's touch, but anything's possible. Maybe it just made sense to her. She knew Milo was here, and—well, she knew Milo."

"If everyone knew he was here and everyone knows he's a forger, why haven't you stopped him by now?" There had to be more to this than met the eye. Hell, if the FBI knows what you're up to, maybe it's time to retire to that cozy little villa in the south of France. Or, better yet, someplace without an extradition treaty.

"We haven't been able to connect him to any of the forgeries floating around on the market," said Jane. "Before I can get a warrant, I need some concrete evidence linking him to the works. And there's been a major hurdle in the way."

"Which is?"

She pushed her empty glass away—a little regretfully, I thought. "There's too much out there," she said. "At any given moment, there are maybe fifty to a hundred people worldwide engaged in creating fake paintings attributed to major artists. We don't usually know the names of those forgers, but there are things that give them away. You can't be famous in secret, after all, but you also don't want to advertise what you're doing. So a lot of them develop some small hint in the work that points to it being theirs."

"Like the cows," I said, remembering Ali.

Jane was startled. "The *cows?*" she asked.

Wow, had I really said that out loud? "Nothing. Just a thing—a clue, I guess—Ali noticed in Midsomer Murders," I said uncomfortably.

She was still looking blank.

"It's a British detective show," I said desperately, wishing I hadn't brought it up. "In one of the episodes, there's a forged painting, meant to be a copy of a piece by some famous local painter. But someone noticed the cows in the painting weren't native to that area or hadn't lived there at the time it was supposed to have been painted, or something like that, I don't remember what. In the same painting, they'd arranged the farm hands going out to the field to look like the Beatles on that album cover." I was definitely floundering. "Ali brought it up. With Caroline, I think. Said that's what he'd do if he were passing something off—just a little inside joke."

"Like an Easter egg in software," said my father surprisingly.

"Easter egg?" My turn to stare.

"Yes, don't you know? Software engineers nestle some piece of code inside the application they're creating. It can be a booby trap or maybe something gentle and silly."

"Like a hidden signature," I said, and he nodded.

"Anyway, in this episode, it was all about the forger laughing at all the people who were bidding big bucks for this particular painting at auction. Because they'd dissed him when he tried to sell his own work." I looked at Jane, realization dawning. "I just described Milo Griffin, didn't I?"

"Pretty much," she agreed. "But he can't be doing it by himself."

"Who else, then? What about Rhys?"

"Rhys Whitney isn't a great artist in anyone's mind but his own," said Jane scornfully. "Rhys Whitney couldn't host a beginner's painting show on public television. What he does is derivative, mundane, and poorly executed. But he is a brilliant businessman, and he understands things about the art world most of us forget."

"Like what?" asked my father.

"That magician's tricks always work best when the audience actively wants to believe," she said. "It's sleight of hand, smoke, and mirrors. Listen, you look at these artists, these dead artists, and you look at their lives. And where they were when they were painting something. And sometimes, there's a gap in the timeline. Someone producing six or eight paintings in six months, but then a year and a half of nothing."

"Yeah, so?" I was getting a little impatient again. I took a swallow of wine. "Why's that significant?"

"Because we *want* it to be significant," said Jane. "Maybe the artist had run out of inspiration, or they got sick, or they were getting a divorce—there are myriad reasons for dry spells. But to the art world, well, there's a gap. And we all want to fill the gap. So if everyone's always been expecting to find these lost paintings, then it makes it a lot easier for someone to step in and say, behold! Here are the lost paintings. And everyone rejoices." She shook her head. "It's almost too easy," she said.

"But isn't provenance difficult to prove?" My father was getting adept at talking about art, tossing expressions like that around with ease.

"Everyone *wants* these works to be real," said Jane. "You don't understand—it's not just about the money; it's the prestige. To be the person who found the lost Gaugin, the Matisse we all knew he must have painted... even the Hawthorne no one realized was hidden in Provincetown. To be that person, famous in the right circles, that's priceless, especially for someone like Rhys, who God knows tried hard enough to attain fame on his own merits. And

Rhys always finds something to hook it all onto. There's always just enough truth in his stories to make them believable."

"So you've seen him do it before?"

"We had one… possibility," she said. "It fell through. He hadn't tried to sell the piece yet, and he hadn't had Milo—or whoever was doing his stuff at the time, anyway—he hadn't had them sign it. So he could say it was a straightforward copy; it was just a practical exercise. A lot of artists do that, not just art students. It's legal to do—it's even legal to *sell* a copy of someone's work, as long as you represent it as a copy."

"Does the signature matter?" asked my father.

She nodded. "Signing someone else's name is the definition of intent to commit fraud." Now she sounded like FBI, falling into the law enforcement jargon. Ali did that, too, sometimes, without thinking. They have a different communication manual from the rest of us.

And it was oddly reassuring to hear her talk like that; it made the whole surreal past few days feel a little less surreal. There's a part of me that never grew up, that's a complete rule-follower, that believes the police are really there to help us out—and it felt good that an authority figure was engaging with something I knew nothing about. It was a validation of sorts, I suppose, but nonetheless welcome, for all it said about responsibility.

And responsibility… "Damn!" I pushed away from the bar and spilled my wine simultaneously. "What time is it?"

"Almost noon," said my father. "Why?"

"I have to run," I said. "I'll catch up to you, I promise, but I have to go."

I had suddenly remembered I actually had a real job, I wasn't actually a detective, and I actually had a meeting at the other end of town in fifteen minutes.

Breathe. Just breathe. "I think I need to call a cab," I said.

***

The Provincetown Inn sits far in the West End of town, across from the Murchison estate where Ali and I had pretty much met. Or at least had together avoided getting shot. Which always feels—well, *memorable.*

The inn couldn't be any different from the Race Point Inn if it tried. It was built sometime after the First World War (though they'd been steadily adding sections since then, including trucking in four acres of landfill to build an extension of the property to build a new motel-type structure, along with a swimming pool shaped like a pilgrim's hat, no mean feat). The Race Point is a baby in comparison.

If you visit the Provincetown Inn in the winter—when it's closed to guests—you'll catch a particular Stephen King vibe, long empty corridors, and a sense of being watched from the framed sepia photographs on the walls. But those aren't the walls you should be looking at.

In its heyday, the place was a town unto itself. In lobby after lobby crafted to look like the town square, with shops and other amenities opening out into them—a barber shop, two gift shops, clothes boutiques, a beauty salon, sundries shops… I'm probably leaving out a whole lot. Guests could play shuffleboard, go bowling, shoot pool, or play ping-pong, all under the same roof. There was once a nightclub, a lounge where famous crooners came to croon, several bars, several restaurants, a ballroom, an indoor swimming pool… the list goes on. Much of it's gone now: there's still one restaurant, and pop-ups occasionally commandeer the stage in the old lounge; the building surrounding the pool is gone, and if you want to get your hair cut, you have to go downtown. You can still see the "storefronts" where many of these shops once were, and it lends a nice old-time vibe to the place.

But by far and away, to my mind, the murals are the best part of the Provincetown Inn.

There's a wonderful story about a fellow who hitchhiked to P'town sometime in the sixties and, unable to come up with the cash for a room, instead bartered his artistic prowess for a summer's lodging. He created stupendous murals throughout the inn. It's apocryphal, of course, as many great stories lamentably are; the murals are, in fact, the work of a local artist, paid in much the normal way—but they still impress. Based on old postcards and vintage photos, they depict many familiar scenes around town and include faces that were recognizable to viewers at the time, which must have been rather fun.

I always tell visitors to make sure to include a visit to the Provincetown Inn while they're here; if the swimming pool doesn't attract— and, come on, who doesn't want to be in a swimming pool shaped like a pilgrim's hat?— then the murals are sure to.

I was here for something rather more prosaic than sightseeing; there was a wedding coming up in April, and it was a big one—all hands on deck, as it were. One of the two brides was the daughter of a senator, and she was marrying the CEO of some sort of investment company—my eyes glaze over when anyone starts talking high finance to me—but the point was, these were high-powered, wealthy women. And they knew exactly what they wanted.

What they wanted was a wedding ceremony under a tent up at the Pilgrim Monument (if you're noticing a theme here, it's because there is one: when the Mayflower arrived in the Wampanoag world, it stopped first in Provincetown before heading on over to Plymouth; the Mayflower Compact was written by the pilgrims and others on board right here at anchor in Provincetown Harbor); they had invited four hundred-odd people. I had no idea where all these people were going to be seated; thankfully, that wasn't my problem.

They were starting their day with a lavish brunch at the Race Point Inn, heading up to the Monument and Museum for the ceremony and champagne toast, then on to the Province-town Inn for a catered meal under yet another tent, followed by music and dancing. The Mayflower trolleys and the town pedicabs were all being pressed into service to transport all these people to and from the various venues. They had reserved all the rooms at the Race Point and most of the rooms at the Provincetown Inn. And because it's never too soon to start planning something with that many moving parts, the various events coordinators—me, Alan from the Provincetown Inn, and David from the Pilgrim Monument and Provincetown Museum—were starting to work out the broad-stroke logistics.

Well, I'd *said* I was looking for a challenge, right?

At least I was the only one who didn't have to deal with the stress of putting up a tent; we don't have the large expanses of grass offered by both the Provincetown Inn and the Monument, so I didn't have to make sure chairs had been duly delivered, microphones and speakers all worked, music arranged.

We have a lovely string quartet we use for occasions such as this, and they were easy to work with, all of them musicians from the Cape Symphony; flowers would be provided the day before by Wildflower, and food and alcohol by our kitchen and bar, respectively. I definitely had lucked out; except for the sheer numbers, this was something I coped with regularly. And I didn't have to even think about the weather, which in April can go in nearly any direction.

I grabbed a coffee in the restaurant before heading outside to where Alan and David were already talking; I really didn't need them scenting wine on my breath this early in the day. Which, of course, made me late, but I wasn't going to worry about it; I had plenty of other things on my plate to worry about.

"…and we have Angel Foods doing the catering for the champagne toast," David was saying when I joined the two men, standing on the lawn and looking meditatively around them. The pool, I noted, was still going strong, even with the storm forecast, and Beyoncé was belting out from the speakers. "Hey, Sydney."

"Hi. Looks like everything's still in full swing. When are you guys bringing in the pool chairs?" The sun was ridiculously still out, but there was an edge to the air. Even if you didn't know something was coming, you'd know something was coming. "Hey, David."

Alan raised his voice to compete with the music. "As soon as they can get peoples' butts out of them, I think," he said. "Do you guys want to go inside?"

"We don't need that much time; I can hear okay," said David, and I shrugged. "I live upstairs from a nightclub," I said. "I can take anything."

Alan returned to his list. "We're doing a Cape Cod clambake kind of thing," he said. "Tent here—" he gestured, "—and buffet style. Raw bar first as they all get settled in. It's gonna take a while to get everyone down from the Monument in all the various vehicles, then herd them all out here. Then when everyone's in place, we'll have lobsters, clams, corn on the cob, salads, and coleslaw. Wine and beer and a full bar setup."

He passed some photocopies of the lists to us; we had to know about the whole thing since, invariably, people would ask. "They're going to spend the day eating and drinking," I said, not for the first time. "Food at the Race Point. Food at the Monument. Food at the Provincetown Inn."

"It's what they want," said Alan.

"If I ate all that, they'd have to cart me away in a wheelbarrow," I said.

"Then, the next day," Alan said, keeping a firm grip on the here-and-now, "breakfast wherever they're staying on their own, then over to the pier for the Dolphin Fleet whale watch, back here for lunch and Art's Dune Tours, then a sunset cruise for just the wedding party on the Bay Lady."

"While everyone else presumably eats some more," I muttered.

"I think most everyone is leaving, just the wedding party staying on. Over to you then."

"Yep," I agreed. "Dinner for twenty at eight-thirty at the restaurant at the Race Point. We're all set for that."

"Sounds like you two have it under control," said David. His was the easy part. The ceremony itself, a few snacks while people waited for transport; one and done, in a sense. But honestly, this wasn't exactly breaking my back, either. My crew at the Race Point runs like a well-oiled machine to use the cliché. We could do this stuff in our sleep. It was almost too easy.

I immediately pushed the thought out of my mind. I had a good job I was good at. Why was I questioning it?

I wasn't. And I wasn't going to think about it anymore, either.

With that firm intention in mind, I fell into step next to Alan as we walked back across the expanse of lawn to the inn. "Good season?" I asked.

He shrugged. "Not bad. Had some good events. You?"

"Yeah, it's been good," I said. *The death of visiting art brokers notwithstanding.* I took in a deep breath; the wind was coming in off the harbor, crisp and clean but still with that bit of menace lurking in the background. You could almost think you'd imagined it. Almost. "You're so lucky to be right on the water," I said.

He grunted. "Won't be so lucky in another eight hours," he said.

"I do see that," I conceded. With its artificial landfill stretching out into the harbor and the motel-style rooms on top of it, it was easy to see how the Provincetown Inn could take a battering.

"It's early this year," said Alan. "We don't usually get anything this big until way into November."

"Climate change," I said automatically, nodding.

He didn't say anything; perhaps we'd arrived at the moment when there wasn't anything to say anymore about the planet. "If you want to come by the office, I can get you the pedicab schedule," he said. "Forgot to bring it out."

"Sure, no problem." I followed him into the building and through a couple of the indoor/outdoor lobbies and corridors, past one of the huge banquet rooms, empty and desolate now.

He'd caught my glance. "Hard to imagine that back in the day, we filled these places every night. The townspeople came regularly for a night out. Dinner dances."

"Where'd you prep the food?" I'd seen the inn's kitchen, which while completely adequate for the catering they did now, would have been hard-pressed to deliver dinners for hundreds of people several nights a week.

Alan laughed. "You folks at the Race Point use your cellar for parking, right?"

I nodded; parking is at a premium downtown and often unavailable during the season; the Provincetown Inn, on the other hand, rejoiced in having a large parking-lot for guests of both the inn and the folks who dropped in daily just for the pool. "I take it you don't?"

"Don't need it," he said, stating the obvious. "What we did need was an industrial kitchen."

I stopped. "You have a *kitchen* down there?"

He nodded, unlocking the door to his office. "I'll give you a tour sometime," he said. "The word kitchen doesn't really do it justice, either," he continued, walking into the office and tossing his keys on the desk. You could tell they had more room out here than we did on the other side of town; Alan actually had a real office with a door. I had a cubbyhole behind Reception. No, I wasn't jealous… "It's mammoth and runs the whole length of the building. Massive machines. We used to do

everything here from scratch, all the baking…
everything. We could handle several different
banquets a night if necessary."

I was fascinated. "When do you use it
now?"

He shrugged, sat down in the office chair
behind his desk, sorted through a few papers,
then leaned back and put his feet up on the
desk. "Never. Last time had to be—oh, I don't
know, fifteen, twenty years back? There was a
guy in town who did volunteer catering. He
used to make stuff and hand it out to the
homeless. He did parties for people who
couldn't afford parties." He sighed. "A lot of
changes in this town, Sydney."

"I'll say." I was trying to imagine someone
giving parties for the homeless and the
screeching of offended neighbors who were
the only ones, in their eyes, entitled to have
fun. It wasn't just the town that had changed; it
was the world. "And now?"

"Haven't been down there in years," he
said. "Here's your pedicab schedule."

I picked it up. "Thanks, Alan. Hope you
survive the storm without too much damage."

"You, too." Feet back on the ground, he
was already calling up an email on his computer. Efficient, that was Alan. I sketched a half-
salute in the air and headed out.

This time, with no pressing appointment, I walked back up the length of Commercial Street. There was a sharpness in the air, but the sun was still giving exuberant September warmth, and the street was full, restaurants' barkers enticing passers-by to come and enjoy a meal or a drink, guitar-wielding musicians wailing about love, bicycles still rushing at a furious breakneck speed up and down the street, people stepping off the sidewalks and wandering without looking into the paths of oncoming cars.

We've had more than our share of bicycle-related accidents on Commercial Street, especially since the relatively recent addition of motorized scooters, electric skateboards, and the ever-present pedicabs. I read somewhere that the Massachusetts Department of Transportation had ranked Commercial Street in the top-five percent of dangerous roadways on Cape Cod. And since these new "vehicles" now comprised so much of the traffic, there was a lack of regulation that made Commercial Street a little like the Wild West.

The Wild West with tourists.

Technology might drive innovation, but it also drives ethics and laws. We don't know how to deal with things that don't yet exist, and then when they do, communities are forever racing to catch up.

But never, I thought, in all these years of confusion and sheer messiness on Commercial Street, had anyone been killed—by a motor vehicle.

I wondered, suddenly, whether the police were talking to Rhys. Had he simply reported the SUV stolen to distance himself from what he was about to do? But why would he kill Caroline? If she was close to pointing the finger at Milo, there were a whole lot of other ways of dealing with the situation, of keeping her quiet. I could think of five or six of them off the top of my head.

I thought of the panic room Mirela had found in the basement of Rhys' gallery and wondered again what was going on between Rhys and Milo. And how Jane fit into the puzzle—was she here for personal reasons as well as professional ones? After all, she had a history with Milo; she obviously had a history with Caroline, but was her involvement deeper than that?

You had to wonder.

I stopped at the Blue Monkey on my way up the street—well, how can you not? The pastries are almost as good as the ones Angus the pastry chef makes at the Race Point, and

Angus wasn't here, and the Blue Monkey was, and the sugar rush I got from it propelled my thoughts as well as my perambulation. As soon as I brushed the last of the crumbs off my shirt, I stopped in front of the library, hitched myself up to sit on the retaining wall, and called Mirela.

"Sunshine," she answered, sounding a little strangled until I heard the loud roar of Lily's voice bellowing and understood why. "Hey, Mirela, bad time to call, huh?"

"It is Lily," she said, stating the obvious. "Why did I have a child?"

"You didn't." Lily wasn't actually Mirela's daughter; she was, technically speaking, her niece. But Mirela's sister had abdicated any responsibility for the child, and Mirela had returned from her family visit in Bulgaria with a baby in tow. "You brought her home as a souvenir."

"Then it is even worse," she said. "Wait, and I will step outside. She does not understand I can still see her through the window. She will stop when she thinks no one is looking."

I waited a moment, idly watching tourists take pictures of themselves in front of the statue called The Tourists, and wondered for about the hundredth time whether it was redundant or a deep philosophical statement, the epitome of meta. "All right," her voice came back on. "Said and done. What is it you call me for?"

It was true the screaming was now considerably and blessedly muffled. "I wondered if you'd seen Rhys," I said. "Or Milo, come to that. They've both disappeared."

"I am not someone looking for something to do, sunshine," she said severely. "I have a canvas to finish and a toddler to train."

"Sometimes I think you have no sense of humor at all," I complained.

"No one with a child has a sense of humor," Mirela said. "They remove it."

I laughed. "Okay, okay, I get it. But—"

"You are still thinking there is a mystery here," she said. It was a statement, not a question.

"Well, yes," I admitted. "There is perhaps something," said Mirela. "But I think it is not a mystery. I think it is a crime."

"They sometimes go together," I pointed out. Crime fiction and mystery fiction— weren't they on the same shelves at the library? But then, a thought occurred to me. "Wait, Mirela—the paintings in the panic room at the gallery—"

"I do not know what this panic room is."

I snorted impatiently. "You know. That room you described. Climate-controlled. The one you broke into," I said.

"Yes, it was not difficult. I did not panic."

"No, that's not it—it just sounded a lot like the rooms some people set up in their homes. In case some intruder comes in. They can hide there until the police arrive." The more I talked about it, the more ridiculous the practice sounded. "It's just a shorthand way of referring to it," I finished, a little lamely. "I know the one at the gallery isn't a panic room. Okay, I'll call it storage, locked climate-controlled storage; is that better?"

She paused. "I see. I do not mind what you call it, sunshine. And you wanted to say something about this room?"

Sometimes talking to Mirela could be exhausting. "Yes. Um, you were talking about crime, and I wanted to know if you think any of those paintings were stolen. I mean, there was the one missing from the Isabella Stewart Gardner—"

"You are as much in love with that story as everyone else," said Mirela dismissively. "Paintings are stolen from museums often. I do not know why this one is special."

"Because it was the biggest theft ever, I think," I said, racking my brains for anything I remembered about it. "Thirteen pieces, all at once? And because it's *our* museum, in a way, you know, us in eastern Massachusetts—I used to live in Boston, it's my hometown, so, of course, I pay more attention. Whatever makes you famous, I suppose."

"You want to be famous for art theft?"

"Okay, never mind that," I snapped. These conversations could sometimes feel a little circular. But it was hard to get those empty frames out of my mind. Because the museum was bound by Gardner's will to not change anything, the pieces were gone, but their ornate gold frames were still on the walls, framing nothing.

It reminded me, achingly, of something I'd read back last winter when I was taking a seminar on the literature of AIDS… I think it was in Rebecca Makkai's book, though I could be wrong. The image was of a woman visiting museums, but instead of seeing what was there, she was looking at what in her mind were empty frames, frames that should have held the great works of creative genius that never came to fruition, the paintings never made by a generation of artists wiped out by the epidem-ic. The hole created by absence, the emptiness of loss.

There was a sigh on the other end of the line; Mirela was bored. I scrambled back to the present. "Do you think that painting you saw in the room—what was it—"

"Rembrandt," said Mirela. "Christ on the Sea of Galilee. A storm. It is a very frightening painting."

I wasn't getting dragged down another figurative garden path. From across the street, I could see Francesco waving at me from behind his easel, his daily project painting the library. On canvas. A *lot* of canvases. I waved back and pointed to my phone in case he thought I was being rude. "Do you think that was the one stolen from the Gardner?" There was no reason, after all if Rhys and Milo were forging paintings, that they couldn't also receive them as stolen goods. They'd have to be middle-men—I couldn't see either of them slipping around museums at night, dressed in black, armed with flashlights—but it seemed plausible at the very least.

Diversification. That's what keeps a lot of boats afloat in an uncertain economy.

Mirela laughed as the image hit her as well. "I do not see them as cat burglars," she said. "Rhys would need to stop and admire his handsome self in any mirror they passed."

"Yeah, you make a point." I sighed. "So—you said it was a crime. What crime?"

"Rhys," said Mirela, "needs money."

I found that a little hard to believe. He ran one of the most successful galleries in town and had another in Boston or New York and yet another in Paris. Still, "enough" is an elastic term when it comes to people and their financial situations. For some people, there can never be enough. "What does he need money for?" I asked instead.

"For what? I do not know, me. I am not his confidante." She sounded irritated. "But I am also not stupid. I see the paperwork. There is a second mortgage now on the gallery, and he has been telling me to finish more paintings, quick, like that."

"Doesn't necessarily mean—"

"Sunshine, you do not know him. He runs through money. Everything he inherited, everything he has, he spends. You do not see it here because he is not gay. He spends his money in different places. When he is in Paris, there are women, there are luxury hotels, there is always a new car or a Rolex or nice drugs. He spends and spends, and then he tells me I should paint faster. Well, I do not work in a factory, me."

"Maybe he's getting Milo to do more," I suggested.

"And—what? Paint all day, every day? How do you make someone work that much, work that fast? One person cannot do this. I do not think that Milo is the answer to your mystery, sunshine."

"But you still haven't told me what crime he's committing. It *is* Rhys you're talking about, right?"

"I do not know!" She sounded frustrated. "This is not new. All summer, I have wondered."

"And you didn't tell me."

"I did not know. I still do not know. I know only that for months he has been different—worried. He has been difficult, and I do not know why. I see him creating special storage—what you call the panic room, Sydney. I see him—well, no, perhaps I do not say this after all."

"Say what?"

She sighed. "If you were to ask me what is Rhys' problem, I would remind you of the story of my Uncle Nicolay. This man started a business outside of Sofia back in 1990, when communism was over, and it was, they said, the dawn of a new day."

"Right," I said. "The fall of your Comrade Zivkov."

"You do remember things, after all," she said admiringly. She might not have a great sense of humor, but she certainly could layer the irony.

"I am a woman of many talents," I agreed. "What about Uncle Nicolay?"

"He started a business. And he took on a partner, then two partners, as the business grew. They were making heavy machinery, sunshine—construction machines that excavate. Do you know what I am describing?"

"Sort of," I said cautiously.

"Well, it was Uncle Nicolay's company, you understand? He named it. He built it. But slowly, it seemed more and more of the decisions were taken by his partners, by the people they had brought into the company. They were younger men, men with plans. After a time, they made it very clear they did not need Uncle Nicolay anymore."

"Okay...," I said again. Unless she was planning to give me a quick lesson on hydraulics, I wasn't seeing where this was going.

"Well, it is that Rhys looks like Uncle Nicolay looked before he was made to retire from his own company. He is losing control of something, sunshine; I just do not know what it is." She took a deep breath. "I have been reviewing my contract with the gallery."

That sounded reasonable; Mirela had the talent and the following—and commanded the price-point—that any gallery would be delighted to represent. And Rhys? Losing her would be a blow for sure—there are just so many oysters one can sell, after all—and it sounded like he was already someone losing control. There's a saying about some kind of creature being at its most dangerous when it's cornered. I couldn't remember the animal offhand—tiger? Alligator? Mole rat?—but I was sure I'd read that somewhere.

Was Rhys dangerous?

"I do not know if it is Milo making him feel this pressure. I do not know if it is someone else and if there are people who are behind the scenes. But I know Rhys is frightened."

"And the crime?" She was the one who'd used the word, after all, not me.

"It is forgery," she said. "I was not sure, but I am sure now. I just do not know who is doing it, how many people. It is not just one person, I am sure."

"You weren't sure two days ago!" I protested.

"You have made me think, sunshine. And remember things. Like scenes from a movie, I remember things. Things he has said. And things I hear. When I close my eyes at night, I hear your voice, and then I remember."

I thought about it. "Do you think Caroline knew about it?" I asked.

"I do not know!" Impatience breaking through.

"Okay," and this time, I said it soothingly. "Where's Rhys now? Do you know that?"

"I do not, and you do not want to see him, Sydney."

"Of course I do," I said, with more enthusiasm than I felt. What *was* that animal? A bear? A snake? Rhys cornered sounded a lot like any of them. Well, maybe not the mole rat. "Caroline's dead," I said.

"And you do not owe her anything," said Mirela.

"I want to see that room," I said.

"No. You do not."

Short of turning this into a playground taunt—*yes I do, no you don't, yes I do*—I couldn't imagine where else to go with the conversation. Of course, I wanted to see that room. Rhys' SUV had killed Caroline. Rhys had sold Glenn a painting that might or might not be an original Hawthorne. Rhys had more paintings like that in a specially constructed room in his basement, not to mention possibly one of the most famous stolen paintings in the western world. Rhys was feeling pressure from some- where and was most probably in a battle for dominance of his illicit trade with Milo.

It was actually coming together quite nice- ly.

It occurred to me that while in the past I had, in fact, been a sort of seaside Miss Marple, a lot of the time, I'd allowed events to just carry me along in their current. If I couldn't be enthused anymore about bridal parties and champagne toasts, then at least I could take the reins of an investigation and have some agency in figuring out what was happening.

And this was the perfect opportunity. "You have to let me into the gallery," I said.

"This will not happen, sunshine. In fact—" and then whatever she was about to say got subsumed into a particularly loud bellow. Lily. "I must go," she said. "It is Kid Zivkov again."

"The gallery?" I snapped. "What about get- ting me into the gallery?"

"Good-bye, Sydney."

Frustrated, I stared at the phone. I wished I knew something—anything—about breaking and entering. My education had been woefully inadequate in that area.

"Excuse me?" The woman had been trying to get my attention for a moment by the time I looked up hazily from my thoughts. "Excuse me? Can you take a picture of me in front of the statue?"

"Sure." I hopped down from the wall and took her camera from her. Across the street, Francesco was laughing gently, but only because he does everything gently.

I took the picture.

Ali and my father were playing chess in the small bar when I got back to the Race Point, still having no idea how I was going to break into the gallery. And I was going to have to do it soon if the sharpness in the air meant anything.

The storm was coming. A perfect time to go snooping around, I told myself.

There was no one behind the bar, so I went over and helped myself to a ginger ale. I had a feeling I should probably keep my head fairly clear. "Who's winning?"

"I have him on the run," said my father. Ali just smiled his lazy cat-that-just-got-the-cream smile. "He has a lot of my pieces," he acknowledged. In chess, that may or may not mean anything; but I'd played Ali, and I knew. Still, he was being nice to my father.

"Uh-huh." I sat down at the table with them. "I've been thinking about—"

"Shhh!" My father looked at me. "Can't it wait until we're finished here? I need to concentrate."

"Okay." I slid down in my chair, the picture of a piqued adolescent. I felt like I ought to be doing something but had no idea what that was.

I'll never understand how people can watch chess matches. Seriously. After about an eternity (or, more likely, two minutes), I got up again. "I'll be around," I informed them.

Neither man responded.

I considered calling my mother, but that might set a dangerous precedent, not to mention the fact that I had nothing to tell her she'd find interesting. I decided to chip away at the other mystery and went looking for Mike instead.

I found him outside, arguing with the guy who maintains the pool. I pretended to watch the few hardy souls who were mostly standing about in the water, chatting together. It was still warm, but not that warm. Still, they'd probably go directly from the pool over to the spa, where they could bask in heat from the sauna and the steam room. We really do offer something for everyone.

Mike came over, clearly annoyed. "He's *moving*," he said. "Can you believe that? Before he drains the pool for the off-season, he's moving off-Cape. And good luck to *us*, being abandoned like last year's fashion and trying to find someone new at the end of the summer."

"What *is* last year's fashion, anyway?"

He relented and smiled. "They all just pass you by, don't they?"

"I have my own fashion sense," I said airily.

"Okay, if that's what you want to call it."

I came to the point, as this conversation was clearly going nowhere. "Have you talked to Glenn?"

He tore his eyes from the retreating back of the recalcitrant pool guy. "Why? Did you? What do you know?"

I shook my head, and we stood there for a moment, siblings joined in worry about a parent. "When's he going to Amsterdam?" I asked.

"Monday morning."

"Monday—*this* Monday? Day after tomorrow?"

He nodded. "He wants to see us before he goes."

"Us, as in separately, or us, as in at the same time?"

"He just said, 'you and Sydney' to me, so I'm guessing it's a meeting. Why?"

"He's firing us and closing down the inn," I said, Anxiety Girl emerging. She was never far from the surface.

"Don't be ridiculous," said Mike. "You need to calm down, Sydney." He pulled out his phone and started pressing keys. I turned away, the panic really rising in my chest now. *Breathe, Riley. Just breathe.* "Oh, hey, Sydney, I almost forgot. Detective Agassi wants you to give her a call."

"Why didn't she call me directly if she wants to talk to me?"

"You asking me? Do I look like her social secretary?" He went back to the device.

Sighing, I took my phone out and strolled away. "Julie? It's Sydney."

"Of course it is. Wait a minute, okay?" I could hear muffled voices on the other end as she covered the microphone, and then she was back. "Okay. Here's the thing. Caroline Harrison's body has disappeared."

"Wait. What?" I mustn't have heard that correctly.

"A private ambulance company picked it up at the hospital in Hyannis," said Julie. "I've been trying to reach her sister, but she's not answering calls or texts. Do you know where she is?"

"No, I just got back to the Race Point myself," I said. "I was in a meeting out at the Provincetown Inn and—"

"All right. I'm sending someone over." She wasn't interested in where I'd been, what I'd been doing.

"Wait!" I exclaimed; her words had started to really sink in. "Someone stole her *body*?" And it wasn't even Halloween yet.

"It was removed by the private ambulance company," she corrected me. "The state police are obviously very interested in finding it."

"I can imagine." In Massachusetts, the state police are the law-enforcement arm of the district attorney's office. If there are any questions about someone's death—and clearly, there were a lot of questions about Caroline's death—it becomes their purview.

Difficult to do *without* the body, of course.

But on what planet did this make sense? Who would want a dead body? Surely we weren't going to add necrophilia into the mix here, were we?

Another thought occurred. "Why are you telling me this?" I asked.

"Because you seem to be in the center of it, as usual," she said. "Your inn, your father—"

"It's not my inn."

"—your friend Mirela," she was continuing.

"What does Mirela have to do with Caroline's body disappearing?" I demanded.

"Because," said Julie, "Caroline Harrison was texting with the owner of the gallery where she shows her work. For about five days before she arrived in Provincetown."

That was news, but I had something else to find out first. "And so? That still doesn't say Mirela's involved," I said.

"Involved in what, exactly?" Her voice was mutating into its official tone. So she *was* questioning me, after all.

"In whatever's going on," I said. I wasn't sure I was ready to tell Julie about our suspicions because that was all they were until we had some proof. Proof the forgeries were happening, and proof that tied them somehow to Caroline's death. The disappearance of her body was something I wasn't ready to take on board yet.

Besides, if I told Julie anything, she'd have cops out looking for Rhys and Milo, maybe visiting the gallery. And that would be extremely inconvenient for someone who was planning to break into said gallery. Namely, *moi.*

Julie wasn't finished with me. "What do you think's going on?" she asked.

"I have no idea," I said. "*I'm* not a detective." I could hear a snort on the other end of the phone. "I just want to make sure Mirela's not in trouble. You know her. You know she's honest. So why do you suspect her?"

"Suspect her of what?" she countered.

Was every interaction this weekend going to go round and round in circles? I was still dizzy from my last conversation with Mirela. "Of anything," I said impatiently. "You're the one who brought her name up, Julie. Like she's connected to my father being here and Caroline being murdered—"

"No one has said she was murdered."

"Okay, then, whatever," I said a little helplessly. "If she wasn't murdered, why did somebody steal her body?"

"I'm the one who asks the questions," she said a little austerely.

Then start asking the right ones. But I didn't even know what those right ones might be.

Did Caroline's disappearing body add to the mystery or explain it?

I clicked off and closed my eyes. Time to lay it out and see if I was actually losing my mind here.

Rhys Whitney had come up with a way to authenticate forged paintings and show a believable provenance; some of these forgeries were (probably) done by his associate Milo Griffin. They may possibly have been stealing artworks as well—who knows? I couldn't get the Gardner heist out of my head. Only the most famous art escapade outside of fiction; of course, I had to think about it. (I mean, how cool is that? Solve the biggest mystery of them all?)

It tied in a little too conveniently with the appearance of an FBI agent who investigated art theft (and who also just happened to be the sister of a possibly murdered art expert who was connected to the possible forger himself). That was all just a little too close for comfort.

Rhys reports his SUV stolen, and a day or so later, it is used in an incredibly improbable "accident" on Commercial Street that kills the art expert who had been showing interest in his (alleged, okay, Julie?) forgeries. An art expert whose body then—*disappears?*

The paintings were being stored in a special room at Rhys' gallery, well out of sight and well-protected from anyone but Mirela, who—unbeknownst to me—apparently had mad lock-picking skills.

Rhys was the common factor in all the little bits of the puzzle floating around. And I was more than ready to cast him as the villain—I'd never particularly liked him and only did any work for him in the gallery during the winter as a favor to Mirela (and my own occasional sense of Race Point Inn claustrophobia). Rhys had always struck me as arrogant, rude, and generally unsympathetic. So it wasn't a great mental leap to go from that to considering him a suspect.

But if he had killed Caroline… why? What did her death do for him? And would he then have stolen her dead body? Why?

There was something here I was missing. I was laying all my cards down on the table, but they weren't adding up quite right. There was a joker somewhere in this deck that changed everything, and I had no idea who or what that joker was.

And that was probably not a good thing.

***

The first person I saw when I got back to the inn was Special Agent Jane Pfeiffer.

I hadn't factored her into my card game, and I wondered, now, if she wasn't the joker I'd been looking for, ripping right through the deck. She and Caroline had been up to something—otherwise, they wouldn't have lied about both being in Boston at the same time. She'd appeared suspiciously quickly as soon as Caroline was in a car accident, and she didn't seem overly grief-stricken to hear of her sister's death. And they both had a past connection to Milo, who was (I surmised) the artistic intelligence behind whatever it was Rhys was up to.

I couldn't wait to see how calmly she took the disappearance of her sister's body.

I slipped into my cubbyhole before she had a chance to see me; I didn't know how much my face would give away, and I needed time to work this through a little more.

What if Jane already knew about Caroline? What if she were responsible? The body had disappeared, after all, *after* Jane had arrived on the scene. And while I couldn't imagine hiring a private ambulance was cheap, her clothes—and willingness to check into the Race Point, not the least expensive inn in town by a long shot—indicated money wasn't a factor. Maybe the FBI paid well.

Maybe having something on the side paid even better.

But… assuming just for a moment Jane *was* responsible for Caroline's disappearance, I couldn't see exactly what she got out of it.

Unless there was something the body would tell the medical examiner and, therefore, the state police—and therefore, the district attorney—that Jane didn't want them to know. What would the body show that might point to Jane's involvement? What didn't she want the coroner to see? What was it she didn't want law enforcement to find out?

She was sitting in one of the lobby's easy chairs, reading a newspaper. As calm and collected as if she were a regular guest and this was a regular visit. Not the portrait of someone whose sister had just died.

Not really the portrait of someone who'd killed her sister, either.

And it was Rhys' SUV. Jane hadn't been in town when it was stolen. Of course, *stolen* was possibly an elastic term here. Maybe she and Rhys were in this thing together, then. It wouldn't be the first time someone in law enforcement went over to the other side. Love, money, there were lots of reasons she may have been seduced into doing something illegal.

She could even have been the one doing the seducing.

My iPhone did its little dance, and Ali's picture appeared on the screen. Sighing, I turned away from the lobby and swiped to answer. "Hey, babe."

"*Cara.* Just the person I was looking for."

"Apparently so, since you called me." I could feel myself smiling. I really, really liked this man.

"Listen, are you planning on weathering this storm here at home or at the inn? Because I need to go out for a while. If we're staying there for more than a day, I need to pack a few things."

"I hadn't even thought about it," I said, a little helplessly. "I'd really rather be at home, but with my father still here. . ." My voice trailed off a little helplessly.

"Are you there at the inn now?"

"Just got here. Why?"

"Because your father is packed and ready to leave. He's been asking where you are."

"Wait, what?" Leave? I step away from the inn for five minutes, and everything changes. Caroline becomes a missing person after death; my father decides to hightail it out of town. "He hasn't tried to reach me."

"Just telling you what he told me, *cara.*"

I took a breath. "He can't leave. There's a nor'easter coming."

"Yes, well, that's still a few hours out, isn't it? And it's just three hour's drive for him to get home. I think he's had enough of art and artists for a while."

"When did he decide this? I can't believe it!" Damn it, I should have kept up with him better. I'd assumed he could figure things out for himself. It was an odd role reversal, me feeling like I had to take care of my father.

Ali heard what was behind the words, as he usually did. "He's a grown-up, Sydney. He can make his own plans. And he's right: there's still time, but only if he leaves now. You should probably go find him," I said faintly. "I should have been here with him before. I've been out and about. . ."

"If you asked me," Ali said, "I wouldn't worry. I think you'll find it's not you he's missing; it's your mother."

We each took a moment to reflect on the wild improbability of anyone missing my mother. Like I said, there was some weird secret sauce in that marriage. "Okay," I said at last. "I'll track him down. And—oh, I don't know. Let's just get a room here at the inn. There are a lot of vacancies, no one will mind, and there's a generator if the power goes out."

Jane was waiting patiently for me to finish the call. "Detective Agassi said she told you about my sister."

"She did," I said. "I'm so sorry. I don't really know what to say." Disappearing dead bodies being outside of my experience and all…

"It's very odd." She shivered and pulled her cardigan more tightly around herself. "I thought I'd seen a lot, I'll be honest, but this… is baffling."

I stopped and looked at her. "Baffling?"

She wouldn't meet my eyes. "There's no reason for anybody to—"

I grasped her elbow and steered her to the settee where my father had been sitting earlier. My father… I had to catch up with him. And Glenn. Suddenly my dance card was filling up, and that was without including my planned surreptitious excursion to the Whitney Worthington gallery. "Jane. You know there's always a reason, right? Someone somewhere had a reason to—do what they did." I couldn't manage to say, "steal your sister's body."

Also, I wasn't sure why I was suddenly lecturing the FBI on criminal psychology. Granted, my own encounters with her colleagues in the past—I'd been doing my junior Miss Marple thing for a few years now, and encountering the FBI had not been the brightest stars in that firmament—had been anything but cordial, but even I had to admit they'd never have looked as lost as she did now.

Then again, none of the other special agents who had graced this establishment had just lost a sibling and *then* heard said sibling's remains had been secretly and unceremoniously carted away. Not sure even Miss Manners (or her next-generation etiquette equivalent, the experts at the *Were You Raised by Wolves?* podcast) had a whole lot to say about how to gracefully deal with that.

Jane wasn't looking at me. "What could they hope to do with her? What could they learn from her?"

The questions were clearly rhetorical, which was just as well since I hadn't a clue. Come to that, not only did I not know what "they" were doing, I didn't even know who "they" were. I cleared my throat. "Listen, I have to do some things. . . but I'll be around later. We're spending the night here at the inn, and we can talk if you'd like. . ." My voice trailed off uncertainly. I wasn't sure what I was offering. Comfort? Company? The benefit of my allegedly razor-sharp mind? A glass of red wine? "I mean, I get it if you don't want to be alone. Maybe you can join us for dinner later. . ."

She turned to look at me then, focusing. "Agent Hakim will be there?"

"Well… yes," I said.

"Yes," she said, as though reaching a decision. "Yes. I need to talk to him."

"Well, okay. He's probably on his way over by now. I just need to see my father and—"

"I think I've figured out what's going on," she said.

I'd been debating how to gracefully take leave of her without seeming unsympathetic; now, she had my complete attention. "What?" I asked.

She lifted a shoulder as if deflecting my interest. "He'll be able to tell me if I'm right," she said. "And, anyway, it doesn't explain anything about Caroline."

She wasn't getting away from me that easily. "Wait. There's an art scam going on involving people trafficking?" I asked.

There was a long moment of silence. Jane looked away, a faint frown on her face, clearly processing something. Maybe she was reassessing her take on my intelligence. "Yes," she said finally. "Yes, I really think so."

And here I'd been wondering if Jane hadn't been behind the disappearance of her sister's body.

She'd thrown a rock into the pool of my investigation, and the ripples started showing up right away.

13

Naturally, the first thing I did was call Ali. "Do you *know* this woman?"

"No." He sounded distracted; I'd interrupted something. "What's she talking about?"

"She won't tell me. I'm not in the law enforcement cool kids' club."

"Had she talked to Julie?"

"I don't know," I admitted. "But I don't think so. I mean, it was like she was working something out right then and there while we were talking."

"About what, principally?"

"Caroline. Or, to be more exact, her disappearance." Had she been killed, I wondered, in order to *get at her body*? Was the murder about the theft and not the other way around? But that made no sense, either; we were a long way from the days and antics of Burke and Hare, and I didn't really see medical-school students renting a fake ambulance to grab one particular body from Cape Cod Hospital. That was sitcom territory, surely.

Ali was talking. "She thinks this all has to do with trafficking?"

"I don't know," I said impatiently. "She said so, but then she wouldn't say anything else. That's what I'm telling you. She won't talk to a civilian—i.e., me—about it."

"Okay. I'll talk to her when I get there. I think maybe—well, too soon to tell."

"Maybe what?"

"Maybe there's something to it," he said. "To what Jane's talking about. I've been getting closer to something that's not clear yet. She may have a better picture of it than I do. It would be crazy coincidental, though."

"Coincidences do exist," I said.

"So you're always telling me." A low chuckle. "This could be the time you're proven right, *cara.*"

"*The* time? As in, once in a lifetime?" But I was smiling, too.

"Something like that." He paused. "I'll be over soon. I think I need to have a conversation with your FBI special agent."

"Not mine," I said.

"Better than mine." Wise man, my boy-friend.

"There's that."

I disconnected and went looking for my father, who seemed to be getting pushed to the periphery of my thoughts and attention way too much. I finally found him (bearding him in his lair, as I'd said to Mike, except he was in the corridor outside his room when I finally tracked him down). "There you are. I checked the bars first."

"Sydney! Where've you been?" He pulled me in for a perfunctory hug.

"More to the point," I said, "where are you going?"

He looked, if anything, amused. "Home, of course."

"You do know there's a nor'easter coming, right? That hadn't escaped you?"

He was checking his pockets. "Where did I put that card key?"

"Dad. The storm," I said, recalling him to reality. My reality, anyway. "You don't need to turn in the card. They make new ones at Reception anyway. Are you sure you want to be out and about in it?"

"In what?" He gave up looking for the key and hefted his carryall. "I'm fine, Sydney. Truth is, I'm feeling a little… out of place." He smiled. "Maybe the world of fine art isn't for me, after all, though I do like your boss' painting upstairs. But I haven't played golf in a week, and. . ."

"There's a golf course in Truro." It wasn't the point.

"That's not the point," he said, agreeing with my thoughts. "Don't worry about me, Sydney. You have enough to worry about here; I can see that. And you know how I am."

"I'll take that." I grabbed the bag from him, and we started walking down the corridor. "But the weather—"

"Sydney," he said, stopping and facing me so that I had to stop, too. "What did I do before I retired?"

"Sales," I said.

"Which I did in my car," he said. "I'll be home before the storm even hits the Cape, and I'm driving inland the whole way, up Route 495. I'll be safe as houses."

We reached the end of the hallway and started down the stairs. "I'm sorry it hasn't been—as much fun for you, this visit," I said.

He laughed. "The last time I was here, you nearly got killed out at that old Air Force base," he said. "I like visits where my daughter doesn't come that close to death."

Then I'd better not tell you what's next on my agenda. "But you loved visiting the Air Force base," I pointed out instead.

We had reached the lobby. "Sydney," said my father, "I'm going to be safe. Make sure you are, too. That's all I ask."

I tried one last-ditch appeal. "Aunt Germaine's going to be furious at you for taking Ma away from her." Because, knowing my mother, there was no way she would leave my father in peace. Once she knew about his intentions, she'd be racing to get home before him. He would probably prefer a couple of quiet days alone, but that was never going to happen as long as my mother was alive and kicking.

He was watching me. "I'll just have to take that chance, then." There was a glimmer of amusement there; my father and my aunt were not what you'd call the best of friends. Thwarting Aunt Germaine would have definitely put his day in the success category. "Now give me a hug."

"All right, all right." I complied with a quick hug—my father isn't exactly touchy-feely. "I can walk you down to your car."

"I can find my car." He was still obviously amused. "Go on, go find out whatever it is you want to find out about these paintings." And before I could say a word, he added, "I'll text you when I'm safe home." A quick kiss on my cheek. "Bye, pumpkin."

Pumpkin. He hadn't called me that in years—no, decades. Not since before Alexandra… disappeared. That was when he'd changed. Maybe Ali finding out what happened to Alex had freed my father from whatever he'd been feeling all these years. I started to say something and then realized he was already out the door.

Well, that solved one problem, anyway. I didn't have to worry about him being too shaken after the—well, I could hardly call it an accident now, could I? Accident victims don't have their bodies stolen. I'd been right from the beginning. It was murder.

And everything was pointing to Rhys Whitney as the murderer.

***

Whatever Jane and Ali between them were thinking about, I was on my own quest. The answer had to lie with the art Rhys had stashed away in his panic room; that would be where the stolen art, or the forged art, or some combination thereof, was stored. I was in no doubt about that—Mirela is no idiot, and if she (who was usually the voice of caution whenever I was off on one of my wild tangents) thought there was something wrong, then there was something very wrong indeed.

And to be perfectly frank, I really just wanted to see them. Imagining being in such private proximity to a Rembrandt was enough to get my pulse going. I've never known much about art beyond the obligatory class or two in college, but I was certainly making up for that lack now.

First on the to-do list: call Mirela. "What are you doing right now?"

She sighed. "Sunshine. You are very persistent."

If she hadn't liked my persistence before, she wasn't going to be crazy about what I was going to ask her now. "Um—I'm wondering if I can borrow your key. To the—um—gallery." There was really no way to dress it up. I was willing to try breaking in, but I'd have to find out from Mirela first what anti-theft devices Rhys had put in place, so I might as well start with the easiest way to circumvent them: a key.

"You are not serious."

"Really? You're asking *me* that?"

A sigh. "You know it is against—"

"—the rules," I finished impatiently. "I know. You don't have to be there, okay? You could have lost your keys. Anything can happen. Maybe you left them at the inn or something."

"And instead of returning them to me, you went to the gallery?"

It wasn't impossible; I could make that work. The Whitney Worthington was one of the handful of galleries that occasionally paid me to open up on winter weekends. I could work with that, I decided. Say something, anyway. "Come on, Mirela, even if they find out you gave me the keys, what's the worst that can happen? They'll fire you? Give up representing one of the most popular artists in the world? Not in a million years, and you know it."

"I am not that very popular, sunshine."

"False modesty never works," I told her.

"I am never too modest."

I felt the impatience rising in my chest. "Will you just give me the key, Mirela? Please?" I paused, listening to the silence, trying to gauge its quality, what she might be thinking—or deciding.

She sighed again. "Why is this so important to you?" she asked. "No, wait, do not answer; you must listen to me first. It may perhaps become an important issue for the world of art, yes, but it is not very important to the *world* in the grand scheme of things." She spoke the words carefully, as though they were capitalized: the Grand Scheme of Things. "Why is it that you care?"

It was a good question, actually. From one point of view, Caroline was dead, and common shared humanity cried out for justice if not revenge. The truth was I really *was* pretty good at figuring things out and unsettled when I didn't know the answer.

But beyond that—well, Mirela was right. My own life wouldn't be terribly impacted if someone wanted to pass off fake paintings as the real deal. Nor even if someone was setting themselves up as one-stop-shopping: Forgeries, fakes, thefts. I'd still go to the Stop & Shop, have a coffee at Far Land Provisions, sit in the Little Green Car in the Harbor Hotel parking lot gazing out at the bay, and listen to the piano bar at Tin Pan Alley. Why *did* I care? Enough to risk getting caught doing something illegal and enmeshing my best friend in my illicit activities?

If I were being honest with myself, part of it was boredom. I'm never going to set up shop as a private investigator. That said, I have had occasion to—as they say in all the detective shows I watch on Britbox—"help the police with their inquiries." (And even on occasion go ahead of them in said inquiries). Whenever this happened, I've felt I was doing something important. Something meaningful. Something that answered, at least in part, the questions that present themselves on sleepless nights, questions about the fundamental unfairness of life and lack of justice, questions about the meaning of life and what the hell we're all doing on the planet.

Like my life made a difference somehow.

Weddings are lovely; don't get me wrong. Weddings can be—and frequently are—the most important day in somebody's life, and my facilitating that romantic magic to happen helps make them beautiful and memorable. It's all fun and games, isn't it? But since statistics show about half of these couples will end up separating, it's hard to take my role as Cupid enabler very seriously. If the job were challenging as well as meaningful, even with the limited amount of meaning I could squeeze out of it, then perhaps I'd be more engaged. After all, everybody loves a challenge.

I often have a lot of wild thoughts in the night. It wasn't just flight from a faceless bad guy invading my dreams. It had been easy to ignore my sister's brief life until the kidnapping in Provincetown surfaced her presence for all of us, and now she wouldn't leave me alone. What did my life really mean? Was there a reason she had been the one to die and I had been spared? Was I alive just so I could live out my life on this spit of land... and arrange for people to get *married*? Was that all there was?

I'd felt called to Provincetown. This was where I could be happy. And I had been. Was I still? Or was this just some sort of early-onset midlife crisis?

A few years back, one of my brides had been French. Provincetown stories delighted her, and I soon figured out why. She came from the farthest west one can go in France, a department in Brittany called *Finistère*. The name, she explained, was given by Roman traders overrunning the land in the first century. In Latin, it was known as "finis terræ," the end of the earth; the traders dared go no farther. *Beyond this be dragons.* "We have something in common," she told me. "Only the strongest make the choice to go to the end of the world to live."

Except that, lately, I hadn't been feeling so very strong, had I?

Was that where this sudden passion to uncover devious goings-on in the art world had come from? Helping me feel stronger, more needed, more necessary? Giving me something meaningful to do with these particular moments of my life?

Mirela was still waiting on the other end of the phone.

I could see what was coming. This investigation was going to turn out to be what most of life actually was: messy, incomplete, and barely comprehensible. We all want an orderly arc to our lives, don't we? And none of us gets it. I had a lot of half-formulated ideas about what I was doing and why I was doing it, and none of them answered Mirela's question.

So I told her the truth.

"I don't know," I said. "It's just—what they're doing is wrong, isn't it? You were right from the start. You were the first one to notice, and you were absolutely right; you even talked about unintended consequences. So maybe we can minimize them. Maybe we can make sure people don't get hurt." I hesitated. "Or maybe I just like being the white knight riding in on my champion steed to rescue the world."

There was a sound on the other end of the line that—if I didn't know better—I could have sworn was a muffled giggle. Mirela cleared her throat. "You want," she said carefully, "to keep people from suffering. This is good. Do you know who those people are? What you are saying, sunshine, is you want to save wealthy collectors from buying a false painting. Is that really what you want?"

Put it like that, and no, I really didn't. One of the reasons I was lukewarm about my father's interest in collecting art was because I didn't think he should. I hear the words "art collector," and I tend to see red in more ways than one. My true belief is that people should be *prohibited* from owning great art. Art is part of our cultural heritage. Art should belong to everyone, placed in museums where anybody can go in and see them. Hell, England's best museums are *free*. Yet every year, great art disappears into private collections—and the world never sees it again. These people—I can't bring myself to say "owners"—keep it in vaults where it does nothing but sit and appreciate in monetary value, surely the least valuable of commodities.

So if a fake van Gogh or Titian or Vermeer were to make its way through the auction houses or the art markets and subsequently get walled up in one of those expensive tombs, then more power to you, O forger.

Which put me squarely in the middle of my own argument.

But there was a Rembrandt, possibly even a real Rembrandt, taken from a beloved museum, which already a generation of people hadn't been able to see. If that were the painting in the basement of Mirela's gallery, then hell, yeah, I wanted to do something about it.

"If we know what's down there," I said to Mirela, "then we'll know what to do about it. If they're fakes or forgeries—"

"You know the difference?"

I swallowed. Okay, fine; I hadn't listened to Caroline for nothing. "A forgery is a copy of an existing painting," I said. "A fake is something done in the style of the artist. And signed, of course." The coup de grace, that signature.

"So which are you so angry about, sunshine? That there are fakes? That there are forgeries?"

"What if it was you?" I demanded, choosing a new tack. "What if someone were imitating your art? How would you feel about it then?"

She was definitely getting a kick out of this conversation. "Sunshine," she said, "I would like to see someone try."

"You're not taking this seriously!"

"It is you who are not serious. You want to go see this room to ascertain what, exactly? You are such a fine art connoisseur that you can tell just by looking who painted these pictures? And then what will you do? Tell the Provincetown police?"

I know I had a pained expression on my face. Sadly, a pained expression does not work well over the telephone. "Of course not," I said, though Julie Agassi would be flailing me alive if she'd heard my response. "But at least we'd know—"

"I know already, Sydney," she said. The banter was gone.

"What? What do you know?"

"I am not an idiot," Mirela said. "There are paintings there that should not be there."

I nearly lost it then. "And so what? What've you done with that information? Who do we complain to?"

"You tell me, sunshine. I do not see a path forward."

"I still want to see them," I said stubbornly. "Listen, Mirela, no one needs to know. In another six hours, we'll be in the middle of a nor'easter. No one will be going anywhere; there's no way anyone will see me. There'll probably be power outages; there always are. No one will know I'm there. Just say you left your keys at my house, and you won't get blamed, even if I'm caught. But I won't be."

The voice came from behind me. "Caught doing what, exactly?"

It was Jane Pfeiffer.

14

I turned around slowly. She was standing behind me, and I wished I'd made the call from Mike's office, or Glenn's office, or anywhere but the lounge where I'd assumed I'd be alone. Too late for that, anyway.

I said to Mirela, "I'll call you right back," and disconnected before she had a chance to say anything.

"So," said Jane, folding her arms casually, looking smart, elegant, and thoroughly interested.

"So," I echoed. "Ali's not here yet if that's what you're wondering."

"What I'm wondering," she said, "is whether I can go with you."

I stared at her. "How much did you hear?"

She smiled. "Enough. You're going to go ascertain what paintings Rhys Whitney has hidden in the cellar of his gallery in a climate-controlled locked room."

I let out the breath I didn't know I'd been holding. "Let me get this straight," I said. "You're in law enforcement, and you want to break into someone's property."

"Well, technically, we wouldn't be breaking in," she said. "Trespassing, certainly."

"You're the funniest FBI agent I ever met," I said, then lifted the phone again. "Hey, Siri, call Mirela." I waited while my electronic assistant rang the number.

"What is it, sunshine? Have you come to your senses?"

"Not noticeably," I admitted. "Anyway, Mirela, the party's grown."

"There is no party."

"Oh, yes," I said, watching Jane. "I think there is."

***

We almost made it out of the inn. But I made the mistake of answering the phone after finishing with Mirela, and it was Mike. "Sydney, can you come to the office?"

I glanced at Jane, who was waiting, her raincoat over one arm. "This isn't a good time, Mike."

"It has to be. It's for Glenn."

My stomach did a couple of fast turns. Now we were going to find out whatever it was that had been bugging Glenn. . . and suddenly, I didn't want to. I didn't want to know, didn't want to face whatever it was he was going to tell us. Didn't want change, didn't want to lose him. . . "You have to come, Sydney."

"Okay." I disconnected and turned to Jane. "I need a few minutes," I said.

She nodded. "I'll wait for you in the lobby."

"Fair enough." My heart was beating way too fast. *Breathe, Riley. Just breathe. Nothing bad is going to happen. Nothing bad is going to happen.*

Please, God, don't let anything bad happen...

Mike was leaning against the wall beside my cubbyhole behind Reception. "Has he said anything to you?"

I shook my head. "Nothing, just he wanted to meet."

He shrugged and pushed himself off the wall. "Let's go solve the mystery," he said.

For one absurd moment, I thought he was talking about the gallery; but then I looked past him. To the door to Glenn's office. Which was closed.

"What was that you said before?" I murmured. "We who are about to die salute you?"

"Don't be so cheery," he said and reached past me to knock on the door.

Glenn's office was in many ways the double of Mike's: it had windows on Commercial Street, it had a fitted carpet, and a big desk. The similarities ended there: Mike's was very much a working office, with file cabinets, bookcases, stacks of papers, and a safe. Glenn's looked like a movie set, some director's idea of an office. The books in the bookcase were leatherbound for show. There was a comfortable leather couch and matching easy chairs. A few regular chairs were ranged on the client side of the desk.

Glenn himself was sitting behind it, his presence immense both by virtue of his size and my concerns. "Come in, come in, both of you. Sydney, close the door behind you."

I obeyed and came to stand next to Mike, the two of us facing him for all the world like guilty schoolchildren on the carpet before the headmaster. Or Mother Superior, depending on which school you'd attended.

"You'll have noticed I've been distracted lately," he said, then abruptly gestured toward the chairs. "Sit down, sit down, both of you. You make me nervous hovering there."

I slid into one of the client chairs. "Distracted? That's one word for it," I said.

"Don't be cheeky," Mike said to me.

Glenn was smiling. "What word were you thinking of?" he asked.

"Scary," I said.

He seemed to like that. He looked down at his iPad and swiped through a few pages, finally finding what he was looking for and swiveling it around so we could see it. A photograph of a large man—large in muscles rather than fat—with a dark beard and a big smile. Behind him, a line of terraced houses painted gay colors. "André," said Glenn.

"He looks nice," I said. He did, too. Damn him.

Glenn said, "It's been a while since Barry died."

We both nodded. Not much you can say in response.

Glenn cleared his throat. "He's a university professor," he said. "And an artist. We've been seeing each other."

"Discreetly," I said. Sometimes I can't help myself. Mike jabbed me in the ribs with his elbow.

Glenn sighed. "I'm saying this because I want to make some changes around here," he said. My stomach did a slow flip-flop. *Here it comes.* "I want you both to step up a little here. I know I've been taking advantage of you, just leaving you to run things when I'm not here and doing it without a lot of recognition."

Mike said slowly, "It's what we do." I sensed he was as puzzled as I was.

"Yes, well, I'm going to be spending more time away," said Glenn. He looked down at his photograph of André. "And I know you're going to keep running things smoothly here while I'm gone, just the way you do now— well, no, not just the way you do now." He paused and looked back up at us. "I want to give you both more—recognition. And a raise." He cleared his throat. "Okay. Let's make it official. Sydney, you're the manager now. Hire someone else to do weddings. Mike, you're the executive manager. New titles. And I'm bumping up both your salaries."

Mike and I looked at each other; we couldn't help it. "That's very generous," Mike said slowly.

"Are you sure you're okay?" I asked Glenn.

The twinkle was back, the twinkle that had been missing these last days, and thank God for that. He was suddenly, again, the Glenn I recognized. "Why?" he asked.

I shrugged. "No one in their right mind would give me a raise," I said.

"Got that right," said Mike under his breath. My turn to jab him with *my* elbow. Not for the first time, I thought how much we behaved like siblings, given half a chance.

"Take it," said Glenn, ignoring our interplay. "Listen to me. I'm fine. I don't have some exotic life-threatening disease. I love the Race Point Inn, and I'm never selling it. The two of you, along with the team you've put together, are the best in the business. I want you here for as many years to come as you want to stay. But I'm also tired. I stepped into all this not knowing what I was doing, and the two of you made sure I was successful, and I'll never forget that. And now there's a part of my life, a big part actually, that's in Amsterdam. I want to know when I'm away that the inn is running just as well as when I'm here—no, better than when I'm here. It's what I can still do for Barry."

Before I move on. The thought was there, even though no one had spoken it. Glenn couldn't move on to another real relationship until he felt he'd honored his first love. I got that. I tried one last stand anyway. "I don't know much about running an—"

Mike's voice cut across mine. "You learned how to do events," he reminded me. "You'll learn whatever you need to know." He smiled, anticipatory; I could have sworn he licked his lips. "I'll teach you."

"Something to look forward to," I responded automatically, without thinking. What I was really thinking was, *why the hell couldn't he have said this a week ago?*

Reading my mind, Glenn said, "I didn't tell you until now because I wasn't absolutely sure everything was lining up." He paused. "And to be fair, you've been pretty busy yourselves." He looked at me with sympathy. "It hasn't been the best time for your father," he added.

"Point taken," I said. "So what is your plan—I mean, now?"

"I'm leaving today," he said unexpectedly. He made a gesture, and I saw the roller case and the gym bag behind him on the floor. Closed. Packed. "I'm going to Amsterdam for a few weeks. Spend some time with André." I could swear every time he said the name, he looked happier and happier. "Give you time to explore your new roles without me looking over your shoulders."

"You know there's a storm coming, right?" I demanded.

"Which is why I'm telling you now. Jack's flying me down to Connecticut, he has a fare going there anyway, and I'm hitching a ride. We'll be well inland before this thing hits. I've booked a flight from there to Miami. André's meeting me there. We'll take a few days' vacation on the beach and then head over to Amsterdam. You kids can run things starting right now."

Mike and I exchanged glances. I wondered if he—or even Glenn himself—had noticed the word *home* in that sentence.

Mike rose to the moment, literally and figuratively: he stood up and reached across the expanse of desk to shake Glenn's hand. "Thank you," he said. "We'll do our very best."

Glenn was beaming; he'd look a lot like Santa Claus if you added a red suit. "I know you will."

I stood up, too. "Thank you," I said a little faintly. There was suddenly way too much going on in my world.

There was a tap on the door, and the Kevin from Reception put his head in. "Your car's here," he told Glenn. "Word is they'll be flying out of the airport for another hour, then that's it, everyone's grounded, so Jack says to get moving." He looked at me. "And there's a guest who says she's waiting for you."

"Got it," said Glenn calmly. He stood up. We were dismissed. I thought about hugging him but didn't. I wasn't really sure how I felt.

Outside his office, I turned to Mike. "Did you have any idea?"

He shook his head. "Not about the promotions," he said. He was calm; Mike was already, to all intents and purposes, running the inn—his life wasn't going to change drastically. I wondered how much mine would.

Jane was indeed waiting in the lobby. "Well?" she demanded as soon as I appeared.

I sighed and reached over to my cubbyhole for my phone and my jacket. Ali had called. I held up a finger to Jane, who greeted it with a snort of impatience while I pressed the call-back icon. I'd forgotten I'd told him we could stay at the inn during the storm.

"*Cara.* I'm leaving Ibsen with plenty of water and some dry food, and I cleaned the litter. Do you want me to bring you anything, or are you coming back here first?"

There weren't a whole lot of women whose partners could talk about changing the cat's litter box so naturally. I was lucky. I was telling myself that even as I spoke. "I'm actually going out for a little while," I said. "Oh, and I have something to tell you. About Glenn. But not now." His door was still open, the Kevin from Reception trundling his suitcases out the front door. I supposed that now I was going to be doing more running the place, I'd have to start learning their names. I turned away from the lobby so Jane couldn't lip-read; it would be just my luck if she could. "I'm meeting Mirela at the gallery," I said, keeping my voice low. "Jane's coming along, too. To see what's in the—"

"Stop," he said. "Listen, *cara*, you can't do this now. There's more going on than just a few pieces of stolen art—"

"Aha," I broke in. "You said stolen. So you agree the Rembrandt might be real!"

"I'm agreeing nothing of the sort. I'm saying your little mystery is getting to be a lot bigger than you think."

"Tell me, then."

I heard him take in a long breath and then release it. "Is Jane with you right now?"

"Not far away," I said cautiously.

"Put her on the phone."

"Wait, what? Why?" I paused. "Ali, what's going on? You have to tell me what this is about."

Another breath. "It's not safe. I have—I think there's more to all this than just art fraud."

Something clicked in my head. I said, "You're thinking trafficking, aren't you? Trafficking in art? Here in Provincetown? What does it have to do with—"

He was not happy with me. "It's not at the gallery, anyway," he said obliquely. "I'm trying to track it down now. I'm going out to check something at the Provincetown Inn. You have to wait until I get back. I think—never mind, *cara*. Please just put Jane on."

I gave up and disconnected. Ali had to be wrong. There was no human trafficking going on here, and even if there were, it would have nothing to do with Rhys and the gallery. I knew I was behaving like a spoiled brat, but at that moment, I didn't care. I'd never liked Rhys, and now that it was pretty clear he was a forger and a murderer, I wanted to tie the case up with nice pretty ribbons. And I could only do that if the paintings in that cellar were forged, stolen, or both. Mirela had her suspicions, but Jane would know. Ali would just distract her.

I took a deep breath, turned to face Jane, and picked up my jacket. "Let's go."

15

In the end, all three of us went.

The sun was gone now for good. It had been flirting with the clouds for most of the day, but they'd moved in substantially in the brief time I'd been at the inn. The wind had picked up, too, and I shivered. Just because I wanted to do something didn't mean I *wanted* to do it, if that made any sense.

And it was still weird interacting with an FBI agent who didn't look or speak or act like one. Not that Ali did, either, for that matter: but I was used to him, and I'd sometimes heard him slide into that same law-enforcement voice and jargon; he just mostly chose not to.

I allowed myself to briefly wonder whether Jane might have faked her credentials, then put the thought out of my head. She and Ali had spoken; he'd know if she wasn't who she said she was. And having your sister killed and her body stolen could make you rethink the whole do-things-by-the-book concept. If I'd been Jane, I'd have been closer to throwing the book than to following it.

I had a feeling she was on the same page.

Mirela was clearly unhappy and making no excuses for it. "This is ridiculous," she said as we met her in front of the gallery. "This will not help anything."

"Then give me the key, and go home," I said, my hand out, waiting.

She made a gesture of impatience. "If I am not with you, you will do something stupid," she said and unlocked the door. I wondered, fleetingly, what she thought she could do to stop me; I am often the master of doing something stupid, and this could well be one of those times. And I'd be just as stupid with or without her.

There was a keypad discreetly on the wall to the left, and Mirela punched in some digits and then opened the door wider for us. "Come on, quickly," she said. We trooped in, and Mirela closed and locked the door behind us. "Do not turn on a light."

"Which way's the basement?" asked Jane. There was a flashlight in her hand; I hadn't noticed when she'd picked it up.

"This way," I told her; I'd never actually been down there, but I'd been minding the gallery one wintry afternoon when an electrician needed access, and I knew where he'd gone.

"This is a terrible idea," announced Mirela.

"Probably," I agreed. Jane had already found the light switch and was starting down the stairs. "Come on," I said to Mirela. "We'll be quick, I promise. Just let her take a look, and then we'll know for sure what we're dealing with."

"Sunshine, you will owe me for this." But she followed us down the stairs anyway.

There wasn't a lot to the basement. When you're on a flood plain, as Provincetown is, you're always running the risk of flooding from a particularly heavy rain or a particularly high tide. From that point of view, it made perfect sense to construct a sealed space where artwork could be stored safely.

Even when said artwork was completely legitimate.

There was shelving storing a lot of artsy junk; I had no idea what all the cans were for, or the stacks of canvases, or any of the detritus all around us; Rhys wasn't, it seemed, the neatest of people. But the door at the other end of the room was all Jane seemed to notice. "Can you open it?" she asked Mirela.

An exaggerated sigh. "Of course, I can open it," Mirela said scornfully. "I told Sydney already this is not a very good lock."

"Probably never thought anyone would come down here and look," I suggested.

She didn't spare me a glance. She had been right about the lock, anyway—well, that, or else she was an expert safebreaker because it took her less than two minutes to open the door.

The panic room—sorry, climate and light-controlled art storage space—was a good deal larger inside than I'd assumed, or even that it had looked like from the cellar stairs. Mirela touched a switch, and the room was flooded with harsh LED light. Inside, framed works were stacked perpendicularly in racks; a few were propped up on the counter space that ran along two walls. Under the counters, shallow drawers I knew stored unframed paintings.

I saw all this from the doorway; it took Jane about two seconds flat to be in. She'd gotten rid of the flashlight and was pulling on some plastic gloves. I followed more slowly. I could hear the sound of the dehumidifier now.

It worked well; there wasn't any sense of moisture in the air. There was a heat source, too, keeping the room cool but not cold. All the comforts of a museum, in fact.

"What are we looking for?" I asked Jane. I hadn't thought to bring gloves; I slid my hands into my jacket pockets. "I'll try not to leave fingerprints anywhere," I added belatedly.

Jane gave a snort. "Leave fingerprints anywhere you want," she said. "Just don't touch the *art*."

Mirela, having apparently now decided *in for a penny, in for a pound*, pulled aside a long dark drapery at the end of the room, flicking a switch on the wall as she did.

And there it was. Churning foaming waves, dark stormy skies, and sheer shimmering terror coming right off the canvas. Suddenly, brilliantly come to life, the lights above it picking out the shadows, the fear, the storm.

The Rembrandt.

I think I gasped; Jane made an odd noise in her throat and stepped away, almost instinctively, to get the full effect. The painting drew you in; I couldn't stop looking, feeling a tugging someplace inside me. My heart? My stomach? Who knew?

"He never did any other maritime painting," breathed Jane.

That snapped me out of it. "So you think this is the real thing?" I asked. "Not a forgery?"

She shrugged. "Who knows? We'll test it," she said. "I don't know if it is or not; that's above my pay grade. But it's one hell of an amazing copy if it isn't." She sighed softly. "If it's real, we've been looking for this one for a long time." She hadn't taken her eyes off the painting. I remembered her saying the family hobby was talking about the Gardner heist and exploring theories, something she played at with her sister. "Oh, yes," she said, almost reverentially. "If it's not real, it's the forgery of the century. Any century. Look at how he lowered the viewpoint so you can feel the weight of the sky, the weight of the waves, and the panic they were feeling. No one else in the early 1600s could touch that. No one but him."

"There's a fellow getting sick over the side," I said. I hadn't noticed that prosaic detail when I'd looked at the online images of the painting.

Mirela scowled at me. "Only you would notice that, sunshine," she said. I shrugged. Sydney Riley, mistress of the inconsequential.

"And there's Rembrandt himself, right in the thick of the action," said Jane, pointing. "It wasn't unusual for painters to put themselves in their paintings, but only ever as an onlooker to a scene. Here he's right in the middle of it. It's unique in so many ways, this painting." She hadn't once taken her eyes off it since Mirela had opened the curtain. "Look at how the brushstrokes are wild, broad, windswept splashes across the canvas," she said. She had lowered her voice as if we were in church.

As, perhaps, in a way, we were.

I was probably showing my inexperience as an art connoisseur. Still, I really did prefer this style, pictures that looked like what they were meant to portray, rather than the mad splashes of color Mirela and her colleagues at the gallery—oysters notwithstanding—were moved to create. This was… magnificent.

And, if it *was* the real thing, last seen by the public in 1990.

I took a deep breath. "Are the rest of them here?" I asked, and Mirela shrugged. "I did not look especially," she said. "This one, it is hard to miss. Rhys believes he has a private museum here."

"It certainly is hard to miss," said Jane. She *still* hadn't taken her eyes off the painting.

"Okay, so what else is here?" I asked. The storm on the canvas was reminding me of what was brewing outside and that time was short. We were there to gather evidence and then get the hell out. I tore my own eyes from the canvas and turned to the racks. "What else was stolen from the museum?"

Jane said, without looking away from the Rembrandt, "Three Degas sketches," she said. "A Manet. A Vermeer. A Flinck. A couple of smaller Rembrandts. A Napoleonic filial."

Well, at least we knew the filial wasn't here; I couldn't see anything in the room but canvases, some framed, some not. "One of the guys they suspected came from Cape Cod," I said slowly, remembering. I'd seen a documentary on Netflix or someplace like that.

"He was in prison when the paintings were stolen," said Jane.

"Maybe he had accomplices," I said. "Listen, that makes the most sense, doesn't it? After all, now we know the painting's fetched up here. Maybe someone brought it to him, and now that you have evidence, you could confront him."

"He's dead," said Jane, her voice flat. "We've wondered… we did send people to look at his property. We thought maybe they were buried in the backyard. We completely dismantled his shed, his house, everything." She shivered. "No one believed they weren't lost forever," she said. "Let's not get ahead of ourselves. The probability is this is one of Milo's."

Mirela stirred. "Milo is very good," she said slowly. "But is he that good? I do not know."

"There's something about it, something that… oh, I don't know," said Jane. "It *could* be Milo." But she sounded doubtful. She had turned back to the Rembrandt—if indeed it was—and seemed to be going into a trance.

"Let's look through the rest," I said to Mirela. "We've lost the FBI again."

Mirela moved over to the rack and started shuffling canvases. "This looks like a Vermeer," she said, but her voice was hesitant. "It is not one… I know about."

So not one of the Gardner pieces. The only Vermeer painting I knew much about was the Girl with the Pearl Earring, and that was only because somebody had written a novel about it. This canvas showed a woman standing next to a rough table, pouring something from a jug into one of the tankards on the table. A man was sitting at the table, food in front of him. They were both watching what she was doing. "So, is it real?" I asked Mirela. "Or a forgery?"

Jane had decided to join us. She narrowed her eyes at the painting and then, to my surprise, smiled. "Well, well, well," she said appreciatively. "What you have here, ladies, is a genuine van Meegeren."

We both looked at her, waiting. I'd never heard the name before; Mirela looked as though her command of English had gone off the rails.

"Han van Meegeren," Jane repeated with some impatience.

Okay, I'll bite. "Who?"

She made a gesture that could have meant anything. "One of the greatest art scams ever," she said, almost reverently. "He did Vermeers, lots of them. During World War Two, he sold one of his fakes to Hermann Göring—as an authentic Vermeer. But then the war ended, and the Dutch authorities arrested him for treason. Well, for all intents and purposes, he'd apparently sold one of the Netherlands' cultural crown jewels to the Nazis, and so they were going to execute him. But he said, no, it wasn't treason at all. He claimed the painting—it was *The Woman Taken in Adultery*—wasn't actually a Vermeer at all but rather a forgery he'd created and sold on to the credulous Nazis because they were all mad for classical art. Hitler was even planning on building the biggest museum in the world to house everything they stole."

"Everyone knows that," said Mirela impatiently. She was doing everything but peer at her watch.

Jane smiled. "Well, van Meegeren claimed it wasn't just that he wasn't a Nazi collaborator; he was actually, in fact, a national *hero* because he'd traded his fake Vermeer for two hundred original Dutch paintings Göring had seized at the start of the war. There's a movie made about it. It's on one of the streaming services."

"What happened to him?" I asked, fascinated. I was loving this dark side of the art world.

"Well, they didn't believe the painting was a fake. They said no one could paint like that, and so forth. So he offered to paint a Vermeer"—she sketched quotation marks in the air—"right in front of the court. And that's just what he did, to everyone's astonishment."

"Didn't that land him in another pot of hot water?" I asked. "I mean, now he's admitted to being a forger and all. . ."

"The trial took two years," said Jane. "They changed the collaboration charge to forgery, and van Meergeren got one year in prison but was actually tickled pink. My father knew him around the time he was released. He told my father that, back when he started out, he'd looked up the prison sentence for forgery, and it was two years, so he was delighted to only get one. He said, 'I'm sure about one thing: if I die in jail, they will just forget about it. My paintings will become original Vermeers once more.'" She sighed. "It shook the art world, I can tell you. You have to understand. All these great experts had authenticated his work—art historians, connoisseurs, museum directors, unscrupulous dealers—they'd all been in-volved. So all the contemporary methods of evaluating the work of master painters required a profound reconsideration, even a kind of catharsis."

"And this is one of his?" I tilted my head to the side to consider the picture. No way could I tell one way or the other. That was, of course, the point.

Jane was looking at it, too, and smiling. "I do think so," she said. "There were a couple of his paintings in our house growing up. My father was rather proud of his association with van Meegeren."

Which reminded me… "You and Caroline were both in Boston last week," I said. "But neither of you wanted to say so. How come?"

She didn't even flinch at her sister's name. Her dead sister's name. Her disappeared sister's name. Her probably-*murdered* sister's name. "It's nothing," she said, her voice abrupt. No trespassing. Not that I'd ever been stopped by someone's unwillingness to talk to me. "Was it something to do with your father?" I asked.

"It was because—" Jane said, and she never got further because, at that moment, the heavy, steel-reinforced, no-one-will-ever-break-in door slammed shut behind us, and we could hear the bolt falling down into place.

And then the lights went out.

***

Interestingly, none of us screamed. If this had been a TV show, we'd all have been screeching and banging on the door. But we were apparently made of stronger stuff than that.

Or maybe we just didn't want to ruin our manicures pounding on a steel-reinforced door.

We could still see; the cold overhead workshop-style lights were off, but the warm spotlights over the possible Rembrandt stayed on, and after our eyes adjusted, we could see quite well.

Mirela spoke first. "I knew this would happen," she said. "Now Lily's nanny will never work for me again. I promised her that I would be home soon. She is very strict."

"Soon is a relative term," I told her. The conversation was absurd, but it made as much sense as anything else, given our situation. What would be a better conversation to have? Wonder who locked us in? We knew who locked us in. Wonder why he did it? We knew why he did it.

"It's Rhys, isn't it?" I asked rhetorically. "It has to be. Damn, we should have posted a lookout." *A bit late to think about that, Riley*, I thought. *And why hadn't the FBI thought of doing it?*

Jane said, "This is good. It shows we're on the right track."

"So glad to know it," I snapped. "How are we going to get out?"

She actually smiled. "What, you think they're just going to leave us here? You're afraid we're going to be entombed—with that?" She was looking at the painting again. She didn't sound overly fussed at the thought of being entombed with it. She took a deep breath. "They'll be back for it," she said. "And for the rest. They haven't got all this stuff here just to sit. He'll be moving it along."

"But not necessarily right away," I objected. I wondered how long we could stay in the
panic room without panicking.

And—naturally—now I needed to use the
bathroom, possibly simply because I couldn't.

Mirela was fiddling with her phone. "There
is no signal," she announced. "The gallery has
wi-fi, but I cannot find it."

"The room's blocking the signal," said Jane
practically. I didn't like how she'd said it: she'd
made the room sound like a malevolent being,
an evil entity that wouldn't allow us to escape.
And didn't have a built-in toilet.

"How does this help Rhys?" I demanded.
"So he's got this stuff here, maybe some of it
stolen, all of it illegal, he's going to have to sell
it eventually to someone. What's he going to
do with *us*?" There were three of us and one of
him. Taking us prisoner maybe hadn't been the
brightest move. Thinking that made me feel
better. We were smart; we'd figure out a way
around this.

And, worst come to worst, either my boyfriend or Lily's nanny would come looking for
us.

Eventually.

I didn't much care for the other alternative
that had come to mind: we knew about the
paintings, and maybe it would be better if we

weren't around to tell the tale. But there was a very big step between stealing—or forging, or faking—fine art and murdering three people. Not to mention one of said people was an FBI agent.

If that happened, if Jane got killed, *they* wouldn't let go of it, ever. Rhys would be on a Most Wanted poster in every federal building in the country.

So I was going with a rescue. Something that would preferably happen sooner rather than later.

You couldn't hear anything from inside here, but I imagined what would soon be going on outside, the wind picking up, breaking tree branches, cutting off power lines. I wished I had actually looked at a forecast. The storm hadn't started when we'd set out for the gallery, and I wasn't even aware of how long we'd been in there. It could have been five minutes, and it could have been an hour. Who knew what was happening outside?

Of course, if the storm was hitting now, that might be a good thing for us—*if* this place were dependent on the one electrical line running along Route 6A into Provincetown. But I had a feeling people smart enough to put in a panic room were also smart enough to have a generator that would keep it safe in case of an outage. *Are you trying to reassure yourself, Riley?*

I remembered Mike's voice calling me Anxiety Girl. At least I was reacting true to form.

I was anxious, Mirela was cross, and Jane was the least ruffled of all of us; she seemed more intrigued than anything. Maybe she knew something we didn't. "Did you have Rhys on your radar for this?" I demanded. A conversation, I felt, would be helpful. Anything to keep whatever was bubbling up inside me from surfacing. I was starting to feel like I couldn't breathe, which couldn't be a good thing.

She managed to tear herself away from the maybe-Rembrandt. "Rhys?" she asked. "No, I don't think so."

"It's his gallery," I pointed out. "He installed the panic room. He has—all this." I gestured around. "It has to be him."

"Oh, I'm sure he's involved in all sorts of art fraud," she said easily. "And obviously, if this is real, I'd love to know how he connected with the Gardner heist. Especially if he has access to any of the other pieces." She smiled. "Aside from the most important consideration—that they can go back to the museum and thousands more people will be able to see them—well, it certainly won't hurt my standing with the Bureau to be part of their return."

"You think the forgeries and fake paintings were done by Milo," said Mirela unexpectedly. She was frowning, still thinking the issue over. Mirela doesn't like being wrong. "I did not believe he was good enough to do it."

Jane nodded. "I think he did some of them," she said. "He has the skillset and the need to thumb his nose at the art world. He's a talented but way underappreciated artist, which, as you both know by now, is a pretty exact profile of a forger. But he didn't do it alone."

"Rhys?" I asked. I really, really wanted it to be Rhys.

She clicked her tongue impatiently. "Look at how many paintings are in here, and who knows what's already been sold. There are a whole lot of Hawthornes, which I'm not sure is worth Milo's time. He probably did a few for practice and then handed them over to someone else. And there are higher-end artists in here, too. We're looking at hundreds of millions of dollars in this room alone, and he may have more storage somewhere, probably in a freeport somewhere."

"Freeport?" I repeated until I remembered. Ali had told me about one in Geneva—a place to store valuables. In secret. "Ali said—"

"Yes," she interrupted eagerly. "I want to talk to him. He's been working on the traffickers doing crypto."

"Yes," I said uncertainly. I wasn't sure how much I was allowed to say here.

She took a deep breath and nodded. "That's the connection," she said. "It's a smaller operation than the crypto scam, but I think they've got at least someone else working on these paintings, someone really good, so maybe kidnapped—"

"Wait," I said. "They're trafficking in *artists*? That's absurd."

"It's not. They're not holding anybody in a cell anywhere, making them sleep on mattresses on the floor—these are people with sophisticated skills. It's a specialist market. And it's so easy, really, if the talent is there, and someone has connections. . ." I must have been looking skeptical because suddenly—incongruously— she laughed. "Okay, don't believe me. But first, I have to tell you another story."

"Go on, then," I said in resignation. It wasn't as if we had anywhere else to go. Mirela was prowling around the room; Jane seemed as ruffled as she'd have been at a tea party. A singularly boring tea party.

"John Drewe and John Myatt perpetrated what's been called the greatest art fraud of the twentieth century," she said. "Drewe was a con artist; Myatt was a struggling painter. They connected, and Drewe basically gave Myatt a pittance for what he was creating. Modglianis, I think, and some Picasso and Rosetti. They weren't great fakes, even, so ridiculous—he was using the same kinds of paints you use on the walls of your apartment, but it made Drewe very rich and set Myatt to prison." She paused. "So think about it. What if he'd had *five* Myatts? Struggling artists like Myatt—he was a single dad trying not to be evicted. And, of course, once it started, Drewe had complete power over him. There are starving artists like that all over the world. Offer them a good job, then make sure wherever you take them, they can't leave. Maybe in a country where they don't speak the language. Maybe somewhere they're undocumented. Whatever. If all goes well, you could make a lot of money."

"Someone would know," I objected. "All those people living together? There's no space for anything like that in Provincetown. Everyone would *know*."

"We're not talking a thousand people here," said Jane. "Even just one or two, besides Milo—if they're good, they could make you a fortune. Of course, if you found a forger who already had a lot of work. . ." She paused. "I don't know Provincetown well, but you do. Someplace where they could come and go and blend in. There has to be someplace you could hide a studio and a whole lot of artwork without being noticed. Without interfering neighbors, you know?"

Anywhere, I thought. We have more artists' studios than anywhere else I've ever lived. In the winter, there are about two thousand people who live here. In the summer, that goes up to sixty thousand. You could hide a marching band in those crowds. "Where, then?" I asked, almost rhetorically.

Mirela said, "I know where."

We both turned to look at her.

She shrugged. "I did not think it was important," she said.

"Mirela, it's important," I said.

"He asked me. Milo asked me. A place he could rent. Something larger than just a studio, someplace people could live, too. So I told him there are some suites at the Provincetown Inn, and it's very easy to come and go there. I do not know if this is what he did, but it is what I told him to do." Her voice implied that anyone with half a brain would follow her instructions.

Ali's voice came back to me. *I'm checking out the Provincetown Inn.* That had to be it: and Mirela was wrong. It wasn't one of the suites; it was the long-abandoned kitchens stretching out under it. It had to be. Plenty of space and solitude: no one went there. People walking around on the main floor never dreaming that beneath their feet. . . "We have to get out of here," I said.

"No kidding," said Jane.

Mirela said, "There is a code."

I was getting very exasperated with her. "Wait, you knew how to get out this whole time and didn't say? We had to listen to Fake Art History 101 and all the time. . ."

"I am not sure it will work," Mirela said. She was looking exasperated, too. I almost expected her to echo my mother's *do not take a tone with me.* I couldn't blame her, not really; I was the one who'd insisted on getting her stuck down here. "It is a number Rhys had written on the back of his hand. He does not remember numbers. That is well-known."

"Who cares?" I asked rhetorically. "What is it?"

"And, more importantly, where's the key-pad?" Jane wanted to know. She was already running her hands over the door's metal frame.

It took us another twenty minutes, but Mirela found it at last, down at mouse height behind a stack of canvases. Rhys might be bad with numbers, but Mirela has an eidetic memory. "Eight-four-six-nine-seven-one-eight," she recited solemnly, and Jane keyed it in, and the door clicked open. It was almost anticlimactic.

Beyond was darkness.

Mirela was fearless, or perhaps it was just that she knew the place better than we did. "Come on," she said and felt her way across the cellar to a light switch by the door. "It is not working."

"The power's probably out," said Jane.

We felt our way up the staircase and through a door, listening at first to make sure no one was there. A silly enterprise; all it told us was no one was actually speaking. But when Mirela opened the door, we were into the gallery proper, and we were alone.

16

The world outside was a few shades of gray short of fifty, but not by a whole lot. The rain hadn't started yet, but the once-blue sky was overcast, and the wind was whipping down Commercial Street like a freight train. We stood in front of the open gallery door and contemplated what to do next. My hair blew across my face, and I lifted a hand to get it out of my eyes and mouth.

Somewhere behind us, a sign creaked, and I nearly jumped out of my skin.

"You must call the police," Mirela informed me. "We do not have time for this. And Lily…"

"My car's still parked in front of the inn," Jane said to me. "We can take it."

I hesitated. Now that we had a sense of what was happening, it was starting to feel like a job best left to steely-eyed professionals. Ali was already onsite if he'd followed through on our phone conversation, and he wouldn't go into a dangerous situation alone—or so I fervently hoped.

Jane was FBI, but Jane had already lost a sister to this enterprise, and she also had made it clear her career was going to shoot into the stratosphere if she delivered thieves, forgers, and traffickers to the unit.

"There is no hurry," Mirela said. "We are safe now, and soon it will—"

Jane cut her off. "Someone knows we're onto them," she said. "Don't you see? Why do you think they locked us in that basement? It was to buy time. Move the operation and move whatever else they have stored at this other inn you're talking about, and then they'll be back for what's downstairs. And then they're gone—the whole operation, the paintings, everything."

"Ali's on the case—" I began, but she cut me off. "And he's out there alone," she said. "Is that really what you want, Sydney? To leave him to deal with Milo and Rhys by himself? People have killed for a lot less than what's at stake here!"

"He probably called in—" I was still trying to find a good reason to stay put.

"They're not flying helicopters into this weather, so there's no specialist team getting here anytime soon, and it would take hours to dispatch anyone from Boston. We're it. Are you coming?"

I gave up. "I am," I said. "Mirela, go home, take care of Lily. Call Ali and tell him, okay?"

She was looking murderous. "And leave you? I am not that kind of girl."

Jane said, "All right, all right. I'm getting the car. Wait inside. You're calling attention to us staying out here."

After she left, we went back inside and closed the front door. I said to Mirela, "This may end your relationship with the gallery, you know."

She shrugged; when you're as good as Mirela is, you don't worry about trifling details like the closure of your primary place of business. "This will end the gallery," she said. "It is not my problem."

No, I could see that. I shivered and then remembered my earlier discomfort. Seize the day and all that. "I'm using the restroom," I told her.

"You are not," she said.

"Yes," I said. "I am."

The restroom was tucked into an alcove at the back of the second display room in the gallery. There was more storage space and a small, efficiency kitchen about the same size as the one in my apartment with a table, chairs, and a toilet. I closed myself in with a sigh of relief—why do heroines in novels never have to pee?—and had finished and rinsed my hands when I could hear Mirela talking to someone. Jane was back with the car, I thought; she'd been quick. I opened the door and found myself looking straight at a gun. Pointed in my direction.

I sighed as I took in the velvet jacket. Blue, this time. "Milo Griffin," I said.

He inclined his head; the pistol didn't move. "Sydney Riley."

"Looks like you're still not ruthlessly faithful to the original conception of art," I said, remembering his pretensions. "But aren't guns just a little obvious?"

Rhys' voice came from the front gallery showroom. "Is she there?"

"I've got her," said Milo. The eyes weren't the eyes of someone about to shoot, though; they were still bedroom eyes. I could see why both of the artsy sisters had fallen for him. To me, though, he still looked like an extra in a Johnny Depp movie. "Come on, let's go," he said, gesturing to the showroom with his free hand. The gun never moved.

Mirela was in the front room with Rhys, though standing well back from the big plate-glass windows. Not that there was anybody out there to see anything. "This is not a good time," she was telling him. I wondered what she was on about; it sounded as if he'd asked her to tea. "It is not just me. It is not just Sydney. There is an FBI agent, and she will be here soon. If you leave now, you will not have to be arrested by her."

Rhys didn't say anything, but Milo smiled a slow, satisfied smile. "It'll be good to see Jane again," he said. The way he said it, he might as well have been saying, *It'll be good to sleep with Jane again.* He kept his eyes on me, including me in the remark. It all felt far too intimate like I was being invited to join a threesome. "Let's go downstairs," he suggested.

"With you? Not a chance," I said.

An eyebrow arched gracefully. "Sydney Riley, as much as I would treasure time alone with you, I do have other things on my mind just at the moment," he said.

I took a deep breath. "Like Christ on the Sea of Galilee?"

The smile never wavered; he'd already known I knew. So he was the one who'd locked us in. But then… why was he back so soon? *Rhys* was the one who might suspect Mirela knew how to get out of the panic room; maybe Milo hadn't known she had the code. But neither seemed very surprised to have found us there.

Rhys and Milo. It wasn't an either/or; it was a both/and.

I remembered Jane's voice less than an hour ago. *Drewe was a con artist; Myatt was a struggling painter.* Drewe and Myatt; Rhys and Milo. But I was still trying to wrap my head around the two activities, which seemed to me to require vastly different skill sets. Fakes and forgeries required obsessive attention to detail—creating a provenance, sourcing the right materials that would stand up under investigation, and having significant contacts in the international art world. Not to mention the need for real, pliable, gifted artists.

On the other side of the equation was art theft: the ability to penetrate a museum, gallery, or collector's home, nerves of steel, a means to exit quickly and unobtrusively. Obsessive attention to detail might be the only thing the two had in common; the Gardner heist, after all, had been meticulously planned. If any of it was still around.

If any of it was in Rhys' panic room.

So was Rhys some kind of mastermind who could do it all? He hadn't struck me that way, somehow—a middleman at best. Maybe I wasn't giving him enough credit. Maybe he really was the busy spider at the center of the web, weaving provenances out of nothing, finding buyers, negotiating with art thieves, kidnapping forgers. God knew I'd been wrong about people more than a few times before, and this could well be one of them.

But it still didn't seem quite right.

He spoke to Milo. "No need," he said. "They'll just get in the way. We're supposed to have this all cleared out by now." He, too, I noticed, was carrying a handgun. For a state like Massachusetts, with strict gun laws, all this weaponry seemed a little excessive. Still, it was persuasive.

Rhys said to Mirela, "go back and bring out a couple of chairs," he said. "One at a time, and slowly."

Mirela didn't move. "You are not in charge," she said.

"What do you think this is?" He waved the gun a little wildly. "Looks like I'm in charge here, honey. And, by the way, I think your art is overrated."

She was almost smiling. "You said *we are supposed to have this all cleared out,*" she said. "So, who is it? Who is giving you orders, Rhys? Who is it that's your boss?"

He rounded on her and did something clicky with the gun that didn't fire a bullet but didn't exactly sound reassuring, either. "Listen, bitch, I've put up with—"

I didn't think he needed any encouragement. "Mirela," I said urgently. "There's absolutely no need to speed things up here."

"This is amateur hour," said Milo. "Let's get them both in the back room. Then they won't be in the way."

I fervently hoped it was the living me he didn't want in the way, not my body, and because of that hope, I wasn't as crazy as Mirela seemed to be about antagonizing anyone. I turned and went. Back by the sink and the table with the microwave and the mini fridge were a couple of chairs; it was what passed for a break room at the gallery. Milo had followed me. "Sit down," he said.

I sat down. Mirela was right behind me, discretion having apparently won out over valor, and she sat across the table. That left the two men in the doorway holding guns and looking faintly ridiculous.

Mirela hadn't given up. "If you plan to do anything, you will need to do it very quickly," she said.

"As long as it's not shooting us," I muttered under my breath.

Everyone ignored me. "There is a storm on the way," she informed them.

"Yeah, we were actually aware of that," Rhys said. He stuffed his gun behind his back into the waistband of his jeans. Sadly, it didn't go off. "Stay here with them," he said to Milo. "I need to get the canvases packed up in the tubes."

"Be careful there with the Rembrandt," I said, trying to sound mocking. I think I probably just sounded scared.

"Shut up," said Rhys and headed down the stairs. I waited until we couldn't hear his footsteps anymore, then turned my attention to Milo. "So what's the plan? Grab the paintings and run? What about all the people you have working for you? Can't shoot them all, can you?" Belatedly, I realized that, yes, actually, they probably *could* shoot everyone. Us. Jane. The artists they'd trafficked. My heart lurched at that thought. Ali had been on his way to find the trafficked people. Ali…

Don't think about Ali. Breathe, Riley. Just breathe. And while you're breathing, think about how to get out of this.

There was the rat-a-tat of someone pounding on the front door. "Don't look now," I said to Milo, "but that's probably the sheriff and his posse here to round you up."

"It is the FBI," said Mirela. She's never really gotten into the concept of light banter. Maybe they don't do repartee in Bulgaria. I'd have to ask her about it later—assuming there was going to be a later for either of us.

Rhys didn't waste any time. Within seconds he was back up at the top of the stairs. "I'll get it," he said. "You watch them."

"It's Jane Pfeiffer," said Milo, in much the same way as he would have said, "it's the postman" or "it's time for coffee." Apparently, he could turn off the charm as easily as he could turn it on.

"I know," said Rhys impatiently. "Let me take care of this."

His footsteps echoed across the gallery, through the smaller space, and out into the front. The sound of the lock turning. A crisp voice. "Rhys Whitney? I'm Special Agent Pfeiffer, FBI."

"The gallery is closed today," said Rhys.

"I'm not interested in the gallery," she said. "I'm meeting some friends here."

There was a pause. "You should move your car," he said, finally. "It will get towed. Your friends aren't here. Maybe they went somewhere to be safe? I gather there's a nor'easter on the way."

"All the same, I'd like to see for myself," she said.

I was thinking she needed information, and probably the most important information was that we were alive. "Jane!" I yelled. "We're in the back!"

"Shut up!" Milo hissed violently. He drew back his hand and hit my face, hard, with the gun, knocking me off the chair. Everything seemed to go very red and very fluid for a moment or two; my cheek hurt like hell, and I wasn't positive I hadn't lost a tooth. The red segued briefly to black as consciousness ebbed; the next thing I remember was someone pulling me up and pushing me back onto the chair.

By that time, Jane was in the room with us, sitting in the third seat at the small round zinc table. A café table, I thought irrelevantly. Perhaps we could order an apéritif. *You're losing it, Riley. Breathe. Just breathe.*

Okay, then: for as long as they let me, I was going to keep breathing.

I tried to pull my attention back to the room, though it was feeling less and less interesting to me. Whatever was going to happen was going to happen. My body was sending me strong signals: lick your wounds, deal with the pain, and let the world do what it's going to do anyway without you.

Mirela hadn't gotten that memo. Maybe because she hadn't been a target for Milo's rage yet. She was looking at Jane calmly. "The FBI does not carry a gun?" she asked.

"It's in the car," said Jane. She had a cut on her cheek, too, and it looked as though her eye might be bruising. That whole side of her face was red and swollen. No doubt a mirror image of mine.

In short, I thought, these guys weren't kidding.

Everything still seemed a little blurry around the edges. I tried to look at Mirela but couldn't gauge her expression; hell, the state I was in, I couldn't have gauged the Mona Lisa's expression.

Rhys was in one of the front showrooms, apparently on the phone. Bits of dialogue drifted back to us. "No… not yet. We've had our hands full, in case you hadn't noticed. . . Yeah, we got them all out. Nobody even knew we'd been there. Don't worry about it, I told you, it's all fine. . . Well, what did you expect? We didn't know. . . Look, I'm sorry, but we're doing what we can do now. . ."

I looked at Milo. "Sounds like somebody's in trouble," I said.

"Shut up." All the sexy élan, all the *sous-entendres*, even all the pretentious artsy verbiage was gone; Milo was not in his happiest moment. I felt absolutely no sympathy for him; neither was I.

And I *had* lost a tooth.

"At least now we know exactly who you are," Jane said. Her voice was a little slurred. She was, I saw, coping with a rapidly swelling lip. "You're just the worker bees, aren't you? Somebody else has the power."

"Shut up." He really needed to work on his vocabulary, I found myself thinking. *Really, Riley, you're held at gunpoint, and you're worried about syntax?*

Jane was undeterred. "So, who is it?" she demanded. "My guess is you're clearing out the gallery and meeting them somewhere else to hand over the paintings. You giving up all of them, Milo? Even the beautiful Hawthornes you did for local consumption? You should get credit for those, at least."

"I'll have credit for a lot more," said Milo. "No thanks to you."

"Oh, I'm sorry. Is law enforcement getting in your way, Milo? I wouldn't worry. You still have time to get out of here with your Rembrandt. It *is* yours, isn't it? But you must have—"

Milo cut her off. "We're doing fine," he said. "You always leapt to conclusions, didn't you, Jane? See, some things never change. Don't worry about us. Soon we'll be out of this so-called art colony, and I, for one, am never coming back." He gave an elaborate theatrical shudder; Milo was obviously feeling better. Something in the last couple of minutes had reassured him.

I wondered what it was.

What I really wanted was for the room to stop moving. I'd been knocked out before, but not like this, with reality coming and going seemingly at will. Everything is in focus one moment and swimming away into the distance the next. Maybe I could just black out and not be around when the shooting finally started, as it now seemed inevitable it would. You don't feel getting shot if you're already unconscious, right?

Then I focused on Mirela. I didn't have strong feelings about Jane one way or the other, but I wasn't leaving Mirela alone.

There was a fair bit of noise coming from the basement; Rhys, no doubt, finishing packaging up the paintings. There was the sound of the flat-file drawers opening and closing, the roll of glassine paper falling once in his haste. I could imagine him covering them before rolling them and fitting them inside the archival tubes stacked in the corner.

Stacked, I recalled blearily, right beside the keypad Mirela had used to get us out of the panic room. Rhys had to have known we'd get out. So what had been the point of locking us in? To buy time before we raised the alarm? That made no sense: we'd been in there a few minutes, but there was no way for anyone to know that Jane would use the opportunity for a lecture on art forgers…

Unless *she'd* known.

If what she and Milo were doing now was some elaborate show for us to believe they were on opposite sides of the fence here, it was pretty much wasted on me. I had a suspicion my mind wasn't working at exactly one hundred percent. I moistened my lips, which suddenly felt too dry to speak. "Jane," I said, articulating with difficulty, "are you in on this?"

She was staring at me. "Does it *look* like I'm in on this?" she demanded. "Maybe you didn't notice which side of the table I'm at here? Milo and I may have a past, but it doesn't look too good for the future."

"Not for your future, anyway," said Milo. He was warming to this evil villain role. Next time around, he'd be sporting a monocle and stroking a fluffy white cat. Next time around, I was going to have to pay more attention; sometimes bad guys do look like Captain Jack Sparrow.

Next time around? Do you really think there's going to be a next time around, Riley?

Rhys dropped something downstairs and swore loudly. "Hope that isn't your Rembrandt," I said to Milo. "The Saudis will want it in pristine shape."

"What Saudis?"

I shrugged, which turned out to be a bad idea. "Whoever you're selling it to," I said. "They're the first that come to mind. Didn't they buy that da Vinci portrait of Christ?"

"It wasn't a da Vinci," snapped Jane. "It was done in his workshop. The crown prince got taken for hundreds of millions."

"Won't be a problem here," said Milo.

"You could always return it to the Gardner," said Jane. "There's a substantial reward offered. They wouldn't question whether it's real or not. You could just say you found it— wherever it is, you found it."

"Oh," said a voice from the doorway, "I don't think Milo even knows where it came from. Nice suggestion, but we have other plans."

I recognized the voice before I even had the opportunity to try and turn around.
Caroline Harrison.

17

"But you're dead," I said before I could help myself. One of the world's Stupidest Remarks Ever.

"Apparently not," Caroline said. She came farther into the room, which was starting to feel very crowded indeed. She was wearing a raincoat and high heels, still had that coastal grandmother vibe, and was very much alive.

Jane was staring at her sister. "I should have known," she said slowly. "Milo couldn't have done this on his own."

"No, he couldn't, could he?" Caroline was sounding very pleased with herself. She flicked some moisture off her sleeve, and it hit me squarely in the face. Milo had taken a step back to accommodate her in the space, and now she leaned over and kissed his cheek. "Is everything under control, darling?" she asked.

I was still feeling like maybe my concussion was worse than I'd thought. "You got hit by an SUV," I said. "You were transported in an ambulance."

"Hit by *Rhys'* SUV," she said, nodding. "He's quite an amazing driver, as it turns out."

Mirela said, her voice unexpectedly loud, "You took something. A poison."

Caroline glanced at her. "I knew you were bright," she said. "Too bad a little slow to get there."

"What are you talking about?" I asked Mirela.

She shrugged, or at least it looked like she did. She, along with everyone else, still seemed a little bleary to me. "It is a substance. It is illegal. It slows down a person's vital signs," she said. "I have heard of it used before. In my country."

"Like hypothermia," said Caroline, nodding, "except without the cold. They declared me dead on arrival. No pesky emergency room, just a gurney in a corridor for hours, because the hospital's understaffed, especially on a Friday night. Pretty easy to leave when no one's looking. And then, *voila*, not only is one dead, but one also doesn't even leave a beautiful corpse behind."

I felt there were probably a lot of snappy rejoinders I could make to that remark; only the part of my brain that formulated snappy rejoinders was apparently on vacation. Pity. "So what's the plan?" I asked. Might as well cut to the chase here.

"We have to part company, unfortunately," said Caroline. "I won't pretend I didn't enjoy the time I spent with your father, Sydney, but I fear my consultant days are over. I am about to become part of the leisure class." She raised her voice. "Rhys!"

"Almost done!"

"Okay." She wasn't standing particularly near any of us, even if we'd been able to formulate a plan to take her on; besides, Milo still was holding a gun, and I had no reason to believe he didn't know how to use it. Even if he shot wildly, I thought, he would surely hit someone with all these targets in such a small space.

Pity it couldn't be Caroline.

"How did you get the Rembrandt?" I asked. "Come on, it's the least you can do; tell us that. We were all amazed to see it." Understatement of the century.

"I knew Myles Connor," she said. Milo gave her a sharp look, but she ignored it. "He used to live next door to our auntie in Harwich."

"He was in jail when the artwork was stolen," said Jane. "It wasn't him. He was ruled out."

"Just goes to show how little imagination the FBI has," said Caroline. "Unless, of course, it *is* a forgery. What do you think, Janey? Is it, or isn't it? We used to talk about it all the time, remember? Is it one of your art frauds? Or one of the most magnificent paintings ever created?" She allowed herself a laugh; the questions weren't meant to be answered. She raised her voice again. "Rhys?"

"Yeah! Don't rush me!"

Caroline sighed, but Jane wasn't finished with her. "Where's the rest?"

"From the Gardner? Who knows?" Caroline seemed unconcerned. "Out there somewhere, maybe. Or destroyed. Or buried in someone's backyard. These people, they don't give a damn about art."

"They could have fooled me."

"It's a *commodity* for them," Caroline said. "Not like it is for us. Not like the way you and I love it, Janey. Not the way Father taught us to love it."

Jane was nodding. "He's why you're doing this, right?" she said. "To prove something to him?"

"Don't be ridiculous. No one's ever proving anything to him. He'll never think highly of either of us. Don't fool yourself. Joining the government didn't help you any, Janey, did it? Make him respect you more now that you're a big illegal art expert? Don't make me laugh. We could never have pleased him, no matter what, no matter how hard we tried. We're too different from him. Too different from each other."

"I don't know," said Jane. "We both work in art fraud, apparently."

Caroline liked that; she even spluttered with a little laughter. "That's clever, Janey," she said. "I'll have to remember that." She paused. "At least now he'll see I'm as important in the art world as you are."

"Wait," I said. "What are you saying? You're doing all this because of some crazy sibling rivalry? Is that it?"

Jane said calmly, "There's more to it than that."

"But not a lot more," said Caroline.

"So that's the stuff in the gallery," I said, not needing to hear more about this dysfunctional family's dysfunction. "Who's been doing all these forgeries?"

"That's Milo's department," she said, her voice flippant.

"Couldn't have done it without me, darling," he chirped.

She gave him a look. "Don't exaggerate your contribution, Milo," she said, and there was steel in her voice. I had a sudden vision of her in full dominatrix regalia. It even fit. Coastal grandmother by day, dungeon master by night. "Where are they?" I asked.

"Long gone," said Caroline. "We have to thank your boyfriend for that, Sydney. You're smart to latch on to him. He knows what he's doing."

I felt my stomach lurch. Was he dead? Was I responsible? "What exactly does that mean?"

"The Provincetown Inn never even knew we were there," she said. "No one opens up those kitchens anymore. It was the perfect place. I even stayed there when I was— between existences, shall we say. Uncomfortable but quite safe. Until Agent Hassim came along."

"What have you done to him?" I think I was screaming at her. It sure felt that way from inside my skull.

"He's fine, don't be melodramatic," she said briskly. "We cleared out this morning. The artist and a hell of a lot of canvases he's been working on for years. With some help from Rhys, we should have plenty more Hawthornes where those came from. And a couple of Pollacks, too. I do like Provincetown artists."

Rhys himself appeared at that point, his arms full of cylinders, the cylinders presumably full of art. "You were supposed to meet us in Hyannis," he said pettishly to Caroline. He sounded tense. "You were supposed to follow the plan. We agreed. You're completely out of line here. I don't know what you expect me to do about all this. Just once, you couldn't do as you were told. Just once. Now there's a storm and—"

"Oh, for heaven's sake," said Caroline. In one fluid movement, she turned to him, pulling something sharp and bright out of her pocket as she did, her arm up and then down as she plunged it into his neck. He made a gurgling sound and went down hard. A geyser of blood spattered everything, including my face. Milo gasped and found his voice. "What the hell was that for?" he yelled at her. "He isn't—"

"He isn't irreplaceable," she snapped. "Want to see if that works for you, too?"

Was she planning on stabbing everyone in the room? I looked across at Jane. As the current representative of the FBI, she must have some idea about what to do in a situation like this one, but she looked as shocked as I felt. Rhys' blood was on her, too. Maybe seeing your sister kill someone in front of you isn't covered in the agency handbook.

Caroline had rounded on Milo, the knife—a big one—still in her hand and literally dripping with blood. "No," said Milo, and raised both hands in what seemed an automatic gesture as though to protect himself.

The gun jumped in his hand and went off, and Jane slumped onto the table.

I didn't scream; I was too busy staring at the pistol, which Milo had let go of when he moved away from the crazy lady with the knife; I grabbed it, the action reflexive rather than brave or thoughtful. I swallowed hard, stood up, and held the gun out with two hands, the way I'd seen it in the movies, trying to cover both Caroline and Milo with it. "Stay where you are," I said, though I didn't have a clue what should happen next.

Caroline laughed. "Don't be absurd," she said, raising the knife and taking a step in my direction. "You have no idea how to use that thing."

"No," said Ali's voice from behind me. "But I do."

And then he shot her.

***

Caroline lived; Rhys and Jane didn't. It seemed a dismal end to things.

The storm had moved in since we'd been downstairs in the gallery, but Julie was on hand with a couple of police cars, and once the EMTs had checked us out, her people drove us all back to the inn. Well, except for Mirela, who was still talking about the nanny never forgiving her. I resolved to try and get along better with Lily in the future.

Ali had his arm around me and wouldn't move it for anything. The ambulance guy had to work around him.

"Just make sure you hold onto her this time, won't you?" I could hear Julie talking to the ambulance guys, who were none too pleased to be told their business. But she had a point. Milo, on the other hand, she sent off in one of the squad cars, heading toward the police station. It had been moved into a bigger, newer building recently; I trusted he'd be reasonably uncomfortable there.

The Race Point Inn was brightly lit, dry, and sparkling when we ran through the lashing rain to the front door. Mike was hovering in the lobby. "Are you all right?"

I nodded before remembering I had a concussion. Mistake. "I'm fine, Mike."

"Get in here." He seemed to include everyone in his gesture, and we all crowded into the small lounge: me, Ali, Julie, and a couple of her uniformed officers. Mike yelled to someone, and a few minutes later, one of the Kevins appeared with tea and brandy. I thought we were probably supposed to pour one into the other; I ignored the tea and took my brandy neat. A whole big swallow of it.

"You're not supposed to drink alcohol with a concussion," said Ali.

"I do a lot of things I'm not supposed to do." I leaned gratefully into his shoulder. I don't think I'd ever been happier to be with him. "Are your people safe? The artists they trafficked?"

He nodded, turning his head slightly to kiss my forehead. "Person. Just one artist. We're taking care of him," he said. "Don't know how all the art's going to get sorted, but thankfully that's not my department. It *was* trafficking of a sort—Rhys stumbled onto this guy in Boston by accident, and when he told Caroline about it, they blackmailed him with threats to call the police—he'd been making fakes for a while by then. After that, they pretty much kidnapped him—*and* all his finished canvases. Gave them a big advantage on startup costs, that's for sure." He paused for a yawn. "Seems he'd already been on the FBI's radar for a while, and Jane was on the case. When he disappeared, Jane suspected something, though she hadn't put it all together yet. I got the tip-off from another source, and… well, there was too much about this story that lined up with everything happening here."

"And no one at the Provincetown Inn even knew she was there?"

"No. There was no reason for them to— the kitchens are locked and haven't been used in years. It was always going to be temporary, just until they could get the provenance sorted and the first batch of paintings sold. He couldn't have stayed there much longer—not once it turned cold, anyway. But in the meantime… well, Rhys didn't trust either of his partners and wanted to keep the operation where he could be in control."

"Well, he got the part about not trusting Caroline and Milo right, anyway," I said. Even to my own ears, my voice sounded exhausted.

Mike was watching me, and he turned to Julie. "Can we do the rest of this later? They can tell you the whole story—"

"That's not why I'm here," Julie said.

There was something in her tone. Some echo of something dark and threatening. "What?" I said.

She swallowed; I'd never seen Julie on the back foot before. "I have to tell you—I'm sorry to tell you—there was a flight to Miami crashed on takeoff from Bradley Airport," she said, her voice as flat as if she were reciting a lesson.

Mike made a sound I'd never heard anybody make before.

Unlike TV detectives, Julie didn't keep us in dramatic suspense. "Here's the thing. I got a call from Jack. He flew Glenn out of P'town," she said. "He knows me and works dispatch at the station part-time. He'd dropped his guys off and was refueling at Bradley International before heading out on the next leg of the flight, so he was still at the airport when it happened. A jet bound for Miami stalled on takeoff and crashed." She hesitated for a millisecond. "It was Glenn's flight," she said. "Jack said there's no way there were survivors; it was carrying a full load of fuel. He said it was a horrific fire."

Her eyes were on me. "I didn't want you to hear it on the news."

There was a moment of stunned silence, and then Mike turned and walked out of the room unsteadily, like someone who is drunk. I could hear him being sick in the lobby.

"No," I heard myself saying. Somehow I was standing up. "No. He was going to Amsterdam… he was going to be happy again."

"I'm *so* sorry," said Julie. I'd never imagined her voice could be that gentle.

Mike was back in the doorway, looking white. He had an envelope in his hands, one of the Kevins over his shoulder, curious. "How did he *know*?"

I tried to pull myself together; Mike was in as much pain as I was. This wasn't my moment. "Call Ed," I said. Ed was Mike's veterinarian boyfriend.

"Know what?" asked Ali.

Mike ignored my suggestion. "Glenn left this," he said, holding the envelope out to Julie. "But how could he have known?"

"Known what?" I asked blankly. I had no idea what he was talking about.

Julie took it. "This is an envelope addressed to Michael Madison and Sydney Riley," she said. "Do you want me to read it?"

Mike swallowed and didn't say anything. I sat back down and gripped Ali's hand. "Yes," I breathed.

She didn't take her time, wait for a dramatic pause; those crime shows have it wrong. Julie was all business, though she kept that gentle voice I hardly recognized. She opened the envelope and started reading without even giving it the once-over most cops would have.

"I've never much believed in premonitions, so if I'm wrong about this, we'll all have a good laugh when I get home. But a strange feeling's been nagging at me. I've been dreaming I died, so maybe my subconscious is just telling me to get a move on with things.

I never thought I'd love anybody like I loved Barry. But I'm getting older, and this—André, I mean—is a second chance for me.

I'm taking that chance, which means a lot for all of us. Your promotions are real, but the truth is, if anything happens to me, I'm giving you the inn jointly. Fifty-fifty. Free and clear. My attorney has drawn up the documents, and I've signed them. I didn't want the fuss of arguing with you before I left, hence this note. You can figure out between you how to make things work and keep me out of it.

Hang on to Martin and Adrienne—it wouldn't be Race Point without them. But as for the rest—well, what can I say? If I do end up moving to Europe, or if that recurring dream is right, and I'm not coming back at all, ever—the inn is yours to do as you see fit. There, I've said it.

Mike, you have a home and a partner, and I'm happy for you. Whatever happens with the inn, the income from your share should keep you and Ed more than comfortable for—well, for always."

Sydney, you have got to get out of that closet you call an apartment, so the penthouse is yours. Bring Ali, bring that cat, but maybe use your discretion around the furniture? I've been to your place. Enough said.

I know these last few days I've been a little distracted, even absent. I've been spending a lot of time making decisions, living in my own head. But that doesn't mean I don't know what you've been up to. I hope you caught the bad guys.

Oh, and the fake Hawthorne in the penthouse? You don't have to worry about that one, at least. Turns out, my appraiser confirmed it isn't fake. Can you believe it? If my weird feeling about all this is wrong, we'll find a place for it at the inn. Otherwise, put it somewhere where you both want it to be. And think of me when you look at it.

Love to you both. Whatever happens—or not— know you made all the difference.

—Glenn

And then I began to cry.

No one wanted to be the first to say anything. Julie handed the letter back to Mike, who looked like he was going to be sick again. Ali stroked my hair.

There was a sudden burst of loud music that made us all jump, and after a long moment, I realized it was coming from my phone. "It can't be," I said out loud.

"What?" asked Julie.

I pulled it out of my pocket. "That song's 'In the Hall of the Mountain King.' It's Glenn's ringtone."

Everyone stared at my phone. "It has to be a mistake," said Mike.

"Answer it," said Ali.

I swiped to open it. "Sydney Riley," I said, the words choked but automatic.

A man's voice said, "Hello? I'm wanting a wedding. This week if possible."

"Not a good time," I said, wondering why the phone had bizarrely chosen Glenn's ringtone. "I'll call you back tomorrow."

"But what if we want to get married tomorrow?" It was a different voice.

Glenn's voice.

I froze for a second, everything weirdly shimmering around me. Encased in ice. *Glenn's voice.*

There was a pause, and then, as though he could see me, he said, "Sydney. Focus. Don't hang up."

I registered that everyone in the room was staring. You could have heard a pin drop. "Glenn? Is that really you? Are you *alive?*" I put the phone on speaker and held it out.

"Oh, damn, you already heard. Sorry; I'd hoped to get to you before the news did. Figured you might be busy with the storm. We're all pretty shaken up about it, but I wasn't on that plane."

"Why not?" I was pushing the words out automatically. I wasn't really believing what we were hearing. Way too much, way too fast.

"André met me here—he wanted it to be a surprise. He rented a limo to take us to New York, and he was going to ask me to marry him on the way. He thought it would be romantic to propose to me at the top of the Empire State Building." A murmur of voices on the other end of the line. "Yeah, well, we were still working on getting my luggage re-routed when that plane crashed. Maybe my dream was right after all. A lot of people saw the crash. It's crazy here, with emergency workers and reporters all over the place, and even some relatives. . . It doesn't seem right to go on to the city to celebrate, not after what just happened, and knowing I should've been on that flight… so, anyway, we're heading back to P'town once the weather breaks."

I didn't say anything. I didn't even know if I was breathing.

"I'm sorry, Sydney. I didn't mean to scare you."

Mike found his voice. "Glenn. We're just relieved to hear you're okay," he said.

Glenn said, with an attempt at levity, "Who knew some premonitions really pan out?" He paused. "But we've been talking, and we're not taking any more chances. I'd say we used up all the luck we can afford. So we're getting married. Tomorrow, if the storm blows itself out to sea again, which they're saying it should. So find someone to do the ceremony, Sydney. OK?"

I was starting to feel giddy with relief, babbling nonsense. "You know there's a three-day waiting period," I said. "And things will be messed up for a while once the storm's over. I'll have to make some calls. But we'll figure it out. Oh, Glenn! You're okay! You're alive! And we'll even get to meet your mysterious André!"

"You will indeed. Um—did you read the letter I left?"

Mike and I exchanged glances. "Yes," Mike said. "But we're happier that you're still alive. That's a lot better than—"

"Never mind all that," Glenn said. "What I wrote is what I want. It's not open for discussion. We'll update the paperwork when I get back, so you can take over ownership immediately." There was a murmur of voices, and then he said, more clearly, "We're gonna be living in Amsterdam. It's what André wants, it's what I want, and I refuse to be an absentee owner. The inn's yours."

"And the penthouse?" Okay, so I'm shallow.

"Still yours, Sydney. Stop fretting. Go look for some slipcovers. We'll see you soon."

***

Later, up in the penthouse, when I was nodding drowsily against Ali's shoulder, his arm around me, he cleared his throat. "So we get to live here," he said.

"Yep."

"And you're going to be the co-owner and manager."

"Yep."

"And we don't have to bring that hideous sofa from Carver Street."

"Absolutely not."

There was a long pause. "Does this mean you're not going to be planning any more weddings?" he asked.

"After Glenn's? I guess not." I hadn't really assimilated the whole thing yet.

"Excellent," said Ali.

Not the obvious response. "Why?"

"Well," he said, "It was going to be awkward otherwise."

"What was?"

He squeezed my shoulder. "Planning our own," he said.

Author's Note

As you can probably tell, I'm fascinated by the extraordinary amount of fraud present in the art world, and by how it's done. Most of the players/places referenced in this novel—Myatt and Drew, Han van Meegeren, the Knoedler Gallery, the Geneva Freeport—are real, and the FBI does indeed have an active art fraud division (still optimistically looking for that missing Stradivarius!).

Techniques for identifying fake paintings have improved substantially over the past decade. And yet, despite that progress, the practice continues.

An interesting read, if you, like me, are intrigued by this world, is Samanth Subramanian's excellent article "How to Spot a Perfect

Fake: The World's Top Art Forgery Detective" in The Guardian newspaper (15 June 2018).

As for theft… Late on March 19, 1990, two thieves dressed as policemen walked into the Isabella Stewart Gardner Museum in Boston shortly after midnight. They duct-taped two hapless security guards and escaped with 13 paintings valued today at some 500 million dollars, including spectacular works by Rembrandt van Rijn and Johannes Vermeer. None of these works has since reappeared, and the theft is considered an active investigation with a sizeable award attached to their recovery.

Convicted art thief Myles Conner's name surfaced immediately after the heist, despite the fact that he resided in a federal prison in California at the time; his most famous crime had been the theft of a different Rembrandt, *Portrait of Elisabeth Van Rijn* from Boston's Museum of Fine Arts. He admitted to having cased the Gardner back in the 1970s, and in 2000 he accused two organized crime-affiliated figures of doing the 1990 heist using his plans (security at the museum having not been updated in those two decades). Both those men are now dead; Connor is, as of this writing, living in Massachusetts, though no longer on Cape Cod.

If you want to learn more, check out Netflix's *This Is a Robbery: The World's Biggest Art Heist* to see how the Gardner theft unfolded. For more on Han van Meegeren, you can read *The Forger's Spell: A True Story of Vermeer, Nazis, and the Greatest Art Hoax of the Twentieth Century* (Edward Dolnick). And if you'd like some general background, there's *Art Forgery: The History of a Modern Obsession* (Thierry Lenain). They were all very helpful to me in preparing to write this novel. If you'd prefer something lighter, check out more of my recommendations here: "Taken! 10 Great Heist Movies" in Criminal Element (criminalelement.com/taken-10-great-heist-movies).

The Provincetown Inn is every bit as eccentric and wonderful as I describe here, and there are indeed massive kitchens in the basement, but they have never sheltered artists of any ilk, and certainly, the inn has never been to the best of my knowledge associated with any illegal activities.

Finally, I'm aware that in this book, I've stepped outside the tried-and-true murder mystery formula of a corpse appearing within the first three chapters. This ninth Sydney Riley mystery is introducing a sort of pivot in her life, and I thought it might be fun to broaden the mystery concept a little in celebration of those changes. We'll get back to our regular programming for Number Ten, I promise!

Acknowledgments

Every time I've been tempted to give up, my publisher and friend Arthur Mahoney of HomePort Press has been there to give me encouragement. He has a diffident manner but a sharp mind in showing me angles I might not have considered (a nice way of saying, "focus, Jeannette!"), and I am so grateful for that and all the myriad other things he does to bring my novels from idea to publication. I am blessed and extraordinarily lucky to have both his wise counsel and his friendship.

Big thanks to Christine McCarthy, CEO of the Provincetown Art Association and Museum, who set me on the path—there are wonderful Hawthornes among the museum's treasures, by the way. And art dealer, appraiser, and independent curator Jim Bakker gave me insights into the art world I couldn't have found anywhere else. They were both extremely generous with their time and expertise. Artist Edward Walsh gave me behind-the-scenes insights into the Provincetown art scene. Much gratitude to Bruce Ployer for teaching me about art storage.

So many other people help in so many different ways. My Patreon crew keeps me sustained and focused: Grant King, Barbara Benjamin and Carol Procter, Amy Davies, Jane Cairns, Cathy Knipper, Margo Nash, Corinne Diana, Ann Robinson, Amanda Robinson, Freddy Biddle, Sydnia Czarnecki, Susan Blood, and Chip Capelli. Several of them are beta readers—and we love beta readers!

Others help in ways too numerous to mention: Carem Bennett, Indira Ganesan (for "Pizza and Poirot"), Colin Kegler, Marge Piercy, Michelle Crone, Dianne Kopser, Julie Blackburn, Bob Allen, Edward Franchuk, Anastasia and Jacob Czarnecki, Garr Roosma and Jane MacDonald, Pat Medina, and Rick Miller. Also, in gratitude for prayers from my brothers and sisters at the Iona Community.

Thanks to my own local booksellers, East End Books, and the Provincetown Bookshop, and especially to my wonderful local heroes at the Provincetown and Truro public libraries—

Amy Raff and Brittany Taylor, and Tricia Ford and Justine Alten.

A big thank-you to all my writing students who keep me honest. And to Eric Bomyea for being my fanboy. Thanks to Miladinka Milic for Sydney's amazing cover designs. To Kyre Song, who is so much more than just my web guy, and Assaf Levavy for being my wonderful sometimes writing partner.

My thanks go, as always, to all the beautiful people of Provincetown, who generously allow me to use so many of their own special selves in my books. Any errors in their portrayal are mine.

Thanks to Erin Delaney for her peerless editing and to my wonderful First Readers: Kimberlee Sams, Corinne Diana, Margo Nash, and A.C. Burch. Any mistakes that remain here are mine, not theirs. To the ladies from Jungle Red Writers for their support and inspiration. And to the New England chapter of the Sisters in Crime—well, for sisterhood!

And you, my readers—I am so very grateful you continue to give me so much of your time and your attention. You trust me to take you somewhere you've never gone, and every day I pray I live up to that trust.

About the Author

Jeannette de Beauvoir is a bestselling author of mysteries and historical fiction as well as a poet who lives and works in Provincetown, Massachusetts. Her work has appeared in myriad literary reviews and anthologies, and she's a member of the Authors Guild, the Mystery Writers of America, Sisters in Crime, and the National Writers Union.

Find out more—and read her blog, at jeannettedebeauvoir.com

Did You Enjoy This Book?

If you did, please…

1) **share your opinion** on Goodreads and/or Amazon;

2) **visit my Amazon page** and check out some of my other books;

3) give the book a boost; **tell people about** it on Facebook and Twitter;

4) **subscribe to my newsletter** at **jeannettedebeauvoir.com** for book reviews, short stories, quizzes, free stuff, previews of upcoming work, and more;

5) ask your local bookseller **to stock** Sydney Riley books;

6) make them your **choice for your next book club** meeting (I'll even join you by Skype or Zoom if you'd like me to!);

7) **email me** at jeannettedebeauvoir@gmail.com;

8) and **watch for** the next Sydney Riley mystery from Homeport Press